MARRIED TO THE ALIEN ADMIRAL OF THE FLEET

Renascence Alliance Series Book 4

ALMA NILSSON

Cover designed by Alma Nilsson

Printed in the United States of America

First Printing: November 2019

ISBN-10: 1697322352
ISBN-13: 978-1697322354

Love begins with a smile, grows with a kiss, and ends with a teardrop.

Saint Augustine

Abbreviations

Universal Credits: UC
Instant Communicator: IC
Video Messaging: VM
Video Messaging in Real Time: RVM
Galaxy Court: GC

1

The High Council Reception

Alliance date: 2nd day of the 55th week of the year 18905, Earth date: November 15th, 2636

Jane gazed with wonder at the image Drusilla James had just sent in a message from the Alliance Capital Planet down below. She was on the warship *Zuin* in orbit. But even from orbit, Jane wasn't going to tell James not to wear that gorgeous human dress to her marriage ceremony. It wasn't her responsibility anymore either. James had sworn an oath to Kara in exchange for Kara fighting a duel for her. If anyone was going to be fined for that provocative dress, it would be Kara and her House Zu. Jane smiled, thinking about how irate Kara's husband, Admiral Tir, would be when he saw the dress, as Jane had no doubt that it would be featured in at least one of the Capital City gossip columns as soon as she walked out of House Human. Not because James herself was very famous, but the man she was marrying was considered one of the most eligible men in the Empire.

Instead of RVMing James from orbit, she sent the following message,

James,

You look gorgeous today. I'm am very happy for you and I hope this is your light at the end of the tunnel and that your toughest struggles in life are over. I'll see you the next time we are on the Capital Planet. Enjoy your holiday with your husband.

J

It was at times like these that Jane missed her partner, Jim, on Earth, and her children. But ever since she and the rest of the *Dakota* crew had been taken captive, no correction, 'had volunteered to become Alliance citizens', they had not been allowed to visit Earth or have human visitors, that is unless they married an Alliance man and had at least one child.

Jane had been 38 years old when she had become an Alliance citizen, only two years shy of being ineligible for an Alliance marriage. As such, part of her contract with the Alliance Empire was that she was not required to marry if she didn't find someone suitable, and her status was more undefined, something she understood to be like a widow.

When Jane had first heard these terms, she had thought they were reasonable because, *What man would want to marry an older alien woman who already had three children?* However, she was quite mistaken in that thought, as she, just like the rest of the younger human women from the *Dakota*, had had young Alliance men lining up to court them for marriage shortly after their first Assembly. Jane spoke to a few men, but the problem was that she still loved Jim and her children back on Earth. The men that approached her for courting, she met only out of curiosity more than anything else. Because she knew in her heart that if she were to marry an Alliance man, it would only be to use him so that she could see her human family again. She could never imagine loving anyone else besides Jim and her human children. And she definitely couldn't imagine loving an alien. Even though she had become accustomed to seeing grey faces all around her and quickly fallen in line with their strict religious culture, she knew she would never be able to love one of them the way she loved Jim. Nor would she be able to love a half-alien child the way she loved her human children. And so, she avoided marriage to an Alliance man because she could. And she kept these views to herself as most of the human women in House Human seemed to like their alien husbands and love their hybrid children. Jane suspected this was because she was the only one who had had a real human family with real human children that she had had to leave behind when she became an Alliance citizen.

Although she had done a lot of questionable things in her life, she didn't want to add using an alien man and having a hybrid baby to the list. Nor did she want to contaminate her human family with some of the filthy things she had done since joining the Alliance Empire. And if she was really being honest with herself, she didn't want her human family to see her wearing an Alliance uniform and living a true Alliance life. When Jane thought about what she had become since she joined the Empire, she felt overwhelmed with guilt and shame because she believed ultimately, she had betrayed humanity. Despite her fate being out of her control, she still felt she could have done more and still today could do more, but she didn't. And her inaction made her ashamed of her position now.

Jane had only wavered for a couple of weeks in resisting Alliance cultural assimilation. However, when it became clear that she would never be returning to Earth, she had thrown herself into her new life in the Empire. She had begun to take her positions in the Alliance seriously, first as Head of House Human, which was a mainly pastoral position and second as Chief of Engineering on the *Zuin* an Alliance Warship commanded by her human captain, Captain Kara Rainer. In many ways, after living in the Alliance for over a year, despite her longing for her family on Earth and her struggles with decisions she had made, she was, more or less, content. Content to know this was the best it was going to be for her forever. Like a prisoner in a prison that was not too bad. Jane had accepted that she would never see her family again, but they had VMs and messages. It was a sacrifice but one she could live with.

Jane looked down at her IC and confirmed the time. Tonight, was a special reception hosted by the High Council for all the Heads of Houses in the Alliance Empire. The Empire was segregated by Houses. Each House had members of all three classes, maximum, middling, and slave. Humans had been put into maximum class, as the High Council wanted to begin replenishing the upper echelons of the Empire first. As Head of House Human twice a year, Jane was required to attend the High Council open days for all the Houses, a time when she could make public requests or complaints about individual issues affecting her House and its members. In all the evenings following the open days at the High Council, there were always receptions to meet and greet with all the other Heads of House and important and influential people in the vast Alliance Empire. Jane had attended for her first time last year and had kept a very low-profile. However, this year, she was much more confident and actually was almost looking forward to meeting some of the other women she had had contact with throughout the year. And it was all women, of course. No men were allowed to represent their Houses in the High Council except under extreme circumstances. Men were allowed to serve as assistants and aides, but that was all. On the Alliance planets, women were in charge of everything. Jane balked at this extreme sexism when she had first arrived, but now it seemed so natural, and she even had to catch herself sometimes for thinking, *Well, he's a man, what can I expect?*

However, Jane was in a unique position as were most women who had served on the *Dakota* in the human fleet as now, they were in the Alliance Fleet with the men. Otherwise, Alliance women never left their planets, not because the men forbid them as other species in the galaxy naively assumed. But, because the women deemed the men less necessary, therefore, if they died in space, it didn't matter as much. However, of course, times had changed, and the Alliance High Council understood that for the human women taken from the human fleet, they would have to risk their safety in the galaxy to keep them happy. As such, Jane served with all of her old crewmates and under their same captain, who was married to their small fleet admiral. It goes without saying that the Alliance men she served with were kept on very short leashes because of this. Admiral Tir was an honorable man, but when it came to his wife, Kara, he was obsessive over her. And this obsession spread to all the other human women onboard the *Zuin* as well. As a result, an Alliance man had to be very sure of his intentions as well as be a friend of the Admiral's to go anywhere near one of the human women serving on the *Zuin*. This meant that although Jane worked with a lot of men, it was about as deadpan as working with computers as she didn't really know any of them out of their fear of Admiral Tir.

Jane looked at her clothing and smiled. Three days ago, she had put in a request with the High Council that human women be allowed to wear clothing from Earth 50% of the time. The High Council had agreed but added to the amendment that they would not be allowed to wear this clothing for any religious functions. Jane had consented to this as the Empire took their pantheon of gods very seriously and knew they rarely compromised when religion was involved. She knew some of the women in House Human would be disappointed, as she guessed they would never want to wear the popular functional Alliance dresses that looked like floor-length muumuus with high collars all the time. Still, Jane felt 50% was a huge win considering the conservativeness of the Empire. This was the second message sent out to her wards. She had not even met most of them yet as they had been ill and kept on Space Port One for the last several months under the constant care of Space Port One Chief Medical Officer Doctor Anu. However, they would be released over the next day, Jane thought it would be nice to share this small victory with them before they met:

Ladies of House Human,

I have excellent news; the High Council has approved our request to wear human clothing on the condition that it is only worn 50% of the time and that it is never worn for religious functions. Our clothing conditions have now been changed, and there is a new function on your IC to keep track of when you wear human clothing. If you exceed 50% in one week, you will be fined. House Human is always low on UCs, so please do not wear your human clothes excessively. I hope you are all settling in at House Human with Madame Bai. I look forward to meeting you all in person tomorrow.

May the gods light your paths,
Jane

Jane was already taking advantage of this new rule and was wearing a human dress for the High Council reception. It was the first time in over a year she had worn a human-made dress, and she loved it. Alliance dresses were all very warm and comfortable, but they were mostly of nondescript designs and hung like tents without copious amounts of jewelry to define the wearer's figure. As most human women didn't like wearing all the copious jewelry to signify societal position and rank that their Alliance counterparts wore, as the dresses hung unbecomingly on most of the human women, and it was a constant complaint she had to listen to among the other members of House Human. And most of those complaints were coming from women who were able to wear an Alliance man's uniform most days, which was simply black trousers and a long-sleeved black shirt with a mandarin collar. She didn't want to even think about all the complaints that would flood her account from the 1,000 new arrivals from Earth.

As soon as her request was passed at the High Council, she had gone directly to the Earth Store, in the Immigrant Ring of the Capital City and bought the tightest form-fitting dress she could find for the reception tonight. It was black and had little black beads embroidered in geometric patterns on it. The dress showed off her athletic figure and her long legs. She wore it with human black stockings that weren't nearly as warm as her Alliance ones but complemented the dress better as the stockings had a light shimmer to them. She knew that this would be considered quite scandalous to most of the Alliance women she was going to meet tonight, but she wanted to prove a point.

And that point was, that human women would compromise and conform, but they would always be human in their hearts. They would never be completely broken by the Empire.

Not everything was terrible for Jane in the Empire. Back on Earth, she would have never been able to afford such an extravagant dress, but now that she was an engineer in the Alliance Empire's fleet, she was very wealthy by human standards. In addition, the Alliance had given her a kind of signing on bonus of a considerable sum of UCs, when she became an Alliance citizen, she viewed it as an apology for taking away her human life, her partner, and children. She, of course, sent a lot of UCs back to Earth for her human family, but even what she kept for herself, despite the high prices in the Alliance Empire, the UCs she had provided her with a better material life than she had ever enjoyed on Earth.

Jane looked at her reflection in the bathroom mirror and ran her fingers through her short brown hair. It was supposed to be forbidden for her to cut it, as only those in the slave class who were considered closest to the gods, were allowed to cut their hair, but as Jane was in the fleet and not on planet often, no one had said anything to her about her short hair. It also helped that her captain, Kara, still cut her hair. Otherwise, Alliance citizens of maximum class, never cut their hair, regardless if they were men or women. And it was the style in the maximum class to wear their hair in elaborate braids and adorn the braids with jewelry. Jane had never had long hair and didn't want to have it now, so she was always grateful for the small reprieves granted to her in this conservative culture. She saw her short hair as one of the last things that genuinely made her human.

Jane put on one necklace, her ID. It was like a dog tag

that everyone in the Alliance wore. It let people know who you were and where you belonged. This was all very important to Alliance people. Jane's tag said, 'Jane Head of House Human.' Then she put on a ring, and it signified that she was in the military and an engineer. She could put on a lot more jewelry to make these rankings even more apparent, including the ship she served on, but that was the last thing she wanted to do. She wanted to feel as human as possible tonight, and that meant wearing the least amount of Alliance jewelry as she could get away with at such a formal occasion.

"Mirror," Jane said as she walked out into her living quarters and a full-length mirror appeared. She looked at her reflection and said out loud, "Yes, this is the Jane, I know. Human Jane. Computer, capture the image, and send it to Captain Kara."

"Sent," the computer responded in an even male voice.

"Close mirror," Jane said and then left her quarters aboard the *Zuin*. She went to the hangar bay where an Alliance pilot and transport was waiting to take her down to the Capital Planet. There were two other men there, security guards. "I don't need any security," Jane said dismissively to the men.

"Sorry, Chief, Captain's orders. After what happened with Doctor Drusilla, I mean Doctor James," Captain Kara had officially changed her name, as Kara had said that 'Drusilla' was an unfit name for anyone in the galaxy, "Captain said she wasn't taking any more risks with her humans."

"Her humans?" Jane asked rhetorically with a little laugh. "Last time I checked; I was Head of House Human." Jane knew though that Kara carried a great deal of guilt for all of the human women forced to live in the

Empire. Although she had never been a member of House Human, she was constantly helping its members in one way or another.

The security guard who had been speaking shrugged.

"Fine, come on. But I feel sorry for you both as I expect this to be a boring High Council reception and security will be tight anyway," Jane said as she entered the transport with the guards silently trailing her.

Jane and her two guards arrived at the High Council Assembly Rooms in the Administration Ring of the Capital City a quarter of an hour later. Jane had attended the party last year but had been so overwhelmed with all the newness of everything she had not been able to properly admire the sheer vastness of the rooms. They were, without a doubt, spectacular in both size and quality. The outside of the building, as were the interiors, were all made out of yellow stone, which was the preferred building material on the Capital Planet. And the Grand Assembly Room was lit only by artificial candlelight that flickered throughout, casting strange and gentle shadows on the high stone walls. And along the high walls, the only decorations were massive statues of the gods looking down on all the occupants of the room. As if the gods were truly watching their every move. Alliance citizens had better night vision than humans, so much so that their eyes shown like cats' eyes in the complete darkness and half like cats in the candlelit room now. Jane preferred their appearances this way. It reminded her of their alienness.

Jane confidently walked in the crowded room of grey Alliance people and got more than a few looks from the other women of the High Council. They were not shocked to see her, as they had gotten over their initial surprise that she really was human with pink skin last year, no, they were stunned now because she was wearing a tight-fitting human dress and human makeup. And probably just now realizing that her hair was still the same length as it was last year.

Jane was not alone for very long at the reception as the Head of Imperial House Zu, a permanent member of the High Council, came over to greet her as soon as she saw Jane. Kes and Jane got along reasonably well, which was good because House Zu and House Human were interlinked by her captain's marriage to Admiral Tir and, more recently, to protect Doctor James. As Jane was inexperienced in managing her house and that House Human's ranking was so low, it had been decided that Doctor James would be moved to House Zu for protection. As a result, Jane was indebted to House Zu for the moment. That move had saved Doctor James's life and House Human from being seen as a weak target open for bullying in the Empire.

Kes smiled as she saw the human representative walk in. Jane of House Human was an honorable woman, and Kes liked her. She only wished that the other human women were as respectful of Alliance ways as Jane, especially her daughter-in-law. Kes couldn't really believe that Jane and Kara were friends as they were so different, and Kara was so impulsive, "Jane, the gods are shining their light on you tonight, even in that ghastly human dress. Whatever possessed you to buy it and then wear it? Are you ill? It looks so uncomfortable."

Jane smiled, "I must admit, it feels so good to wear some clothes from Earth again. You should try it sometime. You must have a stunning figure."

Kes snorted, "No, I think Kara pushes the boundaries enough for my entire House. And now," she reached for her IC and showed Jane an image from one of the most popular Capital City gossip columns, "Also, Doctor James is marrying in this revealing human dress from my House, and I know that Kara has seen it and done nothing as I recognize her little hand there in the side of the image. I assume you didn't have time to tell Doctor James that no human clothing could be worn for religious ceremonies. Right?"

"Is marriage a religious ceremony?" Jane asked, innocently. Smiling to herself remembering the image of James in the sexy silk sequenced dress with embroidery.

Kes gave Jane a sidelong look and thought, *Humans are so sneaky*, "Of course, a marriage ceremony is religious. But then I forget, you still are learning about our religion. And there's only so much we can expect of humans."

Jane ignored the racist comment, nodded, and took a ceramic cup of zota, the preferred alcoholic beverage of the Alliance, from a passing slave. "Doctor James might already belong to House Vo as we speak, so the fine will go to them anyway, isn't that correct?"

Kes laughed, "I doubt it. You know traditional Alliance marriages take some time." She leaned in closer to Jane to speak conspiratorially, "And I've heard they will take the ancient binding tattoos, so it'll take even longer. I almost feel sorry for my daughter-in-law having to witness that tonight."

Jane also knew they were taking binding tattoos. James could not abide by the Alliance Empire's system of slave artists. James had been adamant that she could not share a husband, no matter how long he was away in the galaxy. The purpose of the tattoos was to physically bind two people together, so it would be impossible for them to have sex with anyone else, ever in their entire lives, as it was rumored to be irreversible. If a couple who had taken the tattoos tried to have sex with another person, they would at first become physically ill, followed by passing out. Jane thought this was all well and fine for keeping couples from straying sexually, but she could easily see how this would backfire in the event of a rape of a woman. However, she had never heard of any women being raped. There were only a few exceptional cases from years ago, and these were always mentioned with the greatest of concern, so Jane supposed James had nothing to fear from the binding tattoo.

Traditionally, binding tattoos had been a means of keeping fidelity in marriages when Alliance men began leaving the planet on missions for years out in the galaxy. At the same time, lifespans began extending beyond 300 years. However, hundreds of years ago, binding tattoos had been officially abandoned for the culture of slave artists, which were basically free-range prostitutes that worked both on the planet and on starships. Both men and women had access to slave artists, and it was socially acceptable to have sex with them. Alliance people believed that it was unhealthy to go without sex or some kind of release for long periods of time. On planet though, women had to travel to private spas to enjoy slave artists, as far as Jane knew anyway. On the ship, they were readily available and had their own quarters, which no officer, including a captain, was allowed to enter. Jane personally thought the idea of slave artists made a lot of sense and even had a favorite of her own onboard the *Zuin*. "I don't know what Doctor James and Doctor Ket are planning. I didn't get any details as she is no longer in House Human," Jane lied.

"Of course not," Kes said being polite and accepting the lie. "I'm sure Kara knows and, as usual, refuses to tell anyone anything, not in her best interest."

Jane smiled. She wasn't going to be drawn into the ongoing conflict between these two strong women in her life, "I think Doctor James and Doctor Ket are a good match, so it's good for the Empire." It was forbidden to speak about love in polite conversation, so Jane had to say, 'good match' which she thought conveyed the same idea.

"Good for the image of human women," Kes said casually. "Doctor James is a fine example of what human women can accomplish in the Empire if they just open, accept and apply themselves to their new lives here. She has done so well. First in her class at the medical school and a prestigious position on the Imperial Floor of the Capital City Hospital."

"And she wasn't murdered," Jane commented solemnly. She still felt guilty for not being able to protect James from almost being murdered twice as she was alone on the Capital Planet in the brick and mortar House Human.

"She won in the end. The gods showed their justice."

"Thanks be to the gods for showing us justice," Jane replied with the set response. But she didn't really believe that any of the patheon of Alliance gods had anything to do with it. It was human will that had kept James alive among these vipers.

"Thanks be to the gods. How are the new one-thousand?" Kes asked, referring to the 1,000 human women who had volunteered to return with her son, when he had been on Earth last year retrieving his own wife, who had been tried by the human government as a spy.

"I'd say they are integrating as well as can be expected as they should be just arriving on the Capital Planet now." Jane got out her IC and looked for any updates from Madame Bai about the women being transported down, but there were none, yet.

"Ah yes, the quarantine," Kes said sarcastically. "Have you spoken to Doctor Anu about when they will be released? Are you sure it will be today? I've heard there have been some false starts before. You don't want the slaves in House Human to become lazy without anyone to look after."

Jane laughed at the thought of the slaves at House Human being anymore rude or lazy than they already were and then replied, "They are being released into Madame Bai's care as we speak. It's all been arranged with Doctor Anu. Without a doubt, the slaves at House Human will be busier than they ever have been before. They'll be going from one woman of maximum class to look after to one-thousand."

"I'm glad to hear it. We were all beginning to become a little suspicious. And as much as Doctor Anu is a competent doctor, she is no cultural guide. Madame Bai has proved to be an excellent teacher. I only wonder if the rest of you would have integrated more naturally and easily if you would have been forced to remain on the Capital Planet instead of joining the Alliance fleet and being allowed to roam the galaxy with the men."

"Kes, now would you really want Captain Kara sitting across from you at the evening meal every night?" It was customary that Alliance families lived together and had dinner together every night. As such, breakfast was the most common meal to meet friends for in the Empire.

"No, you're right. I guess I can sacrifice the bad habits of 20 human women for forgoing having the pleasure of looking at my daughter in-law every night over the evening meal." Kes smiled and changed the subject, "And how do you think these new human women will find the Alliance men?" Kes knew that Alliance people were considered only tolerable in appearance by human standards.

"Oh, I'm sure just like the rest of us, they will thoroughly enjoy the men's stunning physiques," Jane said, and this was no lie. Although Alliance people were grey-skinned, they were obsessed with their bodies and took meticulous care to make sure they were as strong and healthy as they could be.

Kes gave Jane a knowing smile, "I must speak to Kada of House Olu now, but I'll find you later to continue this conversation. As I've heard a rumor about one of yours, a Rachel?"

"Yes, find me later," Jane said nonchalantly. Rachel had been playing with fire recently by spending way too much time flirting with their first officer on the *Zuin*, Commander Koz, but never agreeing to courtship. This was something that was severely frowned upon in the Alliance. No one should waste another's time without being serious. The problem was, Rachel was hardly ever serious about anything and despite Jane's warnings she was refusing to be serious about her behavior towards Commander Koz and people were beginning to talk about it.

For the next hour, Jane talked to many Alliance women in the High Council. Most of whom she knew only by sight or quick acquaintance from last year. Now she was finding these women to be not only more welcoming but almost accepting. Jane reckoned it was because she had now been the Head of House Human for a year and had actually had to make quite a few serious decisions about her members' lives. It also helped, of course, that two of her members had married into Imperial Houses. Through all of these conversations, Jane found out a lot of useful information about running her House, all of which she had pretty much been doing by the trial and error method thus far, which meant that she always felt that she was barely scraping by with what was socially acceptable. She was grateful for the connections and the tips these women were giving her now.

After several hours, Jane decided that it was time for

her to leave the reception. Surprisingly though, a tall and strong Alliance man approached her before she could walk to the exit. She could see behind him; her security guards and his security guards were engaged in a very friendly conversation and Jane summarized that they all knew each other. She quickly took in his colossal stature, his long grey hair pulled back in an elaborate braid and his ranking jewelry and immediately bowed. He was Admiral Jei, the Admiral of the entire Alliance Fleet. Arguably one of the most powerful men in the known galaxy, that is, if you didn't know the Empire was actually controlled by the Alliance women on the planet and that Alliance men were second to women.

"Chief Jane, Head of House Human," Admiral Jei said. "I've wanted to meet you for some time now. Thank the gods that our paths crossed tonight," Jei looked into Jane's very human eyes, which were the same color as the daytime sky. He had never seen eyes this color in a being that didn't have some transparent part to their bodies, which he thought was never attractive. As he investigated her appearance further, he noticed that she had the smoothest, cream-colored skin he had ever seen. And that the brown color of her hair that seemed to change depths in the light he thought was more than just a little alluring. He thought her facial features were pleasing and soft, which gave her a younger appearance than her 39 years. And her scent was very appealing. She smelled sweet and heavy all at the same time. He wanted to touch her short brown hair and breathe in her scent further, but he controlled himself, *You're no longer a young man. You've had your children and your chance to be a husband. Treat her as you would any officer.*

Jane looked up into his hard grey eyes and tried not to be intimidated by his size or rank, "The gods have truly shone their light on me that I would be so singled out by you, Admiral."

"The gods are great, indeed," he replied with a bit of humor. He knew that the humans had been forced to accept the Alliance religion into their lives, but he doubted that any really believed in it. As he could not imagine not believing in the gods himself and felt it must be the same going the other way, as being an atheist was probably like being part of a religion as well. Jei didn't believe that one could force oneself to believe or not to believe in religion over the course of a day or a week. Belief in the gods was something that was built up over time.

Jane gave him a little smile. On the planet, women kept to the stringent religious codes of the Empire, the hours of prayer, and times of day one could eat were all held in strict accordance with the gods. The men, on the other hand, were more relaxed about it all, especially onboard their starships. Jane had walked between these two worlds since she took her place on Captain Kara's ship. However, she had never met anyone in the military at a function where she was performing her role as Head of House Human, squarely in the women's world. She was momentarily befuddled as to how she should behave towards the Admiral. On the planet, she, as Head of House Human and High Council Member, was superior to him in societal ranking. However, in the fleet, she was far below him. This was a problematic situation as someone's rank was so crucial in the way you spoke with someone in the Alliance, and now she stood in front of him as an Alliance social ranking impossibility, both an officer, a woman and Head of House. Jane looked at the Admiral and if she was going to guess his mood from his face expression, she would say 'serious,' so she decided to try and keep the conversation as neutral as possible as to avoid any awkward ranking situations, so she asked, "Do you always attend this reception, Admiral? I don't remember seeing anyone from the fleet here last year?"

"Oh no, I just happened to be on the Capital Planet now, so I thought it would be convenient to attend tonight," Admiral Jei's flagship the *Kzi* was being upgraded. He thought it would be prudent to stop by this reception to intimidate some of the High Council members who were blocking his requests to conquer some new territory that he thought would be strategically advantageous in the Huz system. He was tired of waiting. It was an added bonus when he saw Chief Jane. He had forgotten until he saw her that she would be here. Jei had wanted to meet her for a while. He was duly impressed with the way that she had handled House Human over the last year, and he suspected that most of the fleet's human integration rules had probably been written by her, rather than her human captain, who took all the credit. What he had not realized was that she was beautiful. He, of course, had seen Jane's picture before. It was in her file. A plain Galaxy Court, GC, full-body picture with clothing. In that picture, she looked dull, for a human, 'average everything human,' he had said coldly when he had first seen it. But now seeing her in person, in that magnificent human dress, and with the exotic human face paint, he was captivated.

"I see," Jane said, desperately trying to think of something else to say.

"That clothing? It's human? Is that allowed?"

"I had the law passed recently in the High Council," Jane said proudly. "Human women are allowed to wear human clothing for 50% of the time, but not at religious ceremonies."

"Is that right?" he asked rhetorically, pulling out his IC and showing her a picture of Doctor James in her white silk dress. "She's getting married, and I'd say that's a religious ceremony."

"I didn't know what she was planning on wearing for her marriage ceremony, Admiral. Maybe you are unaware, but she's no longer a member of House Human. I've no doubt she was given permission from Captain Kara or someone else in House Zu to wear that dress tonight."

Admiral Jei laughed at Jane, "I don't believe you. But, overall, you've done a good job in your new role. I've been impressed, but you've taken these little things here and there, hoping no one would notice."

"Excuse me, Admiral? What are you referring too?" She asked innocently, knowing, of course, exactly all the little things he was referring to. But she couldn't figure out from his demeanor how he really felt about her transgressions. Alliance people often said contradictory things to what they really believed, believing, of course, they were not being contradictory in their expressions at all. It was still confusing at times for Jane.

"Oh, you know what I'm referring to Chief. The clothing, ranking jewelry, religion, and you continue to cut your hair."

Jane's hand immediately went to the ends of her hair, which was only chin-length but didn't reply.

"How is it that it's the same length now as it was when you arrived over a year ago? I'm certainly no expert on humans but I think that's odd."

Jane didn't reply. She just looked into his grey eyes, trying to figure out if he really did want an answer.

"From now on, Chief. You won't cut your hair. I don't care what Captain Kara does, as you know, it's difficult for me to enforce anything with her as Admiral Tir has her so well protected, but you. You're mine just as everyone else in the fleet is, and you'll comply, or I'll publically punish you myself. Understood?" His mind, quite out of his control, swirled then, visualizing himself physically punishing her, and he almost felt aroused. Something that took him by surprise as he was a man of 206 years and had a regular slave artist that resided in his quarters onboard the *Kzi*. It wasn't like him to waste his time chasing sex or romance. He was too old for that. And he had already done his part for the Alliance. He had married and had children, and they had had children and so forth. His wife had died some years ago, and as there was a shortage of women, Jei had already decided that he would never marry again. And he liked having Vran in his quarters, he wouldn't want another wife. Yet, here he was infatuated by this young human woman before him.

Jane was intimidated by his strong words, "Understood, Admiral." She believed that he would actually hold her to these rules and the last thing she wanted was a public punishment in the fleet. She had seen some men publicly punished by Admiral Tir and it served its purpose to keep them in line.

Then Admiral Jei turned and left Jane standing there alone in the Grand Assembly Room without another word.

Jane stood there, momentarily, watching him go. A few of the other High Councilwomen came over to talk to her afterward. All with the same message, 'I've no idea how you find the patience to work with men all the time. They are so impulsive. You know he didn't even let us know he was going to come tonight?' After another hour, Jane turned to her security guards, and they returned to the *Zuin*.

2

The Hairpin and House Human

The next morning, Captain Kara returned to the ship. She and Jane had a coffee in her captain's ready room off the main bridge.

"How was the wedding?" Jane asked.

"Nothing like mine, and it lasted forever," Kara complained with a hint of a smile.

"What do you mean? How could it last forever, I thought it was just the exchanging of vows and then the deed and then done." Jane wanted details. After what Kes had alluded to, it must have been really something to see, a marriage ceremony with the ancient binding tattoos. A small part of Jane was relieved though that she had not had to be a witness to it. She still was uncomfortable to the Alliance custom of witnessing a couple having sex as part of the marriage ceremony. She could adhere to most Alliance religious practices, but this was still one that made her feel queasy. Mind you, Jane had done her duty a few times already, but she really hoped all the other human women would make good friends so she would not have to be a witness to any more marriage ceremonies.

"Yeah, well, I guess Doctor Ket wanted to make things more traditional if you know what I mean? He went so painfully slow. I don't know how many times he made her orgasm before the thing was over. I never thought I could get bored watching live sex, but there I was bored out of my mind."

Jane smiled, "That must have been embarrassing to watch." Thinking that the participants' minds were probably far away from the audience they had at the time of consummation.

"Thankfully, I had brought a case of champagne, and I took a bottle up to the bedroom. But, I've to admit, after about 30 minutes, it was like watching a really badly made alien porn. I wanted to yell out instructions, but I controlled myself. They were complete amateurs."

Both women laughed.

"Honestly, Kara, you've got to give her a break. What did you expect? James is so young. And her husband, he may be handsome, but I've met him, and he just doesn't strike me as a man who has spent a lot of time studying the karma sutra or whatever the Alliance equivalent might be."

"I know, but you would think they would at least practice a little beforehand for their wedding night to make a good impression on all of us that had to witness it. Practice makes perfect," she said sarcastically.

"It's supposed to be the first time," Jane said, and then they both laughed at the ridiculousness of that rule. No one really seemed to wait until their marriage ceremony to have sex in their experience of the maximum class on the Capital Planet.

"Well, the first time Tir and I had sex was after we exchanged marriage bracelets," Kara said proudly.

"And you'd known each other for what two hours beforehand?" Jane laughed.

Kara laughed too, "I know. But we must have put on a good show." She referred to the doctor who was their witness who now was a frequent visitor to their marital bed.

"I don't think James was out to seduce anyone for joining them. Especially as they were taking those binding tattoos."

"What were the details from the slave who watched them in House Human? 'A wild frenzy of animalistic human love with fur spilling everywhere'? What I want to know was where was that last night? That would have been so much better than the boring and slow lovemaking I had to watch. "

"Something like that. Oh, the slaves hate that we have hair on our bodies. Who knows what that really looked like as she could have just been focused on James's hair. I guess it's annoying to clean up."

"I just don't understand why they don't use machines to clean?"

Then both Kara and Jane looked at each other and said in unison, "Because it goes against the gods." Then they laughed again.

Finally, when Jane regained her countenance, she asked, "And how did the photograph go off?"

"Well, as we took it before they were naked, I think James really appreciated the gesture," Kara replied. Having a wedding photograph taken of the bride and groom was the only human tradition she and Jane could come up with to integrate into the Alliance marriage ritual. "I hope the rest of the human women begin integrating it into their marriages to bring some humanity to these barbaric ceremonies."

"Good. I'm glad we could add something human that was appreciated."

"Yes, and as you can imagine, the Alliance people didn't like it at all," Kara laughed. "They just get so upset when one little thing is changed without warning."

"Well, it's just the way they come. What always gets me, though, is that Alliance people are fine with almost anything, as long as they are made aware of the change well ahead of time," Jane smiled.

"Yes, it did take them almost a decade to actually act on integrating human women," Kara commented. "Anyway, now tell me, how was your night? Just as boring as mine at the High Council reception I imagine."

"I spoke to your mother-in-law," Jane answered evenly, watching Kara's reaction.

"I know, she told me this morning as I left before breakfast, and she was appalled. Absolutely riveting. It's good that she has a high opinion of you, though. Anyone else worth mentioning? Any good gossip?"

"Not really, I did learn though that I don't have to pay all the fines the women in House Human incur though," Jane had had a real problem with James incurring fines by holding hands or kissing her future husband while they had been courting.

"Oh?" Kara asked only half-interested.

"Yes, I can send them to the High Priestess at the Grand Temple in the Capital City for public physical punishment instead."

"You wouldn't really do that, would you? It's so barbaric."

Jane shrugged, "I can't continue to always ask you for UCs from House Zu to cover the fines. And who knows what is going to happen with 1,000 more women? I need to enforce these Alliance rules no matter how illogical and impractical you and I believe them to be."

"But you wouldn't really, would you? I mean, it's so barbaric. A public punishment?" Kara had only been to that temple once, and she had had to take part in an archaic blood ritual with her husband. "I'm more than happy to spend House Zu's UCs on human women kissing random Alliance men. I think that is money well spent. Besides it's good for the Alliance men, the human women and the Empire."

Jane laughed, "I know you think so and you are very rich. That's part of the problem. But, I'm serious, Kara. These new women must integrate. They have actually volunteered to be here."

"Integrate or what? They're not going to send any of us home. We must stand our ground. We must remain as human as possible," Kara put her hand over her heart.

Jane put one finger over her heart, the corresponding hand signal in the Alliance; she was speaking the truth, "We are all Alliance now."

Kara frowned, "I hate it when you do that, Jane. We can't just wash off our human culture or our human spirit. We can only conform so much. There's always a breaking point. We must always keep our hearts and desires human or else, mark me," she spoke with seriousness now, "We will wither and die here if we give in. Only to be shells of real humans to be only breeders like cattle. I won't let that happen."

"To be Alliance," Jane murmured. "It's our only choice, but you're right, of course, we will never be truly Alliance. It's impossible. But I still don't want the hassle of the fines."

"So says the woman who never has to marry and who still has her husband and children on Earth. And is he still faithful to you even after all this time? Is he true to your human love?" Kara asked almost mockingly.

"It's different, and you know that. We never married, so don't insult me by calling him my husband and you know very well that he still is faithful to me. We met when we were so young, and we have so many memories together. You'll have those memories with Tir, and maybe that is why you are fighting so hard against them? You are afraid of creating such intimate memories together that will forever bind you and I'm not just talking about the sex."

Kara shrugged, "Maybe." She didn't want to talk about this with Jane right now. She was jealous of Jane's relationship with Jim, and Jane didn't' seem to realize. If Kara gave Jane the opportunity to reminisce, she would go on and on about what a great man Jim was and their wonderful children. It made Kara green with envy. She did like Tir, but he would never be human, and a part of her hated that. Kara also suspected that a part of Tir hated that she would never be Alliance too. And they hated each other as much as they loved each other. Their relationship was a constant storm.

Kara and Jane were quiet for some minutes, both lost in their own thoughts.

"Oh," Jane said, remembering after a time, "Admiral Jei was there."

"And he spoke to you?"

"Yes, he gave me a stern warning about cutting my hair."

Kara waved this away, "Oh, pooh."

"He seemed quite serious to me," Jane admitted, still remembering the shiver he sent up her spine, when he mentioned a public punishment.

"I wouldn't even think about letting my hair grow long, and you shouldn't either. What can he really do?"

"Easy for you to say, you are married to Tir. You can do what you want. But who am I? Head of the last House in the Alliance Empire with little power and a few UCs. I'm not going to cut my hair anymore. He said he would publically punish me himself. I'm going to take his threat quite seriously. Unlike you, I don't relish in the idea of a public punishment."

"That sounds like a sexy proposition to me. And I mean he's old, but he's still got it. And I'm sure he's very skilled in the bedroom. Can you imagine. He's probably had sex every week, at least since he's been 20 years old and he's over 200 years old now. Think about all the times he's made women come. He could probably make me come in mere minutes by just looking across the room."

Jane looked at Kara in disbelief, "Honestly Kara, is sex all that you think about? And I'm pretty sure people plateau. I don't think it continues."

"I don't know, I think it's like playing an instrument, the more you practice no matter how old you get, you do get better as long as your fingers and mouth and things work."

Jane's mind couldn't help but race now to imagine Admiral Jei sucking on her clitoris. But after a second she shook those thoughts away and said, "It didn't come off like a proposition and definitely not a sexy one either. It was a threat, and he meant it. Just because it's foreplay for you and Tir to have him punish you in front of his officers, it's not for me, and I doubt it is for the Admiral either." She stopped short of saying, 'And please don't put these thoughts in my head because now I'm thinking about him only in this sexy way.'

"I never thought I would see the day that Jane Johnson

adhered to what an Alliance man told her. You are Head of House Human. How can he tell you what to do, and you take it seriously? Especially when he told you this at a High Council reception of all places. That man has some gall. "

"Well, he's the admiral of the entire Alliance fleet, the most powerful in the galaxy and where do we spend most of our time?" she asked rhetorically. "With the fleet. I feel like he has more jurisdiction over me than just any woman who is Head of any House." Jane looked at Kara, she seemed a million kilometers away. "So I've to give up my one comfort of having short hair? After everything else I've done, it's a small thing to do," she lied. Jane felt that by letting her hair grow she would be giving up another human part of herself. And she hated it, but she wasn't going to admit that to Kara out loud. Jane was typically not a complainer.

After coffee with Kara, Jane returned to her quarters quickly before she was scheduled to go down to the Capital Planet and meet all the new women in House Human. As she entered, she saw a parcel addressed to her on her desk. Sometimes people would send her human gifts from the Earth Store especially when the *Zuin* was in orbit as it was cheaper. However, Frank the owner, always wrapped his gifts in human products. And this gift was clearly from the Alliance.

Curiously, Jane picked up the black box. She had no idea who would send her something that was Alliance made. She opened it and inside was a beautiful silver Alliance hairpin and a handwritten note with precise writing.

Do not cut your hair or punishment will follow.

Jane laughed when she read the note. It was unsigned, but it didn't matter because she knew who had sent it. There was no doubt in her mind. This was from Admiral Jei. Jane smiled and then put the hairpin back in the box and closed it. Then, without another thought about the hairpin, she grabbed her IC and left her quarters to attend to her duties at House Human.

Admiral Jei's squire Den walked into the *Kzi's* conference room where he was working alone before a meeting and said to Jei, "It's done."

"Did you give it to her directly?"

"No. She wasn't in her quarters, I used your override and left it on her desk."

"Was there anything out of the ordinary about her quarters?" Jei wanted to know everything about this Jane. He hadn't stopped thinking about her since he left her at the High Council reception last night. Unfortunately, all he could find out about her, he already knew. She really had nothing personal of herself anywhere on social media. And although he had not added her as a direct contact, he had checked her social page today to see if she posted anything from being on the Capital Planet or the hairpin, he had given her. A typical Alliance woman, whether she was romantically interested or not, would have posted the hairpin to her social media account as a sign of her desirability and worth in the Empire. As the hairpin came from the most famous jeweler in all the Alliance Empire, and it was a one of a kind. Also, it was from him, and even though he was a great-grandfather, most older women would be happy to receive his attentions as he was Admiral of the Fleet.

"No," Den replied, not really knowing what the Admiral meant by his question. "It looked like any officer's quarters." Den was 15 years old and had just taken this post less than a year ago. He knew very little of courting and women. And he knew nothing about human women except that they were like Alliance women but different colors and acted a bit strangely. If truth be told he had hurried out of Chief Jane's quarters as soon as he had left the gift as he had been afraid to meet her by surprise.

"Dismissed," Jei said, annoyed the young man didn't snoop around Jane's quarters, but he had expected Jane to be in her quarters, so he hadn't instructed him to snoop and Jei knew most young men Den's age needed to be told to do it. Jei wondered then, *Maybe she considers me too old? I must force myself to stop thinking about her. I made myself perfectly clear with the hairpin, and if she's not interested, there's nothing more I can do. She will make her feelings known one way or another.*

Jane walked into House Human and was instantly reminded again of how bare it was and how much she hated it. House Human reminded her of the dormitories at the human fleet, basic rooms with only a few communal areas to relax. If one could relax sharing sofas and tables and all with other women.

Madame Bai had assembled all the women in the dining hall. All 1,000 of them. Every chair was taken, and Jane suspected all the rooms were full too. The house was meant to hold 1,000 women, and that was how many Admiral Tir had brought back, *How convenient?* Jane thought, knowing full well that nothing in the Alliance was a coincidence.

Jane and Madame Bai walked into the House Human dining hall together. Madame Bai then began addressing the new additions, "Welcome. It's good that you are all here and healthy. We were thrilled that you all volunteered to help us and then devastated when we discovered you had contracted the Zoipli virus while in the spaceport. We all have been saying extra prayers to the goddess of home and of health to bring you to us, and finally, our prayers have been answered. Thanks be to the gods as they allow us to walk in their light."

When the women looked at her blankly, Madame Bai chided them, "Now you say, 'We are not worthy of their grace, but we accept.'"

After all the women said the words, Madame Bai continued, "I'm not surprised that the men that were supposed to teach you about our culture and religion have failed. But don't worry, we will bring you all up to speed. First, I would like to introduce you to your Head of House Human, Jane. She is currently serving with Captain Kara, another human, on the *Zuin*. Now please stand and bow to your Head."

After a couple of seconds of hesitation, the women all stood, and when Jane stood in front of them, they bowed.

Jane stood and began to address the women who had all quieted down for her, "With the gods' permission, mark the date, the 3rd day of the 55th week of the year 18905, Earth date, November 16th, 2636. Welcome to House Human. I'm Jane," she hesitated as she had to drop her surname, and she still was not used to it and she couldn't help but think how ridiculous it sounded as if she were the character Jane from the book *Tarzan*. "Head of House Human. I'm responsible for you all. Madame Bai and her assistants are only your cultural guides. Any problems, you come to me. Any fines will be sent to me as well as, and just so we are clear on that matter, I'll not hesitate to send people to the High Priestess for punishment rather than paying the UCs. Don't be fooled by our connections with some of the Imperial Houses. We are poor and our ranking as a House is low. As you all volunteered to come here, I expect you to be keen to learn and follow all the Alliance customs to the tiniest detail with no deviations. Now, are there any questions you have for me?"

A young woman raised her hand.

Jane nodded, "Yes?"

She stood up and asked, "How can we reach you if you are off in the galaxy somewhere?"

"Good question. What's your name?"

"Petra."

"Thank you, Petra. The Alliance is more technologically advanced than we are, and their communications travel on gravitational waves through space so you can always reach me. Any other questions?"

Another woman raised her hand and then stood when Jane nodded to her, "I'm Babette, and I want to know what happens if we don't find an Alliance man we want to marry?"

Jane nodded, "Unfortunately, Babette, in the contract that you all signed with the Alliance Empire, you must marry either by their choice or by yours. I'd hope for all of your sakes, it would be by your choice alone. I'm not sure what your experiences were like on your journey over but let me assure you that many eligible young men in the Alliance would make excellent husbands and are all desperate to have a wife, especially a human wife. As human women are more likely to give them a daughter. As you are all aware, this is mostly a matriarchal society. The Alliance Houses, especially of maximum class, have few women, which means fewer women to rule."

"Do you represent us in the High Council?" another woman asked.

"Yes," Jane said, taking a sip of water that the slaves had provided for her and Madame Bai. "House Human is not a permanent member of the High Council, but there are a few open days over two one-week periods twice a year when all the Head of Houses are invited to speak about individual issues concerning them."

"When is the next meeting for all the Houses?" the same woman asked.

"This week actually. I'll be attending a High Council reception later. Is there something, in particular, you would like me to petition for? Already we can wear human clothes some of the time. Please let me know before the end of the week if there is something else." Jane had expected these women to be more complacent than some of them were. She had been under the impression from Doctor Anu that the Alliance had used advertisements on Earth with specific subliminal messages to recruit exactly the kind of human women that would most likely adapt to Alliance culture.

"I think it's quite a coincidence that we were released from Space Port One Hospital on the same day that you happen to be on the Capital Planet."

"The gods show us their kindness in many ways," Jane replied, which in Alliance terms meant, 'You're a fool if you think I'm answering that question.' Then when the woman said nothing more, Jane said, "Since you have been in the hospital, many things have happened. Captain Kara has taken command of the *Zuin*, which almost all the former female crew of the *Dakota* is serving on. If any of you are interested and have the right qualifications, we might have a place for you onboard as well."

"And the other crew members from the *Dakota*?"

"One member, Junior Doctor Drusilla, now known as Doctor James of House Vo, remained in the Capital City and is now an Alliance doctor at the prestigious Capital City Hospital. Details of her wedding will be in the Day as she married an Imperial Doctor yesterday." Jane did not want to encourage any of them to see James. She was worried that James would be able to see that their memories had been changed over the last weeks.

"And did this human doctor also think it was wise to wipe our memories?" another woman asked haughtily.

Jane was prepared for this question. "Doctor James was updated about all of your conditions, but when the decision to wipe your memories of the traumatic treatments for the Zoipli virus was made, unfortunately, Doctor James herself was very ill with the Uli virus, so she could not be consulted. However, I can assure you," Jane touched her hand to her heart, "We made the best decision we could at the time. I hope that it is not too disconcerting that those terrible months when you all were ill are lost to you."

"Is it possible to retrieve the memories?" someone else asked.

Jane shook her head, "I don't think so. I'm sorry."

"Who were you to decide for us? We are adults. We could have decided for ourselves."

Jane shook her head and then spoke firmly, "You are adults, but you are now Alliance citizens and apart of House Human. As long as you are in this House, I have the final word on all of your choices. This was part of the deal you struck when you agreed to come here." She let that sink in for the women for a minute, and then when no one else spoke, she continued, "As you know, I have already petitioned the High Council and have been awarded the right to allow humans to wear our own clothing some of the time. If you have other things you would like to see changed, please message me right away or another time and I will petition for it for next year. If you have pressing matters, VM me. Otherwise, I will make a point to drop in every time I am on the Capital Planet and will personally get in touch with all of you to check on your individual progress. Are there any more questions?"

"Are you married?" Babette asked cheekily.

"I am not. It is not in my contract with the Alliance."

"How is it that you don't have to marry?"

"I will only answer this question because it is your first day on the Capital Planet. I'm not married because I was already 38 years old when I came to the Alliance."

"But not too old to still marry," Babette commented.

Jane marked this one as a troublemaker. "No, but as I said, it was not a part of my contract with the Empire. We all have individual and unique contracts with our new galactic affiliation. Now, are there any more questions?"

Another woman stood up, "My name is Mara. Are we at risk of getting another galactic virus? It scares me that Doctor James caught the Uli virus here in the Capital City. I thought we would be safe here."

"Mara, let me assure you, you are all in good hands now. It was rare and unlucky that you were all exposed to the Zoipli virus. Now you have all been vaccinated against any more viruses, and all men coming down to the planet when they have been abroad in the galaxy will be screened to keep you all safe."

"I just don't want to be so ill again. I don't like having months of my life that are missing in my mind either."

Jane could tell that they had all talked about this a lot. She spoke firmly to them, "I can promise you it will not happen again, and the Alliance has the best medicine in the galaxy. Nothing is going to harm you here. Understood?" when they did not answer her, she asked again, "I can't hear you? Understood?"

"Understood," they replied in unison.

Jane nodded, she hoped it was a while before they heard about James being challenged to a duel to the death. "Now, I'll leave you in the capable hands of Madame Bai and her assistants." Jane waited for them to rise and bow. When they just sat there looking at her with blank faces, she remembered that they didn't know what they were supposed to do and chided herself for already falling into the Alliance order so quickly and just expecting them to do the same. "Rise and bow again, I'm your Head of House. You will do this when I leave out of respect."

The women all did as Jane bid, and then she left the dining room, followed closely by Madame Bai. One of Madame Bai's helpers addressed the human women then explaining about their ID necklaces, ICs, and clothing.

In what was referred to as the Classroom, Jane spoke privately to Madame Bai, "Is everything going well so far?"

Madame Bai nodded, "Yes, they are much more pliable than any of you were. I don't know if it is because I have experience with humans right off a spaceship now or if it was because they volunteered?"

"Or because their memories were replaced and who knows what else Doctor Anu and her team added?"

Madame Bai frowned, "Our doctors would never do that."

Jane wanted to roll her eyes but refrained, "I'm only joking. I'm sure it will be easier this time around. You know what to expect from humans now. And as you said, these women volunteered."

"I hope so," Madame Bai confided in Jane, "Two of the women already have bans on them, and I have let them know what that means so there won't be any surprises. I still feel guilty about what happened with Drusilla, I mean, James."

"Yes, I also feel responsible for what went wrong, but we cannot blame ourselves, she never asked for help and always put on a brave face. Still, we must learn from our mistakes and be more vigilant this time."

"With these women, I'll be tracking them in their rooms. Had I done that to you, I would have known James was so unhappy."

"Don't you think that's taking it too far?" Jane would have definitely not wanted Madame Bai and her minions watching her every move in her private room.

"No, I think it is necessary. What if one of them becomes particularly sad, and I miss it again?" When Madame Bai realized Jane didn't follow, she said straightforwardly, "I don't want any suicides. There hasn't been a suicide among women in the Capital City for over a century."

"Oh," Jane said, surprised she even thought something could get as bad as that. "I don't think," she began but then caught herself and said, "Fine, you do what you think is necessary for now. I understand there are a lot of women here, and I want you to feel that you have the situation under control."

"Thank you. I think most of the women will be fine. Some of them, as you have seen, are a bit more difficult. She brought out a small list, I think Babette will be difficult. She seems to ask a lot of questions and not be content with the standard answers."

"Yes," Jane smiled, "but she is beautiful, so maybe she will find a husband quickly who likes to answer a lot of questions. I hope a lot of them actually find husbands after their first Assembly, and then their new Alliance families can deal with them. There are so many."

"I will pray to the gods for it. Expect my first report at the end of the week. May the gods light your path."

"May the gods show you mercy," Jane replied and then returned to the *Zuin*.

Weeks passed by uneventfully as the *Zuin* tracked space anomalies throughout the galaxy and occasionally had to check in on some of the Alliance's colonies. Adhering to Admiral Jei's advice, Jane had let her hair grow. This morning she looked at her longer brown shoulder-length hair in the mirror and put it behind her ears. She had never had such long hair in her life, and she had never expected to have it now, at the age of 39 years old. She sighed and said out loud to herself, "I'm going to have to figure out how to wear it in a braid like the rest of the Alliance soon."

"Jane, would you like me to recommend a hairstyle?" her mirror asked congenially switching on.

"No, mirror off," she replied, and the little mirror light in her bathroom went off. She had become accustomed to most of the technology onboard the *Zuin*, but some things, like her interactive mirror, still annoyed her.

Jane went into her bedroom, a good-sized room that matched her status as Lieutenant Commander and the Chief Engineer. She took off her silver Alliance ranking jewelry, black Alliance uniform with mandarin collar, and put on her blue silk pajamas with a conservative matching robe she had bought for an extravagant amount of UCs from the Earth Store on the Capital Planet. Jane loved these pajamas not just because they were made of silk but also because they matched her eyes and, in the evenings, when she was going through her messages mostly from humans either from House Human or her friends or family from back home, she could at least feel entirely at home wearing something beautiful and human-made.

Jane sat at her desk and began looking at her personal messages. And there was a VM from Jim still there at the top of her list. She had avoided it for days. As it was titled, 'I'm sorry.'

Jane and Jim had been together for decades, they had known each other since they were toddlers, but when she had been taken by the Alliance, she had told him to move on, that she was never coming home. It had been over one Earth year now, as one Alliance year was roughly 1.3 Earth years, and she knew that he finally believed her. She knew by the title of this message that this was going to be the end. Jane always knew this day would come, and she wanted Jim to move on with his life, but it still didn't make it any easier. She still loved him, and if she could return to Earth, there was no question in her heart that she would be with him. However, the reality was unfortunately that she couldn't return to Earth. The human government had marked them all as traitors after Captain Kara's trial last year. Jane had resigned herself to this Alliance destiny after that judgment, she was not a big enough player in the galaxy to have that ever overturned personally just for her. The human government had made a deal with Admiral Tir and had basically sold them to the Alliance for breeding. However, of course, no one could say that, so it was easier to simply say that all the female crew of the *Dakota* were traitors. She had wondered afterward if James had had a premonition about that as she tried to warn Jane about looking too comfortable in the Alliance before Captain Kara's trial. But it didn't matter. From that moment, Jane's destiny had been altered from a human trajectory to an Alliance one, and she had resigned herself to die alongside Captain Kara somewhere out in the galaxy, on an adventure for the Alliance Empire, and nothing more.

Jane took a deep breath and opened the message from Jim. He was at home in the afternoon, in what used to be their living room. It looked unchanged. A few of the children's things were scattered on the floor, and the throw blanket her grandmother had made unfolded on the sofa. Every time she saw this room across the galaxy, her heart longed to be there, and she regretted all the times she yelled at the children to clean up their toys or for Jim to fold the blanket after he used it. Every time this scene hit her like it was the first time, she realized she wasn't ever going to set foot in that house again, smell those familiar house smells of humans and Earth things, hug her children or kiss Jim. She wiped some stray tears from her eyes and breathed deeply while continuing to watch the message. Jim looked handsome, as he always did, with his sandy blonde hair, longer than it should be, sun-kissed skin with a million lines of laughter and light blue eyes. He wasn't smiling now, though. "Jane. I don't know what to say. I know we've talked about this again and again," he ran his hand through his hair, something she knew he did when he felt guilty for something, "and I said that I would never abandon you, but now, with well over a year gone since Kara's trial and your status as a traitor unchanged… I've come to believe that you're right, and I must accept this situation as it is," he paused, looking guilty. "Let me just come out and say it now," he hesitated. "I've begun seeing someone else."

Jane paused the VM. She had tears in her eyes, even though she had told him to do precisely this it still hurt like a blow to the stomach. She felt like she couldn't breathe. She didn't know how she was going to go on with her own life now. Despite the fact that she had told him to move on over the last year, always saying things like, "Forget me. I'm never going to be allowed back. Don't waste your time or the children's pining for me. I'll be okay, and you'll be okay too. You have got a chance at another romance, don't waste it on a memory of me." But the truth was she had never recovered. For a time, she thought she might die of the pain of separation, but as time went on, she learned how to deal with her pain. She did everything in small steps just like she had done through so many other times in her life, wake up, use the toilet, brush her teeth, dress eat, silently rewarding herself for every action, living for every VM from home. Now this reality of Jim leaving her took her back to square one. She wiped her tears and began the message again.

Jim was looking directly into the camera and said quietly, "And the children know her. It's all gone very smoothly, almost naturally, you could say," he looked incredibly guilty now.

Jane stopped crying and wondered, *Who?*

"Sandra has been so good to us since you have been away," he said sheepishly.

Jane stood up and threw her black ceramic water cup across the room, it shattered, and water went everywhere, "My best friend, Jim?" she yelled at the screen.

"We didn't want to say anything to you until we were certain about our feelings and our plans for the future. We've told the children, and that seemed, well, natural too. Sandra has been here for us. Had it not been for her, Ellie would have signed up to become an Alliance bride to be with you. I caught her trying to go to the Embassy in Paris after she saw the advertisement. It's been terrible times for us all," he wiped some tears away himself, "I know it's difficult to hear, but it was time I let you know that Sandra and I are more than friends. We all miss you so very much, you know that." He paused then and ran his hand again through his hair and said, "I'm sorry. I am so sorry for everything, Jane. And you know, I've cried so much for you and I've no tears left, you took part of my heart with you. I'm half dead inside, but I must live for the children and I need to rekindle what I still have of my heart. Sandra helps with that. I wish things would have been different, but you are never coming back to us. We've both said it and known it, and now we must start living it. I will always love you, Jane Johnson. You were my first everything, and the years we shared were the happiest of my life, but the hole you left, I can't leave it empty and survive. I must do this now for myself and the children, or else I can't go on, and no one understands better than Sandra. It's the thing that is holding us all together, our understanding of the loss of you. All I can say is, I am so sorry, but I hope that we can both begin to find peace again in our lives. I wish you nothing but the best, and I always will."

Jane stood up suddenly but didn't know what to do with herself. She just stood there thinking, *How could my best friend and Jim do this to me? Had they always liked each other? How long had this been going on? How are the kids really taking this?*

Jane's three children were teenagers already. She and Jim had known each other almost their entire lives. Jim and Jane had been approved for three children by the human government from the age of 18 years old when they had applied for procreation privileges. She had their first child at 21 years old, and then one followed every couple years shortly afterward. Her eldest daughter, Ellie was already 20 years old, McKenzie was 18 years old, and Brad was 16 years old. Jim and Jane were both engineers, but Jim worked on Earth building the fleet's starships, whereas Jane had always wanted the adventure of being on them. As a consequence of her choice to be on starships, in her children's lives, she had always been away for long periods of time, but now she was gone forever, a prisoner of the Alliance Empire.

It had been the most difficult for her eldest daughter Ellie. When Admiral Tir had asked for volunteers to return with him, she had tried to join that group of human women bound for the Alliance. Jim and Sandra had to physically restrain her from coming. Even though, Ellie was only 20 years old, she knew the Alliance and how they would have loved the propaganda of Jane's daughter joining her. Jane had cried so much when she had heard that. She had VMed her daughter, Earth technology was not advanced enough to RVMs across the galaxy yet and had told her that she didn't want her to come to the Alliance and be subjected to the same fate she was.

Her daughter had messaged her back, "Mom, I don't know why you act as if it might be the worst thing in the galaxy to go to the Alliance Empire. Are they not the most powerful in the galaxy and a place where everyone is treated well? Are you not still serving in the fleet with Captain Rainer as you always were, but on a much better ship with much more exciting missions?"

Jane was terrified that her daughter would volunteer, as she knew the Alliance planned on having an ongoing program to encourage volunteers from Earth. She wanted to make up lies about the Alliance to deter Ellie from ever coming, but as she was sure all of her transmissions were monitored, she couldn't do it. All she could say in the end was, "Ellie, I want you to have a human life. There's nothing greater or more special than that to a human. Don't be drawn in by the material wealth of the Alliance." Ellie did not react well to Jane's VM at all. She swore at her mother, and they didn't speak for months afterward. It broke Jane's heart, but the last thing she wanted was for her daughter to move there and become a second-class citizen, as all humans were in the Empire. And whether Jane admitted it to herself or not, she didn't want Ellie there because she would be a liability. As Head of House Human, Jane was responsible for a lot of women, adult women, but no one could use any of those women as leverage to get Jane to do something. However, Ellie could be easily used against her.

Jane poured herself a glass of scotch and sat down on the floor, thinking. She always thought better on the floor, it was a bad habit. She drank the scotch slowly and thought about how to handle this blow. She took deep breaths and then finished her drink, stood, and said, "Computer delete all VMs and messages from Jim Hughes."

"Messages and VMs from Jim Hughes deleted," replied the computer.

Jane poured herself another drink and sat back down on the floor. She finished that drink and then opened the internal communications, "Kiu, please come to my quarters as soon as you can."

"On my way," a male voice replied.

Minutes later, Jane's door chimed, and she allowed the Alliance slave artist into her quarters. Kiu wore very little clothing over his muscular grey skin, just a small green cloth covering over his genitals. His thick long black hair was tied back in an intricate braid that hung almost down to his slim hips, and he wore beautiful silver ornaments that made a soft chiming sound as he moved. He was Jane's preferred slave artist for the last year onboard the *Zuin*. At first, she had been repulsed by the Alliance's sexual practices, but after some months of being surrounded by everyone having constant sex, she welcomed Kiu's touch. His expertise in sex and didn't think twice about paying for it.

Kiu came in and as soon as the door closed behind him, he began kissing her. His hands in her short hair, similar to the look of a goddess. His tongue was teasing hers. He could taste the human drink on her tongue, and he reveled in the exoticness of it. His hands ran from her hair down the smooth human clothing that he loved to rub his body against. He pinched and rubbed her unpierced nipples through the silky human fabric. Then he moved one hand between her legs and rubbed her fur until she began to moan. Then he whispered seductively in her ear, "Is this what you need, Jane?"

She brought his lips to hers with her hands and then said breathlessly, "Yes, I need this so much. Make me forget what it was like to ever be with a human man."

This was a frequent request that she had for him. He quickly picked her up and carried her to the bed and laid her down on her back. Kiu then stripped off the little clothing, revealing his perfectly toned and muscular body and said, looking down at her with his erect cock in his hand, "Human men have not been blessed with ridged penises," he stroked his large penis as she watched. "And human men have been cursed with fur all over their bodies," he ran his hands slowly from his penis to his chest, "Alliance men are hairless, beautiful and most of all," Kiu began removing Jane's silky pajamas skillfully as if they were melting off of her, "we love the taste of women on our tongues." When Kiu had removed all of her clothing, he began licking her sex up and down, kissing the inside of her thighs and then finally sucking on her clitoris to make her writhe beneath him. He knew exactly how to make Jane come for him and what she liked. After she came, he flipped her on her stomach and covered her body with his, easing his ridged penis into her wet vagina from behind hitting her g-spot perfectly and said in her ear, "And Alliance penises feel so much better. It's the way the goddess intended men to be, not smooth." He slowly moved in and out as her hands grasped the blankets on the bed in pleasure.

Jane paid for Kiu to stay with her all night. They had sex countless times. It was what she needed, but she knew when he left, it wouldn't be enough. Sex with Kiu was hollow. What she really needed was to forget about Jim and the children for a while, to accept her new situation, but she didn't know how to do that. She so often told the other human women that they needed to accept their new Alliance life. She chided herself then and thought, *I need to do as I say*.

The next weeks were uneventful on the *Zuin*. The fleet was in transit towards a new Alliance colony, Leta, that was having issues. As Jane understood it, the citizens of Leta were refusing to accept Alliance rule. Admiral Tir's fleet was joining Admiral Jei's fleet carrying ground forces and diplomats to suppress the new colony's residents.

When they arrived in orbit around Leta, Jane ate the midday meal at the officer's table with Kara. After discussing the official plans, she told Kara about Jim and Sandra again. She had VMed with her children, and it had been heartbreaking how normal it had all been for them. Jane was so hurt. She had wanted her children to have some revolt against Sandra just taking her place in their house, but there had been nothing of the kind. They were all content.

"You should try this amnesia drug called forget-me-not. It's straight out of *Through the Looking Glass.* It'll make you forget Jim ever existed for a while. Apparently, it's how Alliance people get over things faster." Kara was a decade younger than Jane but had been her commanding officer both in the human and now the Alliance fleet. Not only were they crewmates, but they were friends as well.

"I don't think I need to do that," Jane said adamantly, but actually was already wondering how the drug would work and what that would feel like. Jane didn't like to admit defeat, but she did want something to help her, she felt old and betrayed by Jim and Sandra. She had tried to reason with herself that Sandra would be a good stepmother to her children, and that all the children, Sandra's and Jane's, got along well. And that this solution was the next best thing to her being there. But every time she thought about Sandra in bed with Jim, she couldn't move past it. And since Jim had told her, Sandra had not VMed her, and she had not reached out to Sandra. This silence hurt Jane immensely, but she didn't know what to say to her friend either. Every time she thought about them in bed together, she became irrationally jealous and couldn't help but wonder how long it had been going on.

"It's not forever, just long enough that you can move past this. By the time the memories or feelings come back I must admit I don't know exactly how it works, but by the time it wears off, you'll have already created a better life for yourself here, emotionally."

"That might work if it was a true break up, and I had to see Jim and Sandra around every day, but I'm here, and they are there. It wasn't a true breakup," Jane explained.

Kara just shook her head, "It doesn't matter how the breakup happened. It was a true break up as you were never going to get back together with Jim as you are never going back to Earth. But I guess you still had your fantasy that he would pine away for you forever. Go see John in sickbay, he will explain how the drug works. It's the very least you can do. If you don't want to take it after he explains it then just carry on feeling sorry for yourself, I'll listen. I'm not that cold-hearted," Kara said, thinking that Jane just needed to get over Jim, and she was so tired of this conversation. It was obvious to her that Jim and Sandra had probably been having this relationship for a long time and now that Jane was out of the picture, they waited an appropriate amount of time and then came clean. Kara didn't point out that this is probably why the children were so comfortable with it as well, Sandra had been around a lot even before Jane had been relocated to the Alliance.

"I'm not that bad," Jane said quietly, annoyed with Kara for making her out to be some whiny teenager. She and Jim had been together for decades and had children together.

"I know what kind of coffee Jim prefers. You are terrible. You need to forget about him," Kara said just as quietly. "He's moved on and you need to do the same."

Jane didn't have a response to that. She just nodded and finished her lunch silently. Afterward, she went by sickbay. She told herself if she saw John through the glass and he didn't look busy, she would drop by. If he was working, she would just keep going. *It was fate*, she thought and then berated herself, *You're becoming so Alliance, believing in fate*. The Alliance Empire was steeped in religion, requiring its citizens to pray every day, and as a result, many people believed that the gods controlled all of their destinies. Jane had never been religious, as very few people on Earth believed in religion anymore. Still, when she caught herself thinking about fate like this, she did start to wonder if all this pseudo praying, she was doing was becoming real praying. Sometimes she wondered if she would go to pray one day and truly feel that the gods were genuine, and that prayer mattered.

As Jane casually passed sickbay and looked in, John was there with one of his staff and no one else. She sighed and said, "Fate," under her breath, and went in.

"Jane," John greeted her with a smile. They had served together for many years on different starships in both the human and now Alliance fleet. John had even met Jim and her children on several occasions. "What can I do for you?"

"Can I talk to you privately?"

"Sure," he gestured towards his circular glass office in the center of sickbay. When they were both inside, he closed the door and made sure that what they said, thought and did would be completely private. All of John's Alliance medical staff were telepathic, and he never knew when they were listening to his thoughts. John sat down and looked at Jane, she looked tired, "How are you?"

"I'm fine," Jane lied.

"Okay," John said, not convinced at all that she was fine given her bedraggled appearance, "What's happened?"

Jane began to cry as if being with John alone was all the permission, she needed to let her guard down and after a couple minutes, said, "Jim has found someone else. I've been telling him to do that ever since we were deemed 'traitors to humanity,' but for the last year, he told me he would never stop loving me. But now… he told me a couple weeks ago he found someone new and now I'm completely heartbroken as if I were still there and we were still together. I feel like he is cheating on me, even though he isn't. I can't shake the feeling. I don't know why I can't move on." Jane sobbed into her hands.

John just waited for Jane to continue. He knew she was

a sensible woman and that her partner finding someone else was not the issue necessarily, that there was more.

"What's really difficult is that now he's with my best friend, Sandra. And she's moved into our home, I mean, Jim's home now, with her children and is now a stepmother to my children," Jane sobbed. "I feel like I'm a ghost hanging around for any information about them through VMs, and it's turning me into a poltergeist."

John had not been expecting her to say that and had to hold back a smile at calling herself a poltergeist. "I'm so sorry to hear that, Jane. This situation must be so tough. But let me reassure you that I doubt anything was going on while you and Jim were together. He loved you, and you two had a great relationship. He has waited a long time, all the while you telling him you are never coming back. I know you don't want to hear this, but sometimes when people both lose someone they love, that loss brings them together. I suspect that's what has happened with Jim and Sandra. They have bonded over the loss of you, as difficult as that is to accept."

"I don't know, I've been going over everything in my mind, and I can't stop wondering. Was there a look or comment here or there, and I missed it because I was so enamored with him? We had always been together, he was my first love, my first everything." She started to sob again, "I can't stop thinking about it."

John put his hand on her shoulder to comfort her, "I'm sorry. Our situation is not an easy one. Having to give up all of our relationships back home. Have you spoken to Jim or Sandra about it?"

Jane shook her head, "I've been too upset. I didn't want to say something I'd regret to either of them. It was my fault for putting all of us in this situation, to begin with. I'm the one who joined the fleet and who signed up for the war with the Jahay. I knew the risks. If Admiral Tir hadn't taken us prisoner, we'd all be dead, but now, sometimes, I have to admit, maybe that would've been better. This heartache is killing me. I never understood how someone could die from a broken heart," she put her hand over her heart with her fist and said, "but now I know. I know, and it's the most dreadful feeling I've ever experienced, and I don't know if I can go on." She wiped the tears away and looked down at her boots.

John knew that Jane was not a woman of inaction, "So, what have you been doing about these feelings?"

"I've been sleeping with my favorite slave artist and drinking a lot of whiskey."

"And is that helping?"

"You know it's not, or I wouldn't be here," she snapped.

John smiled at her, sympathetically, "Would you like to set up some psychotherapy sessions to talk through all of this?"

"With you?"

"Would you prefer one of my Alliance doctors?"

"No, I'd prefer no one. Kara told me about an amnesia drug, you could give me to make me forget Jim for a while."

"Forget-Me-Not," John said quietly. "It's not really the rational human way to do it. I'm surprised that you, of all people, are requesting it."

"We aren't on Earth anymore; John and I don't want to suffer through this. Jim and Sandra aren't suffering, and I need to VM my children without making them feel guilty about what their father and Sandra are doing," she broke down crying again. "I'm never going to be there again; I don't want to cause trouble from afar because I'm weak. I want to talk to them freely without this hovering over our conversations like a raincloud. I want them to be able to talk to me about everything. Those VMs are all I have left of them and I can't gamble with them. And I know every time I talk to them now, I'm on the verge of ruining those relationships too."

John looked at Jane, considering, "Fine, I'll do it, but only for a few months, less than a year. I know you, Jane, and you'll want to heal naturally from this, not just wish it away. But I also understand that you don't want to make this anymore awkward for your children or jeopardize those relationships when you're so far away. Maybe it's good you set a healthy foundation with the help of the forget-me-not procedure," John stood up then and escorted Jane out of his office to a padded silver medical bed. "Please," he indicated she should lie down.

Jane wiped the tears from her blue eyes, red from crying and drinking, and followed John to the medical bed where she proceeded to lie down.

"I cannot just erase Jim and Sandra from your life, obviously, but I'll dampen them in your consciousness. You'll know them, who they are to you, and remember everything, but you'll feel nothing towards them, it'll be like I'm putting them in a closed jar on the pantry shelf for a while. You'll know you have those memories, but you won't be able to access them. Do you understand?"

"Yes," replied Jane, not really understanding how all of this would work, but she trusted John with her body and mind.

John nodded to one of his assistants, "I'll need Doctor Ko to help me enter your mind and do this. Just relax." Alliance doctors not only had access to superior medicine but were also mind-readers and manipulators.

Jane suddenly felt cold Alliance hands holding one of hers as John programmed a computer. She saw an image of her brain light up on a nearby transparent medical screen.

"Close your eyes," John instructed gently.

Jane obeyed and waited. She felt nothing except the Alliance doctor's hands on hers.

"Jane," Doctor Ko said softly, "I'm in the process finding these memories and separating your emotions from them. As there are many years, and these are deep emotions, it will take some time. Also, I must warn you while you have this emotional separation, you may react to things differently as many of these memories and emotional experiences shaped who you are now. Be wary of being too optimistic or carefree in the next months as it is one of the most common side effects of altering such a vast number of emotions. And you don't want to make too many drastic decisions while your memories are blocked."

"I understand," said Jane, thinking, it would only be a relief to be too optimistic at this point and not really understanding how that could be a negative side effect. Then she thought about all the wild orgies and things Kara invited her to and decided that, Yes, I can see how one could be too optimistic while under the influence of forget-me-not and then regret it later. Her face turned red just thinking about having an orgy with Kara and Tir.

Doctor Ko whispered, "Now you see, that's what I mean by too optimistic."

Jane would never get used to doctors being able to read minds, so she didn't respond. She didn't like to admit that he was in her mind, seeing all of her thoughts, but she needed him to get better, so it was a necessary evil.

Doctor Ko held Jane's hand as she lay on the medical bed with her eyes closed. As the minutes passed, she could feel the weight being lifted from her shoulders, bit by bit.

"You may open your eyes now," John said confidently after about 40 minutes.

Doctor Ko let go of her hands and looked into her eyes, "Chief, don't forget to be wary of being too optimistic."

Jane smiled, "Don't worry, I won't."

John asked, "How do you feel?"

"I feel fine, thanks. I mean really fine. Can I go now?"

John took in her countenance, "Good. I'm glad to hear you are feeling better already. Go back on duty and let me know if you have any terrible headaches. Don't just solve it with scotch or slave artists as the first things you try. Those both only prolong the process of healing."

Jane gave him a little smile, "I won't." She left sickbay and went to engineering. The rest of her day went well. She felt better than she had in weeks and the best part was that she really couldn't remember why.

That evening Jane had just finished a VM to her eldest daughter Ellie when Kara casually dropped by her quarters.

"Do you want to come in?" Jane asked, surprised to see Kara.

"No, you're coming with me to the *Refa*. Tir is having an informal meeting with Admiral Jei and his first officer."

"Why don't you take Koz?" Jane asked. Koz was their first officer.

"Because you need distraction, and he's busy chasing Rachel around the ship. I hope she finally gives in and the long looks of lust across the bridge can finally come to an end once they are both sated." The whole reason human women had been brought to the Alliance Empire was to solve their demographics issues, their lack of women. And on ship, Rachel and Jane were the last two humans not to be married to someone. Rachel was 28 years old and considered to be the most attractive and outgoing among humans. "I want him to settle. Sometimes when he is just sitting there on the bridge, his mind is a million miles away thinking about her. It's annoying and distracting."

"To be newly in love?" Jane asked.

"Not everyone is so sickening about it."

"No, but most are," Jane said nonchalantly. She suspected Kara did love her husband, but she displayed love differently than most. Jane sighed; she did not want to go to the *Refa* with Kara. Informal meetings in the Alliance fleet translated directly into drinking zota, a clear, strong alcohol, out of puzzle jugs which they found absolutely hilarious. "Thanks for the offer, but I really don't need a distraction right now."

Kara looked at her more closely and asked, "Did you see John earlier today and get the amnesia treatment?"

"Yes, and I was given strict orders by the doctor not to be too optimistic in my decisions. Not to say 'yes' too quickly and I think going over to the *Refa* to drink zota would be out of character. So, I'm going to say, 'no.' Doctor's orders."

"An Alliance doctor tell you that?"

"Yes."

"Come on. This isn't being too optimistic. This is following orders. I don't like it any more than you do. And this is an order from your captain."

Jane knew that Kara wasn't going to be put off the idea now. "Fine, come in while I change," Jane had already taken off her uniform and now she needed to put it back on.

Kara entered Jane's quarters and immediately began looking through her things, as was her curious nature. When she spotted the black box from Admiral Jei on Jane's desk, she immediately asked, "Who's been sending you jewelry?" In the Alliance, it was forbidden for women to buy jewelry, and a woman could only receive it as gifts from men. Jewelry was an essential cultural gift-giving practice in the Alliance between men and women.

"What are you talking about?" Jane asked from the bathroom.

Kara opened the simple black box and exclaimed, "Gods," they had all begun using the expletives of the Alliance, "Who sent you something from Juio's?"

Jane walked out of the bathroom and began putting on her uniform, "What are you talking about?"

Kara held up the hairpin, "This."

Jane smiled and replied casually, "Remember when I told you I saw Admiral Jei at the High Council reception, and he was cross about the length of my hair? Well, the next day, he sent me that."

"And how did you reply?"

"What do you mean? I didn't reply. There was no need to send a reply."

Kara gave her friend a skeptical look, "Why do you think he sent this to you, then?"

"I don't know? To be funny. You know as well as I do, probably better, that he is known to act strangely even by Alliance standards sometimes with his humor."

"Did you post it to your social media account?" Kara asked fingering the expensive hairpin.

"Now, why would I do that?"

"To show appreciation, maybe?" Kara asked her friend sarcastically.

"I'm no young woman who's desperately looking for an Alliance husband."

"Are you sure? One might be looking for you. It certainly looks that way to me."

"Oh stop, you misunderstand," Jane tried to explain,

"If you could have heard our conversation, then you would know he meant nothing by this, but to show me he was serious that if I cut my hair there would be punishment and if I didn't I could wear this lovely hairpin. You know how obsessed this culture is with rewards and punishments. That's all he meant."

"I don't think so," said Kara. "I think he likes you in that courting maybe wife kind of way."

"Well, if he did, he's not shown any interest since then, so I think you're mistaken."

"You still have about a year to marry if you want, you know that, right?" asked Kara. "Men still see you as eligible."

"Admiral Jei is over 200 years old. He had a wife; he has children and grandchildren and probably great-grandchildren. He isn't looking for a human wife. He is looking to entertain himself and I firmly believe sent that as a joke or a prize or whatever and I appreciated it but it's nothing more. Now, let's go if you are really making me do this."

"I am. Let's go." As they walked down the hallway together, Kara commented on Jane's wards in House Human, "I hear there is a niece of the Earth Store owner Frank who wants to open a restaurant in the Capital City?"

"Yes, but you know it's tricky because she wants to work only with Frank. Apparently, she hates her aunt Zelda, Frank's wife, but on planet, Zelda has to approve everything. I have got a VM from Jade I've not opened because I know it's going to be just more complaining about her aunt causing trouble for her."

"I don't get it; they all stand to make a lot of money from the deal."

"I know it's ridiculous. I think Zelda is difficult. Jade is young and wants to try this. She should be more supportive, but I think she has lived in the Alliance too long, and the jealousy has gotten to her. I think she wishes she could also open a restaurant, but Jade is a chef, and Zelda isn't."

"Ah, the jealousy. Do you think that will happen to us?" Kara asked, and Jane knew this was her dry sense of humor. They looked at each other for a second as they continued to walk.

"I can't imagine ever being jealous of you," Jane laughed. "I think I might poison Tir if he were my husband."

Kara laughed, "I believe you would. I think it's good the Contract doesn't make you marry. I'm not sure you could be married to an Alliance man. They can be quite subservient in a way that human men aren't. I think it comes from men being so unequal in Alliance society for so long, they aim to please too much, even now."

"I've got a regular slave artist. It's not like I'm a nun, Kara," Jane said defensively. "I'm not completely ignorant of Alliance men."

Kara laughed, "Your slave artist does exactly what you want. That's what he is paid to do. I mean a real Alliance man. I think their wanting to please would drive you insane. It almost drives me insane."

"I'm not sure what you are talking about?" Jane said with a smile as they got into the transport together. Kara often complained to her how Tir took great pleasure in dressing her like a doll or buying the foods she liked or, most annoyingly, checking that she was okay, especially during her first pregnancy. Human women were used to being equal and taking care of themselves. Human men would never do these things as human women would never do for human men. It was understood that everyone took care of themselves, and it worked well. Of course, people did favors for each other, but that was different. Alliance men were actively trying to please women and it just annoyed Kara.

"You know exactly what I'm talking about. I don't think you could take the constant attention from an Alliance man. It is really overwhelming. I had to stop looking at some of Tir's messages."

Jane laughed, "And how well did that work out?"

Kara smiled, "Did we die?"

Jane just shook her head, Kara had missed some critical messages mixed in with the husband messages while Kara had just begun ignoring all of his messages. "Thankfully, you realized that some of those messages were actual work messages before we did all die."

"Yes, thanks to my loyal squire, who now reads through all of Tir's messages and sorts them for me."

"Poor Zin, I feel sorry for him having to look at all that," Jane said sarcastically.

"I know, I really feel sorry for him too."

When they boarded the *Refa*, no one except Tir's squire, Mux, met them. The *Refa's* corridors seemed quiet as he escorted them to the formal reception room. As they followed him, Jane asked Kara, "Where is Andrew?"

"He's here but asleep now with his nanny," Kara replied. Kara and Tir's son lived between the ships as Kara refused to allow him to be on the Alliance Capital Planet as she didn't trust Tir's family to keep him safe. Andrew, or An, his Alliance name, had one Alliance male nanny onboard the *Refa* and one female human nanny, one of the women taken from the crew of the *Dakota*, onboard the *Zuin*. He was over one year old and looked very Alliance with grey skin and green eyes like his father but had his mother's brown hair and devilish smile. "He'll be with me next week, which suits me just fine. Tir loves having him here right now. I think it's that charming age, and Alliance men just dote on him as he tries to walk on his cute little legs."

Jane smiled, "It's true. Even on the *Zuin*, I see the way they look at him. All the Alliance men seem to all want one."

"It's interesting, isn't it? But we can't forget, they see us as the Lost People and hybrid children as the saviors to their race. Of course, they look at him like that." With their demographics issue, religious Alliance people believed that not only were humans the Lost People but that it was humanity's duty to return to the Empire and save them.

Jane and Kara stopped talking as they entered the formal reception room used for just these kinds of purposes. Five men were in the room already, Admiral Tir, Admiral Jei, their first officers, and Admiral Jei's young squire. There were some black sofas and a gorgeous yellow stone table between them.

Tir stood up to greet Kara and Jane.

"Here they are, some of our finest human officers. Captain Kara and Lieutenant Commander Jane, this is Admiral Jei, Captain Ota, and Captain Pan."

Jane and Kara bowed as was the Alliance custom in the fleet, and then Tir took Kara's hand and guided her to a place next to him.

Jane sat down next to Captain Pan, across from Admiral Jei.

"Chief, we meet again."

"Admiral," Jane replied.

"Have you cut your hair since we last met?" Admiral Jei asked Jane seriously.

"I have not," she replied with the same seriousness. Now Jane looked at him in a new light after what Kara had suggested in her quarters about the hairpin. She looked into his grey eyes and thought to herself, *It's a wonder he looks so good for his age.* His long hair that he kept braided back simply was all silver, but other than a few wrinkles on his face, he looked well-preserved. On Earth, he would have easily been mistaken for a 50-something year old. And, of course, his large and robust body was still in top physical form. Her mind wandered further then, *I wonder if he has nude pictures of himself on social media?* Then she caught herself, *Where is your mind running to? He is the Admiral of the entire fleet. He's no slave artist for you to fantasize over. Kara is wrong in this.*

"Good. You are of the maximum class and must have long hair, not short like a slave, only they may emulate the gods," Admiral Jei replied, taking in this human woman's lovely appearance again. He had tried to forget about her after she had not responded to his gift, but he could not. He needed to see her again, so he had specifically joined this mission to meet her. Tir could have easily calmed this uprising.

Tir brought out a puzzle jug and began filling it with zota. They played as they talked about the uprising on the colony.

Jane noticed that Admiral Jei spent a good portion of the night looking at her and asking her questions, not to do with the uprising or engineering specifically, but about working with Alliance officers and even more personally, how she found the Alliance in general.

"I like it," Jane replied, not altogether honestly. "I'll always miss my human children though," she put one finger over her heart to indicate her sincerity in the Alliance way.

"Of course, but after you marry and have an Alliance child, you'll see them again," Jei answered matter-of-factly. He knew he was pushing this personal topic, but he had already decided in the last half an hour, under the influence of zota, that he would pursue her again. He missed having a wife and why not have a wife that he could explore the galaxy with for a while. Jei was a man who liked new things and adventure. He wanted to know what it would be like to be married to a human and someone like Jane.

Jane shook her head, "If the gods deem it so," which everyone knew really meant, 'That is not happening. Ever.' Jane had become accustomed to the hypocrisy in the Alliance of saying one thing and meaning the complete opposite.

Kara gave her a look, "I hate it when you go completely Alliance, Jane."

Then the women looked at each other and shared a laugh, highlighted by the alcohol.

Jei had his answer then. He loved a good challenge, and in that moment, had made Jane his new conquest. He was of course much older than she was, but he still had a good 100 years left in him, if not more, which would be about equivalent to the rest of her lifespan. His children were already adults, and he had adult grandchildren who were married as well with children. Still, it wasn't unheard of, especially in the past before their demographics problem, for prominent and important men to marry again and have more children if their first wives died prematurely. He looked at Jane now, imagining a hybrid daughter between them.

Jane saw the look in Admiral Jei's eyes and thought, *Are you giving me sexy eyes, Admiral?* She pretended that she didn't notice his heavy gaze on her for the rest of the evening, but she couldn't deny she was a bit wet between her legs because of it. When she went back to the *Zuin* alone, as Kara was staying with Tir, Jei insisted on walking her to the transport himself. He didn't say anything as they walked through the *Refa's* corridors, and she was relieved, as she felt she could have easily said something to prove that she had completely misread the entire situation influenced by the zota and Kara's previous comments. She found it difficult to believe that a man who was so important would be interested in a lowly and young human like herself. Over the course of the evening, she had been impressed by Jei's superior intellect and his patience for Tir who wasn't the quickest robot to download the information. But most of all, she was charmed by his witty sense of humor and the look in his eyes when he looked at her. She knew that when she returned to the *Zuin*, it would be her hand between her legs thinking about him.

Jei didn't trust himself not to say anything ridiculous as he had had more zota than he should have, but he had been determined to figure out the puzzle jug, which he had successfully done, and now they all owed him 50 UCs, and this meant he had a legitimate reason to contact Jane tomorrow. But this came at a cost, as he couldn't say anything charming or witty to Jane now. Something to make her think about him as she was alone in the transport back. He chided himself for not thinking about which was the better win in the long term, as saying something to her now would have been much better than winning at the puzzle jug. As it was, he only said, "May the gods be with you," as she boarded the transport. He thought for a minute she might have been open for a kiss in that moment before she boarded, but he hesitated because he thought it was only his fanciful thoughts that imagined that look.

When Jane returned to her quarters, she put on her blue silk pajamas and then looked through her social media. She was shocked that Admiral Jei had already added her as a connection. She added him back and then looked through his profile. She was fascinated. He was 205 years old, and his wife had died in a transport accident on the Alliance Second Planet 14 years ago. He had two grown sons and one grandson who was also an adult, and a great-grandson and so forth. His home and House Rega were located on the Alliance Second Planet, which she knew very little about. Then she dug deeper. He had no new known jewelry, so she assumed this meant he was never planning on marrying again. If he had been planning on marrying again, he would have added to the collection or begun a completely new one for a specific woman in mind, as was the custom in the Alliance. Jane was not surprised to see that he also had some nude portrait pictures of himself on his social page. She loved this about the Alliance, the men were so proud of their bodies; they all had nude portraits done. She noticed that these images were taken a long time ago though, again another sign that he was not looking for a new wife. She said out loud, "You are just flirty, aren't you, Admiral?" She could not help but think as she looked at the pictures, *And probably still very sexy too with that thick cock.* Jane wondered then if he was up for a fling. *Was that even allowed between officers?* They could get married but flings probably not. But then she reminded herself that they were both considered widows, so that was more grey area. She wondered then; *Would I sleep with him then if he wanted to?* And she put her hand between her legs thinking about him and had her answer.

3

Transferred to the Flagship

Suppressing the Leta uprising was even more easily achieved than first imagined. Once the ground forces set down, the colonists immediately surrendered. Then the diplomats were sent in, and after a week, a suitable compromise was struck. Jane had not left the *Zuin* during that time nor seen Admiral Jei again. He had only sent her a short message to collect his UCs for winning the puzzle jug competition. However, on the day they were supposed to depart, Kara called her to her ready room off the main bridge.

When Jane entered, Kara looked angry, "What is it?"

Kara opened a document so they both could read it across her desk,

3rd day of the 1st week of the year 18906

Lieutenant Commander and Chief Engineer Jane Johnson of House Human is to be transferred from the Zuin *to the* Kzi *by direct order of the Admiral of the Fleet, Jei of House Rega, effective immediately.*

"What?" Jane didn't want to leave the *Zuin*. This was her home with her human sisters. She would be the only human on board the *Kzi* and the only woman. "I'm not going to the *Kzi*," Jane stated.

"First, I believe it's pronounced, 'key' and unfortunately, you have to. I tried to tell Tir that I wasn't letting you go, but he said that Admiral Jei demanded it. Apparently, it's not good to have all of us humans together on one ship according to Admiral Jei. I'm sorry, Jane. I did everything I could, but with the arrangements for my son and everything, I cannot push Tir any more right now."

Jane nodded and said sarcastically, "I guess I'll find out now what it is really like to be on an Alliance ship with real Alliance men."

Kara put her arm around Jane, "I'm sure the slave artists will be just as nice as the ones on the *Zuin*. And sooner rather than later, you'll have your very own puzzle jug and think it's such great fun to not spill on yourself," and then both women laughed at the thought.

"I guarantee you, I will never own a puzzle jug," Jane said defiantly.

"Oh, you just wait and see. You've managed to stay in your human bubble here as Tir has kept us all at a distance, and you've only had the best interactions with Alliance people as Head of House Human. You just wait until you are in the thick of it, and you see how they really are. Then you'll really know what integration means." Kara left off saying, 'And then you might be a more empathetic Head of House as well.' As much as Kara was going to miss Jane, she couldn't deny that this move made sense. Jane needed to be more integrated. And of course, Admiral Jei wanted her on his ship, to keep her close. Neither Kara nor Tir missed the connection between the two, but when Kara had asked Tir if he thought anything would come of it, Tir had only replied, 'I wouldn't think so, Jei is quite content with his slave artist, she even shares his quarters. He might only have a curiosity for Jane that will soon fade once they have each other once or twice.'

Kara walked Jane to her quarters as she packed up her few belongings and then walked her to the transport. They chatted about inconsequential matters the entire time, avoiding this goodbye, "Permission to leave, Captain?" Jane didn't want to make this emotional. She just wanted to go. She knew that was the best, like ripping off a band-aid. If she spent too long talking about this with Kara, she might just break down. Of course, Jane didn't want to be the only human out in the galaxy on a warship full of Alliance men and the only other women, Alliance slave artists, but for the moment she knew she had to do this, so it was better to just do it and get it over with. She knew Kara would make the most of an any opportunity to get her back on the *Zuin.*

"Gods, you know you don't have my permission to go. This is worse for me than for you. Now, I'll have to deal with an Alliance engineer. Message me, Johnson, especially if they treat you horribly, and then I'll push Tir to get you back somehow." Kara gave Jane a tight hug and said quietly, "I don't know what I'll do without you. Now go."

Jane tapped Kara's shoulder, "Same, my dear friend. I'll miss you." Then she turned and boarded the transport. When she arrived on the *Kzi*, Admiral Jei's first officer was there to meet her.

"Lieutenant Commander Jane of House Human may the gods be blessed, welcome on board the *Kzi.* I'll escort you to your quarters, and then the Admiral wants to see you directly," Captain Ota said.

Jane greeted him in the set reply but said nothing more, so they walked through the ship's corridors quietly.

She was not happy about this, and she could feel that neither was he. When they reached her quarters, Captain Ota showed her in. They were much sweeter than what she had had on board the *Zuin*, and she was surprised, but then it was that fact that made her wonder for just a minute if her quarters were nicer because the *Kzi* was the flagship. But then she reconsidered that thought when she thought about Admiral Jei's somewhat questionable behavior when she last saw him, and he had walked her to the transport.

Captain Ota watched the human named Jane intently. He could not decide if she had some part to play in this. If she had seen an opportunity to use witchcraft on their Admiral for some kind of powerplay. He didn't trust humans, and he definitely didn't trust this one. She was Captain Kara's confidant, and everyone knew Captain Kara must be a witch. Although, Captain Ota didn't think Jane looked like a witch as opposed to Kara, whose beauty could have only been achieved through witchcraft. Jane looked plain to him except for her different colors, which he didn't find necessarily attractive.

"Captain Ota, this must be a mistake, I've been demoted in rank, these quarters are well above my station. I don't want any special treatment here." Her new quarters consisted of a large bathroom with an artificial light that mimicked natural light, as if one was on a planet with natural light shining through, a small sitting room with a desk and a large bedroom that had a beautifully set window to the galaxy outside. These were definitely quarters for someone with a much higher rank than she held.

Ota looked her in the eyes for the first time and realized that she probably had no part in this. That this tryst was all the Admiral's doing. He had seen the way they had been looking at each other the other week and had just assumed that Lieutenant Commander Jane had maneuvered her way on board the *Kzi*, but now he felt by her demeanor and that question that she probably hadn't been looking to move off the *Zuin*. "No, the Admiral himself assigned these quarters to you. He said that you needed the extra space as you had more duties than just engineering, as you were the Head of House Human, and that human women like to do something called 'yoga' exercises." Ota left off, 'And the Admiral would not want the woman he desires to be seen practicing swords with the men.'

Jane looked at Captain Ota disbelievingly, "Yes, we do like yoga, and this is more than enough space. But this is too much. I don't want to be given anything special because I'm human."

"You don't have a choice. You are human, and these are orders. And you must be treated differently as well because you're the first woman ever to serve on the *Kzi*."

Jane was annoyed, "I'll speak to Admiral Jei about it myself. Now, if you could take me to him?"

"Yes," Ota said, gesturing they leave.

Jane left her bags in her assigned quarters and walked silently with Captain Ota through the massive ship to Admiral Jei's ready room off the main bridge. His ready room was at least twice the size of Captain Kara's on the *Zuin* and much more impressive. Jane felt for the first time now what an honor it was to be on the Alliance Empire's flagship and thought that maybe she should just close her mouth and be grateful for what had been given to her.

"You may leave Captain Ota," Jei said immediately upon their arrival.

Captain Ota nodded and left.

Jane looked at Admiral Jei, behind his desk, and said,

"Gods have granted me this gift, Lieutenant Commander Jane of House Human reporting for duty as requested."

Jei looked up at her face and after a few too many seconds of taking in her appearance said, " Thank the gods. Your probationary period begins now. We have never had a human or a woman onboard as crew, I hope your quarters are satisfactory?" He couldn't help but add the last sentence. It was so wrong, but so was she. She was Head of a House and a woman, he needed to show her that respect even though they were not on the planet. It was an awkward situation. Jei put those thoughts of rank aside for a second as he looked at her and relished the way she looked in her uniform. He could just see the hint of some human curves underneath the black fabric.

"Everything is more than satisfactory. Too satisfactory, in fact. I think I have been given the wrong quarters as they do not match my rank."

"They are yours. You are a human woman, and I want you to have space to do your human exercises."

"That is very thoughtful, but…"

He cut her off with his hand through the air impatiently. "I won't hear any more about your quarters. I set them, and they will remain. Now report to engineering at once. This isn't a human ship, and I won't have anyone lazing about."

Jane gave the Admiral an Alliance bow and then left. As she found her way to engineering through the massive ship, she wondered if everything that had transpired before between them, all the romantic looks, had only been in her head. But she couldn't mistake the way he had just taken in her figure as if she was the first woman he had seen in a century. However, in typically Alliance fashion, his manner and words conveyed the exact opposite. Jane smiled to herself, thinking, *These people are so strange. They love to be contradictory.*

In engineering, she found the Chief engineer and was given some simple tasks to complete. Jane was introduced to everyone and given a schedule. It was all very typical except that it wasn't long before she realized that this would be the first time, she was actually working with Alliance men. Not the men that were so intimidated by Tir, they hardly spoke to her. No, these men were respectful, almost too much so, but also real. They laughed with each other and were annoyed with one another. They were like brothers, and she questioned for the first time as well, *Who really does run the Empire? The men out in the galaxy or the women at the Alliance Empire's core?*

The weeks went by without incident on the *Kzi*. Not surprisingly, Admiral Jei ran a very tight ship. She had seen him only a few times on his rounds through engineering, and he had not acknowledged her at any time. But Jane knew he had read the report her superior had sent about her progress of integration and skill as he had marked it as such, so her probationary period aboard the *Kzi* had ended. She was truly a part of the crew now, and she couldn't help but wonder why he brought her onboard, *Was it really for integration only?*

Report: Jane Johnson of House Human
3rd day of the 20th week of the year 18906
Lieutenant Commander Jane: Engineering

Performed her new duties well and has adhered to all Alliance Fleet rules and regulations. She has been particularly creative when problem-solving and, overall, an excellent addition to the team.

Socially, Jane was slowly getting to know her fellow crewmates, and she had even shared a meal a couple of times with Captain Ota and her commanding officer Chief Hsu. The few officers that were married told her about their wives and even a couple about their sons. For the first time, Jane actually felt the sorrow in the Empire about the demographics issue. She was meeting real men, most of whom, would never have an opportunity for a wife or children, and had not only resigned themselves to their lonely fate but were surprisingly not bitter, and even more surprisingly, these men still had it in them to be happy for those who were lucky enough to marry and have children. Jane supposed it was their deep religious beliefs that allowed them to justify their solitary fates in this way.

However, of course, there were a couple men that she kept her distance from. She didn't need to be telepathic to know that they were trouble. One, in particular, worked in engineering, his name was Lieutenant Nun, and he constantly was asking her inappropriate questions about her relationship with Jim on Earth and her children. Jane was always civil to him, but she never wanted to meet him alone or give the impression that their relationship could be anything other than professional.

Most evenings, Jane was busy messaging or VMing with the unmarried women from House Human, whether it be official documentation or just being moral support, they took up a lot of her time when she was off duty. And when she had time, she would VM her children or Kara. And that was it. Her life was continuing, and as the weeks passed, she really did start to believe that what she saw in Admiral Jei, the flirting in orbit around Leta, all those weeks before, had been just fun and meant nothing romantic, as, beyond her quarters, he had shown her no preferential treatment.

The Chief Medical Officer on the *Kzi* was a different story entirely, though. His name was Doctor Rea of House Edda. He, like the Admiral, was originally from the Second Alliance Planet and was very keen to talk about their home planet to her, their variations in culture and clothing, all of which Jane found very interesting as she thought the entire Alliance Empire was the same, well at least as far as the original Alliance planets went. And it was through Rea that Jane got to casually meet more officers of her rank and get to know typical Alliance men. And after a few months, she decided that maybe the Admiral was right in transferring her to the *Kzi* to mix up humans in the fleet to see how well it would all go.

One night Jane was invited to play a gambling game with some of the officers, and she decided to go. She felt that she was really beginning to make friends. And Jane knew the game so she was confident that she wouldn't make a complete fool of herself. It was a kind of card game, which was mainly just luck anyway, but there would be lots of drinking of zota and banter, so she wanted to go and be social. Especially since Rea was hosting it in his quarters, and they had become fast friends.

Jane showed up and handed Rea a bottle of Italian red wine when he answered the door. She often kept small Earth things such as wine or fruit preserves to give as little gifts for special occasions such as these.

"Is this any good?" Rea asked jokingly. All Alliance people had heard that human-made food and drink was superior in taste to their own.

"Why don't we open it and find out?" Jane joked. She was happy about this comradery. She missed Kara in a way, but she felt she had a more honest friendship with Rea, which was surprising as he was an alien.

Rea opened the wine and poured two black ceramic cups full.

"What about the rest of us?" Ota complained, and Rea filled three more cups, they were five in total.

"To our human officer and the delicious wine, she brings," Ota made a toast, and they all followed suit to Jane.

Jane just nodded and then took a seat at the table where the cards were already out. There was no food as it was not during a designated mealtime, so it went against the gods to eat now.

Rea sat down at the table and began to deal.

And everyone began to talk.

After multiple rounds of cards and Jane almost losing all of her UCS that she had set aside for gambling beforehand, she announced, "Well, that is it for me, I'm out."

"Why don't you bet with something other than UCs?" Ota suggested.

"I'm not taking off my clothes," she said, almost offended.

"Gods, no, please don't, " replied Ota offended she thought he meant that. "I meant how about you bet with what you know about the women in House Human."

"What do you mean?" Jane was confused.

"Well, you know them. We only can see their pictures and read their dull biographies. And you know us. I want to know about some of them in particular, and you can tell me, then I can make a judgment whether or not I should take a holiday to attend an Assembly to meet one," Ota explained.

Jane actually didn't know if she was forbidden to talk about the unmarried women in her care. Madame Bai had never mentioned it. However, from what she knew about Alliance culture and the way they wanted to gamble for information, she suspected that this was at best a grey area and, at worst, forbidden on one level or another. As of course, in the Alliance, there were levels of forbidden. But she knew these men to be respectful, so far, and thought of some women who would be happy to be talked up to these men, so she was going to agree, in five more minutes, that is. "I don't know, it doesn't seem right to share what I know of these women. I'm their guardian."

Rea looked at her and smiled devilishly. He could read her mind easily and knew her game.

"Look, Jane, I'll give you 10 UC if you just tell me about Jade," Ota threw out the offer quickly.

Jane was surprised that Ota wanted to know about her. He seemed way too snobby to want a chef. Someone who was actively trying to be in the middling class, which the Empire had severe reservations about. Jane had already had to fill out documents and send messages regarding her plans. Apparently, the ambassadors on Earth had agreed to her restaurant, but the High Council had not. "Ota, I don't think she would want me to say anything."

"Twenty UCs," said Rea just to make things interesting. He didn't want to know anything about the human women. He just wanted to see how far Ota would go to find out about this Jade, who wanted to open a restaurant. And he was surprised as he thought Ota would rather die than take a human wife, or so he had said last year.

When it got up to 50 UCs, and Jane saw the credits go into her account, she said, "Jade is a lovely young woman who is actually a niece or great-niece to Frank who owns the Earth Store on the Alliance Capital Planet. She is hoping to open a restaurant in the Capital City, where she will serve Earth food. She is currently not courting anyone and does not want to until her restaurant is up and running, or that is what she has told me anyway."

"She cooks, like a slave?" Ota asked rhetorically. "She's not allowed to cook," Ota replied to himself, astonished. "She is of maximum class."

Jane shrugged her shoulders, "You wanted to know about her, and now I've told you."

"Tell me, what kind of jewelry does she like?"

Jane laughed, *Why are Alliance women obsessed with jewelry so much so that that is all Alliance men think about when wooing a woman?* "I'm going to give you a small piece of advice, as she is a chef, I would give her something food-related. I think she would appreciate that more."

Ota looked at Jane in disbelief, "No, jewelry. Women always want jewelry, and then I will know how she feels about me, whether she wants to get to know me better or not at all. What could she do with a dish or cutlery? She cannot show that off to her friends? She cannot show me whether or not she appreciates my attention or not with those things."

Jane shook her head, "Human women are different. I think you should buy her some nice Alliance dishes or something along those lines."

"But how would I know she liked them or me? Like I said, she can't wear them," Ota wasn't a stupid man, but he was one that followed the rules. And he liked the rules of courting, it was all obvious. "How do human men court women if every woman is different in what she wants?"

Jane smiled, "You forget we are equal, and we don't really court each other, we are much more informal, and things just happen naturally."

"What gifts did your husband give you?" Ota asked not fully understanding what Jane was trying to tell him about gift-giving among humans.

Jane paused. It was such a simple question, but she couldn't remember. She knew that she knew, but she couldn't access the memories. Then Rea put a hand on her arm, and she could feel herself relax. He was using his telepathic influence to calm her anxiety about not being able to remember the memories.

"Jane, it's the forget-me-not, that is why you can't remember right now. Don't worry, you still have all of those memories, they are just stored away right now. Maybe it's best to call it a night."

Jane nodded, "Thank you very much for a wonderful evening, and now I'm going to sleep." On her walk back to her quarters, unfortunately she ran into Lieutenant Nun in the empty corridor. They were all alone, and he turned around after they passed and began to follow her. He didn't speak to her though, and she wanted to give him the benefit of the doubt and just assumed he forgot something. Rape was a capital offense in the Alliance.

When Jane reached her quarters and the door unlocked, she went in quickly, and regrettably, he followed. Before she could scream, his strong hand was covering her mouth. She kicked him hard, and she didn't stop kicking him even though it didn't seem to be doing any good. He was a great deal taller and much stronger than she was. Jane knew she couldn't give up. He was a sick man as there was no reason to rape on a ship carrying slave artists unless there was something psychologically wrong with you. She assumed he was after sex because if he had wanted to kill her, he could have easily made something up and challenged her to a duel and have done it legally as she was terrible with a sword. And even though it was illegal on any of the Alliance planets to challenge a woman to a duel or for a woman to challenge a man, as she was an officer onboard a warship, she was fair game as this was a grey area and not one she thought any man, not even Admiral Tir or Admiral Jei would protect her from.

"Humans aren't equal to us, you are lower than slaves, and you should be used as such," he spat in her ear. "We should be keeping you all like the animals you are and just use your for medical experiments. You shouldn't be here among us. You're filth."

Jane didn't stop struggling. She was reaching for her sword, but he obviously knew that and got it away before she could grab it. Then he grabbed his own sword and put it to her throat, and she stopped moving. She was dead still. Waiting. The punishment for rape was death. Jane assumed that if he raped her, he would kill her, so there would be no witness to it. *It would be such a hypocritical Alliance thing to do*, she thought, *But there was no doubt that dead women, can't say for certain if it was a rape.*

When Nun didn't speak, Jane thought about calling security over the internal communications but then thought, *No, he would definitely kill me then as the chance a security guard is right outside my door at this exact moment is nil.*

Finally, Nun ordered, "Take off your clothes and stand over there," he motioned to a couple steps away next to an empty wall. He pushed her roughly when she didn't move. She used that opportunity to pick up her sword, and again he quickly took it from her and threw it behind him. "Don't do that again you stupid little animal. You can't use such a sophisticated weapon, you're nothing. You're not the Lost People. You're a manipulative group of barbarians trying to infiltrate all that we have accomplished. Humans probably started this demographics problem, to begin with. You all deserve to be punished and kept in cages."

Jane couldn't help it, she had to say, "I'm so glad that someone sees reason, and realizes that we aren't the Lost People. It's just too bad you are a raging lunatic." He seemed surprised by her comment, and she didn't waste the opportunity, Jane charged him violently with her whole body and at the same time, yelled, "Computer, call security!"

Nun grabbed the back of her hair and was about to kill her with his sword when a security guard burst in and easily tackled him before he could cut her throat. She escaped with just a small nick on her neck and probably some bruises.

More security guards followed and looked at Jane as she just stood there shaken. "He followed me into my quarters and was trying to rape me," she explained.

"Liar," Nun countered. "She invited me in and then called you. She is purposely trying to get me in trouble. We all know that humans are the most notorious liars in the galaxy."

One guard said, "Lieutenant Commander Jane, you stay here. We will notify you of what will happen from here."

The other guards just nodded and left with Nun between them.

Jane reckoned that the guards believed her over him. Not only was she of a higher rank, but she was a woman, and a woman's word was worth twice as much a man's in the Empire.

Jane went into her bathroom and splashed some cold water on her face and said out loud, "I can't believe that just happened."

Then her mirror lit up and said, "Jane, are you okay? Your heartbeat is over 100 beats per minute. Should I alert the doctor on duty?"

"No, I just had a scare."

"Would you like some medication to calm you?"

"What do you have?"

"Valium," the mirror replied.

"Mirror, you have been holding out on me. Why didn't you ever tell me before?"

"Your heart rate has never been so high."

"Give me the valium," Jane said, and the mirror dispensed the medication. She put on her pajamas, made sure her door was secure, and tried to sleep. But it was difficult. She kept waking up to nightmares of Nun's face pressed against hers, saying terrible things about humanity. The worst part about it was, what he said played on her deepest fears about the Empire. Fears that she tried not to think about. But she had to admit, she and many of the others dreaded the day that human women would be infected with the same issue that was affecting the Alliance women's fertility and then what would become of them? Would they be all sent to a special place to live out their days? Stripped of their jobs and titles? Alone in the galaxy as the human government had made it clear that any woman who volunteered would not be allowed back to Earth as a citizen. And Jane, as the rest of the women from the *Dakota* were deemed traitors anyway, so she could not return either. These were all frightening scenarios that she couldn't shake easily even with the medication.

The first thing the next morning Jane was called into a meeting with Admiral Jei, Captain Ota, Doctor Rea, two of the security guards from last night, and Lieutenant Nun. She had not had a chance to see the doctor, and she had bruises all over her arms and a cut on her neck from Nun, so Jane was looking forward to hearing him trying to convince everyone else that she invited him into her room.

Captain Ota spoke first, "Lieutenant Commander Jane, last night you and Lieutenant Nun were involved in an altercation. As this happened in your quarters, we would like to hear your version of the event first."

Jane stood up, "I was walking back to my quarters after playing cards at Doctor Rea's quarters and I passed Lieutenant Nun in the corridor. He was going the opposite direction as I was, but when he passed me, he turned and followed me. I didn't say anything to him, giving him the benefit of the doubt. However, when I entered my room, he aggressively pushed in behind me. Then he put his sword to my throat and told me to take off my clothes. I took my chances and called for security, and that is when they came in and saw him ready to kill me."

Captain Ota then looked at Lieutenant Nun, "Now you tell us how you think this happened."

"I was walking back to my quarters late last night when I passed Lieutenant Commander Jane. It was obvious she had been drinking a lot, and as she has had no lover onboard, she begged me to go back to her quarters with her for sex. I didn't want to, but when I resisted, she got out her sword and began hitting me." He showed everyone scratch marks she had left on various parts of his arms, face, and neck. "I was only trying to get some control when security came in. You know how I feel about these humans. I would never want to touch one let alone rape one. I was trying to disengage myself from this animal human when security came in. I didn't call security myself because I thought I could deal with a human woman and didn't want to get Lieutenant Commander Jane in trouble. She can't help that she has no control over her primal instincts, humans are just less evolved, and she was drunk."

Ota nodded at the security officers, and the larger one spoke, "When we came in Lieutenant Nun had Lieutenant Commander Jane in such a position, he could have killed her in seconds. I didn't have the impression that he was trying to calm the situation. And when we led him to the brig to cool off, he told us a different story than what he has said here."

"I was drinking," Nun tried to defend himself. "I was upset that I was taken to the brig and not that animal. She was the one who started this, begging me to have sex with her. It was disgusting."

"Thankfully, we also have the camera from the corridor to back up or discredit both of your stories," Ota motioned to a 3D screen that appeared between them all, and they all watched the 30 seconds when Nun passed Jane in the corridor and then proceeded to follow her and quickly push into her room behind her. There was no evidence that she even spoke to him. When the clip finished, Ota said, "Now, let the gods decide, and let the sentence be passed," and looked directly at Jane.

Jane didn't know what she was supposed to do or say. After a full minute of silence, she asked, "Am I supposed to name the punishment, and if so, what is the punishment for attempted rape?" She knew that most personal disputes were handled by individuals, but she had never considered that she would have to decide his punishment this morning.

Admiral Jei spoke up then, "Everyone leave except for Lieutenant Commander Jane."

Everyone obeyed quickly, the security guards holding on to Lieutenant Nun.

Then Jei looked at Jane, "It's within your right to kill him with your sword. It's clear that he was trying to rape you. This is one of the worst offenses in the Empire. Usually onboard it is between two men and the sentence is death for the perpetrator, but this is even worse as you are a woman."

Jane listened and felt that it didn't matter that she was a

woman, rape was rape. However, she wasn't going to bring that up now. "I don't think death is necessary, is it?" Jane didn't think that she could kill anyone without being in the heat of the moment. Last night, when Nun was ready to kill her, she probably could have killed him, but now in the light of day, she didn't think she had the gumption kill him execution style.

"No?" Jei asked incredulously.

Jane looked into his grey eyes and asked, "What is the least punishment?"

"You can do anything you like."

"Anything? I can come up with anything between nothing and death?"

Jei nodded.

"I don't want to kill anyone," she admitted.

Jei looked at her patiently, waiting for her to realize why she needed to kill Nun. He would wait. He didn't want her to make a mistake in this and so he was prepared to lead her to the right punishment no matter how long it took to convince her to do it. Jei was furious that this had happened on his ship and not only that, to his human. When Jane had come into the room with bruises on her face and neck, he had wanted to kill Nun himself right then, but that was not the way justice was carried out. And this was Jane's justice it had to be, or other attacks would follow.

Two minutes passed and then Jane said thoughtfully, "I have to kill him, don't I? Or he will kill me."

Jei nodded, "Yes. He knew the consequences when he attacked you."

"Can I use my gun?"

"No, you must use your sword and do it publically here onboard. Today."

"Today?"

"Yes, and soon."

"Why?"

"So that no one begins to question the outcome of this tribunal. Are you ready?"

Jane looked at Jei as if she was in a nightmare and he was her guide trying to lead her through the chaos, "I don't know. I've never directly killed anyone not in a fight or during war and never with a sword."

"You can do this. Just think of how sad your children would have been to know you died because of this. He would have raped you and then killed you. Of this I have no doubt. Let your children's grief give you the strength of what must be done. Let the gods guide your hands." Jei motioned for her to go out where everyone was waiting and just nodded to Ota. Then they all walked towards the gymnasium.

Alliance gymnasiums were sacred places. Onboard the flagship Alliance Warship *Kzi* it was a regular place of worship while the men trained to the god of justice and the god of war. There was artificial candlelight along the stone walls and streaming banners proclaiming the glory of the Empire. In each corner was a statue of a god; justice, war, honor, and humility respectfully. On the stone floor, there was nothing but some simple lines marking the area of fair play.

Jane waited in the center of the stone gymnasium alone while the security guards brought Lieutenant Nun in and placed him in the middle of the gymnasium. His sword was taken away from him. He was on his knees, begging now, "She did it. That filthy human female is lying. Mark me, humans will be the death of the Empire. They are filth of the galaxy and you have invited them into your beds. You can't let her kill me. Admiral listen, she used witchcraft, she's used it on you. That's why you lust after her dirty body. It's witchcraft!"

Admiral Jei thundered from the sidelines with the rest of the witnesses, "Lieutenant Nun of House Zioz you have been found guilty of attempted rape and murder. Lieutenant Commander Jane of House Human has sentenced you to death by her own hand which will be guided by the gods. Prepare for your punishment and thank the gods for guiding our hearts and hands today." He paused and then added, "And it was proven that the human women have used no witchcraft to seduce Alliance men as the gods demonstrated with the duel involving the human, Doctor James of House Vo. To speak otherwise is blasphemy. Now prepare to meet the gods and explain your misdemeanors to them. Your time with the living is over."

Jei looked at Jane. His grey eyes boring into hers, giving her confidence. He nodded, and she realized she was hesitating. She drew her sword with shaky hands. She had never even drawn blood with it, and now she needed to kill a man with it. She remembered Jei's words to her only minutes before, 'Think of how sad your children would have been to know you died because of this.' It was true. She would have died had Nun succeeded. Jane took a few steps closer and then stood to the side of Nun.

Nun was crying like a child and shaking.

His crying had the opposite effect on her senses, though, as she only thought of her own children then and swung her sword with all her strength. However, as she had never killed anyone with her sword, she didn't strike hard enough or in the right place. It didn't work as well as she had thought, blood went everywhere when she hit his neck, but he wasn't decapitated and didn't die immediately which was disappointing as she wanted this over as quickly as possible. All the men watching gasped when she didn't manage to decapitate him completely. It was obvious that he was going to bleed to death, and it was going to take a few minutes. Jane didn't know if she should strike again, so she didn't. She thought she might just make it worse and was unsure if she could speed it up. She didn't want to look like a crazy murderer just striking him again and again with her sword. So, she just stood over Nun and watched the blood drain out of his body, and the life fade from his eyes as he spat out insults about humanity. Jane had such a strange thought go through her mind at that point, *I've given life through more blood and pain than this one I've taken. I felt so much love in those moments I brought life into the galaxy, equal to the indifference I feel now taking life from this man.* After Nun died, the security guards picked his lifeless body up, and she was told she could report to duty now. It was so ordinary it was surreal.

Jane spent the rest of the day in a daze, not believing that in the last 12 hours she was almost raped and even more shockingly that she killed the man who had attempted to rape her with a medieval weapon as was her right and what was expected of her within the Alliance justice system.

After she was off duty, she went directly back to her quarters, poured herself some scotch, and VMed Kara, the only other woman who would understand this strange situation. Luckily, Kara was available for a live chat, and she accepted Jane's call.

"Day drinking?" Kara asked wondering what was wrong with her friend. Jane was never one to drink during the day unless something was terribly wrong.

"I've had a dreadful day, no, a horrendous 15 hours. I just got off duty, so it's not truly 'day drinking.' It just happens to still be day."

"What happened?" Kara was wondering if it was something with her children or Jim.

"Someone tried to rape me, and I killed him this morning before my shift," Jane just blurted out.

"With your gun? In a struggle?"

"No, with a sword for Alliance justice. Publically," Jane picked up his sword off her bed and pointed to his House's emblem on it. "And now I have his sword to remember the justice I served today by the gods' hands." She said the last bit sarcastically. Jane was traumatized by what she had done.

"Well, he did try to rape you, didn't he?"

"Yes, and he had his sword to my throat."

"So, justice was served. Thanks be to the gods," Kara replied seriously. She didn't believe in the Alliance gods, but she did prefer their methods of justice. It was quick and sensible as long as you were good with a sword.

"Yes, let the gods be praised, indeed," Jane replied sarcastically. "I feel like I'm someone else. Someone I don't know. I executed a man this morning with a sword. I've never felt so alone in the Alliance as I did this morning."

"Were you one of those kids that stopped drinking milk when you found out it came from a cow?"

"Possibly, I don't remember."

"In the Alliance, you have to make your own justice, and you did. If you had let him go, he would have attacked you again and probably killed you. Or even worse, you would have shown that you are weak, and then by association that humans are weak, and then more men would have begun attacking you and other human women because they would know you would do nothing. Don't worry Jane, you did exactly the right thing and you're going to be okay. People die every day and he tried to rape you. He was not innocent."

"I just can't believe I killed that man and then went straight back to work as if it was nothing."

"Did you expect to get the day off? And come on, women have babies and then get on with their lives, why should executions be any different? It's all life and death. Both happen every day. I'm surprised you're so melancholic about this."

"It's just different doling out the justice by your own hand rather than having someone whose job it is to do just that. I know he was a criminal through my own experience, but it was just strange. I don't know what I expected to happen actually."

"Did you expect to receive a certificate and the day off?"

"Stop now."

"Stop yourself, you're being a little ridiculous. Good riddance to him. What kind of man tries to rape a woman when there are prostitutes on board the ship anyway? He was obviously very disturbed."

"He said he hated humans and that we weren't the Lost People."

"Did you agree with him?"

"Yes, and he was so shocked that is how I managed to not die."

"Hilarious," Kara laughed. "Thanks be to the gods for the racist rapist."

Jane wasn't laughing, "And that's not even the worst part. I tried to behead him with my sword, and it didn't work, so he died in a pool of blood in the gymnasium over about ten minutes while we all watched."

"Remind me never to be executed by you. Who taught you that?"

"No one, I saw it in that play about Anne Boylen," Jane said defensively. She wanted to add, 'I'm not killer,' but she would never say that to Kara. It was Kara's strength that had already saved them more than enough times because she never hesitated to kill.

"In the play, that man was supposed to be an expert executioner. The king was doing his wife a favor by using him rather than the usual axe man. But you're a novice with only the gods know what kind of sword? Is it still that piece of crap Madame Bai gave us?"

Jane nodded.

"No wonder. Next time get some tips first, so you don't just watch the person bleed out over several minutes. And definitely invest some UCs in a new sword."

"There won't be a next time," Jane replied quickly.

"Oh, never say 'never' to death, murder and hypocrisy in the mighty Alliance Empire."

Jane heard Andrew scream in the background, "How is Andrew?"

"Oh, you know, he misses his daddy and doesn't want to be with humans right now. It's charming."

"It's just a stage," Jane tried to say comfortingly, not missing having a toddler around herself. "Everything is a stage. He will grow out of this one and then it will be something else. In a couple months it will be all about mommy."

Kara didn't want to talk about Andrew, he was the only thing that made her vulnerable. And she felt that Tir was using Andrew against her and it was working. Kara didn't want to share that with anyone, not even Jane, "I've got to run. Rest easy now. You did the right thing. No one has the right to rape human women. I'll message you later."

Two weeks later the *Kzi* was back at the Alliance Capital

Planet for the most important religious festival in the calendar year. Admiral Jei was being honored by the High Council for his conquering of new colonies and his devotion to the Empire in general. As a result, the *Kzi* was scheduled to remain in orbit around the Capital Planet for a week during the religious festivities. This suited Jane as she had a lot to do with her new human charges, and she would like personally to check in on them. However, before she could disembark at Space Port One, she was surprisingly met by two guards with Alliance uniforms but with purple details that marked them as being from the Second Alliance Planet.

"Jane of House Human?" one of them asked her as she tried to get past them.

"Yes?" she wondered if they were going to ask her directions or if they were looking for Admiral Jei as he was from the Second Alliance Planet.

"We are your security guards while you are on the planet. I'm Gio, and this is Sra."

"Oh, I think there's been a mistake. I don't need any guards."

"No mistake. Admiral Jei gave us orders. We are to stay with you at all times," Gio said.

"That's really not necessary," the last thing Jane wanted was Admiral Jei's personal guards trailing her every move.

"Orders are orders," Sra replied gruffly. "You must speak to Admiral Jei if you want our orders changed."

"Fine," Jane said, and found a console on a corridor wall and to her dismay, found that Admiral Jei had already gone down to the Capital Planet. Jane looked at her IC. She could call him, but she didn't want to sound ungrateful, or be difficult, so she put her IC back in her pocket and admitted defeat. She was reminded then of what Kara told her about Alliance men wanting to take care of women too much.

Jane walked back over to the two guards waiting for her, "The first stop we must make is here to see the Chief Medical Doctor."

The guards nodded and followed her silently.

Jane began walking through Space Port One, when she saw a passing doctor, she stopped her. "Excuse me, Doctor. I'm looking for Doctor Anu, is she here today?"

The Doctor was surprised to be stopped by Jane. "Lieutenant Commander Jane, yes, she's in the medical screening area."

Jane thanked her, "May the gods be great" and changed directions to go to the medical screening area. Once there, she found Doctor Anu in her office. Jane stood at the door, "The gods have been great today that we are both here at the same time."

Doctor Anu was not surprised to see Jane as they had arranged this meeting, but to all ears, it should look and sound like a chance meeting, "Yes, the gods' present many great opportunities for the humble, come in and close the door."

"Have you completed the initial phases of your work?" Jane asked, seriously not wanting to waste any time.

"Yes, but it took longer than I thought because of Doctor Drusilla, I mean Doctor James, Oh, you know who I mean. She began asking too many questions, and then other people began to take an interest as well."

"And the human women? They said nothing to me when I met them right after you had released them from quarantine."

"Good. When I explained it to them initially, they assumed it was all just part of the process of them coming here voluntarily. They all signed the compromises and went through with the procedures. I believe they could also see the logic in it. Afterward, their memories were all erased. They believe they had caught a galactic virus as you know. Don't worry, our skills at changing memories are unparalleled"

"And James?"

"You know she lied about her age?" Anu asked trying to change the subject a little. To sway the argument in her favor.

"What do you mean?" Jane asked.

"Drusilla was only 20 Earth years old when she came here. She is not even eligible to be married to Doctor Ket now by Alliance years. We cross-referenced it with medical records we received from Earth and from the new one thousand. When she began asking too many questions, I told her I would annul her marriage if she didn't back off."

"Did she back off?"

"Of course, she did, she's not stupid, but she is still suspicious and of course she is close with her mother in-law who is the Imperial Doctor to the Empress."

"That's inconvenient."

"I'm surprised she didn't mention it to you?"

"She did mention it a couple of times. I told her that I had been in contact with you and trusted you to make the right decision as your interests were in our best interests too." Jane looked into Anu's green eyes and said, "I don't think she suspects anything more than a little foul play, and even if she did, I don't know that she would be wholly against what we did after her own terrible experiences with integration."

"Well, I don't trust her. I've seen into that little one's mind. She has a tremendous amount of anger that she barely keeps under control. She's the kind of person who could do anything if something were to disrupt that slippery control. And she is too close with Captain Kara, who would definitely see this as a betrayal. Don't you agree?"

It just occurred to Jane then that it had been Anu, not Rez, who had tried to kill James with the Uli virus from Alpha Four and the gravity of the kind of lengths Doctor Anu would go to to get what she wanted. All of which Jane didn't even pretend to know the extent of, "I don't think James is that big of a threat. She wouldn't do anything to jeopardize her marriage or daughter now. I think she really loves Doctor Ket. And as for Kara, I don't know how she would feel about this. In some ways, we are sparing more human women from 'volunteering,' and it's not as if she believes in the Alliance religion, so there is no trouble on that end of betraying the gods. And I think it's really only the religious zealots who would be against this."

Anu just shrugged, not knowing what would happen, "Well, if they discover the truth, who's to say what they will or won't do. And by they, I mean, Captain Kara, Doctor Drusilla and the High Priestess and her zealous followers."

Jane took a deep breath, "But why are we even talking about this. No one will really find out. They're all too preoccupied with other things at the moment, and hopefully, they will just forget about all these few strange things as long as we lay low, and no one's memories come back to them."

"Oh, don't worry, there is no way any of the new 1,000 women are going to remember anything but their boring days being treated in the Space Port One Hospital. My staff have excellent skills in memory replacement."

Jane gave her a hard look, "Have you used it on me or any of the other women from the *Dakota*?"

"Of course not," Anu replied too quickly for Jane to believe her.

Jane just stared at Anu and Anu stared back, after a

minute she said, "Well, there's nothing I can do about it now. Tell me about the human men."

"They were more than willing."

"And their memories?"

"Changed, of course. The men thought they were with slave artists. And don't worry, we found enough men on the planet and pirates nearby who were more than willing to be with some women of their own kind at the time. And it was enough to keep the gene pool healthy, but we will have to monitor the children to make sure none of them marry one another. Perhaps a new law? No hybrids can marry each other." Anu looked at Jane carefully, she looked a million kilometers away from their very serious situation. So she asked directly, "Does he know?"

"Who?" she asked innocently.

"Admiral Jei."

"Stop reading my thoughts. Isn't that against the law?"

"When we are all risking our lives, I'm going to read your thoughts, I'd be a fool not to."

"He doesn't know. Of course, not."

"Do you want to marry him?" Anu asked skeptically.

"No, I'm not even thinking about it like that," Jane said defensively.

"I know your thoughts, you're in love with him. Oh, you are trying to convince yourself it's lust, but it's not. When people are in love, it's like a soft sheen of mild madness that surrounds them. You can't hide it from any doctors here. We can pass people in the corridors and quickly read their thoughts to find out who they are newly in love with. It's like a sickness, Jane."

"That's an invasion of privacy."

Anu shrugged, "I can't help it. It's really one of the only joys of being telepathic."

"Okay, well, I'll tell you then. No, I don't want to marry him, and no, he doesn't know I like him."

Anu smirked, "You don't think he knows you love him? Has he given you a gift?"

Jane didn't answer, but she didn't need to.

"A hairpin from Juio's? And did you post it to your social media? No, of course, you didn't. Stupid human. But then he transferred you to his ship anyway, to keep you close."

"Is there anything else you want to know?" Jane did not want to talk about her love life with Doctor Anu.

Anu smiled, "Oh no, I've enough to satisfy me now. I'm going to enjoy watching this play out," she said smugly. "I'm so glad that the *Kzi* is here all week."

"What is that supposed to mean?"

"I look forward to seeing you two on the military feed. I'm sure the gossip columns are going to pick this up as well. It's romantic, actually."

"Stop. There's not going to be any kind of a romance going on this week. I'm very busy with House Human and I don't even know what he has planned, but I doubt I will even see him. I've got to go now," Jane stood up, and her guards moved forward to meet her.

Anu laughed, "But you've got his with you guards as well, but you don't think you will see him?"

"No."

"Stupid human," Doctor Anu replied.

Jane just sighed, "Thank you, Doctor Anu, may the gods light your path."

"May the gods allow you to be fruitful again," she replied with a grin. "Walk in their light."

Jane left the medical screening area and then went towards the hired taxi transports to go down to the Capital

Planet. She was prepared to take taxi transport, but Gio lead her to one of House Rega's transports.

"Admiral Jei has instructed me that we should use House Rega's transports. They are more secure and have clearance for landing at all the landing pads on the planet."

"Is there anything else he has instructed you that I should know about?" Jane asked.

Gio shrugged, "There is a lot of unspoken information. I guess we will just let it unravel as it comes."

Jane sighed and then said, "We are going to House Human now in Residential Ring Four in the Capital City."

4

Leld and the Promenade

Jane entered House Human and left Jei's guards to find their own place, which they did after speaking to a passing slave. She knew that these guards were not of the slave class by their clothing, but it just occurred to her that she didn't know what class most guards were in nor where they went in situations like this. It was all so confusing because she knew some guards, such as Imperial Guards, could be slaves, but the guards that worked at House Human were not slaves as they didn't wear green, but she had never thought to ask what class they were. It was just another reminder of how much she still didn't know about the Alliance even after being there for over a year.

Jane went upstairs to her old room and the door unlocked simply by her presence in front of it. She walked in, and everything was as she left it, bare. She had nothing personal here except for a few pieces of clothing in her closet. She was glad to have it though otherwise she assumed she would have to stay with Kara or James while she was on planet. Alliance citizens were forbidden from staying in hotels anywhere on any of the five homeworld planets. Jane thought it was an odd law, but one that they followed through on for whatever reason. It was a pity because she would have liked to try one of the modern luxury hotels in the Shopping District of the Capital City. Just as it was forbidden for any aliens to stay in the personal home of an Alliance citizen.

Jane put her bag on her bed and then sat down at her desk to check her messages. None required her immediate attention, so she decided to have a shower. She knew that some of the women in House Human wanted to speak to her, but she thought that would just have to wait until tomorrow. She was emotionally exhausted. She didn't like what she had done to these 1,000 women. Not the procedures and definitely not the memory-erasing, but she said out loud as she entered the bathroom, "Just one more thing to add to the list of, I-had-to-make-the-best-decision-of-a-no-win-situation-in-the-Alliance."

Jane went into the bathroom and was relieved that both the shower and the toilet remembered her, so they were already adjusted to the right temperature and height, respectively. She thought if one more thing challenged her today before she could relax and catch her breath in the shower, even just the toilet she might cry. Jane quickly got into the shower and let the hot water run over her for so long the computer told her at least three times that she had been in the water too long and that it was harmful to her skin. Jane ignored the computer, she didn't care. She needed to think, and the best place she thought, besides on her floor with a bottle of whiskey, was in a hot shower. She thought about what Kara might think if she found out about what she and Anu had done. She considered James's suspicions and wondered how seriously she should consider those moving forward, but mostly she thought about Jei. She couldn't get Anu's words out of her head, 'When people are in love, it's like a soft sheen of mild madness surrounds them.' She had never thought she loved him, an infatuation yes, a little crush, yes, of course. *He was the admiral of the most powerful fleet in the galaxy, who wouldn't have a crush on him? And he had showed her a bit of interest, but that was all,* she thought. And then a little nagging voice in her mind said, *But what if what you feel is real?* And then another voice in her head said, *But what if it's the forget-me-not-drug and they are making me like these Alliance people? That they just didn't pause the memories of Jim but added something about me liking Alliance people because when the Alliance doctor looked into my mind on the* Zuin, *he saw how I felt about his people and wanted to change me. Make me more sympathetic to the Alliance and soften my resentment at being put in this situation.*

Jane let the dryer do its job after her shower and then exited the bathroom. She took out the one formal Alliance dress she owned and set it on the bed. She had not worn it in over a year, and she had only worn it once before. It had been given to her by the Alliance Empire specifically for Assemblies and religious ceremonies. Today she would be attending the ceremony honoring Admiral Jei. She had been surprised to have been invited, but she didn't question whether or not she would attend. She just accepted the invitation on her IC. She looked at the dress and wondered if she should have bought something new instead of talking to Doctor Anu. But then she sighed and thought, *It doesn't matter, all the Alliance dresses look more or less the same to me anyway.*

Her formal dress was of no real shape and was floor length like all Alliance dresses, but what set this one aside as a formal dress was that it had a pattern of dark leaves blowing in the wind that seemed to pleasantly move across the dress with the light. Jane had investigated the fabric when she first saw it and noticed that the tiniest of mirrors had been sewn into the dress to create the illusion. She had laughed then at the irony of going through the trouble to do all that on just a loose-fitting, unattractive patterned dress, but every culture had its own idea of beauty. And now, a year on, she knew that Alliance women craved comfort before style, and this was why their dresses were all so loose but made of the best materials and what set them apart were the designs or the jewelry you wore with them.

Jane put on her thigh-high Alliance stockings and her human sexy black lace undergarments and couldn't help but wonder what Admiral Jei would think of these if he were ever to see them. She was aroused just thinking of him seeing her like this and then what would possibly follow. She thought, *It's such a pity that all this effort is hidden under the loose-fitting conservative Alliance dress.* Human undergarments were forbidden in the Alliance, but she had bought special prayer candles from the Earth Store to atone for wearing them to be placed in front of the goddess of fertility. She would light one on her way out in the small shrine, as she had to pray today anyway. Onboard the warships, prayers were much more casual, unless you were Admiral Tir trying to force your wife to be religious. However, for most officers, unless they were particularly religious, just passing the shrine on their way somewhere in the corridor was considered prayer. However, on the Alliance Capital Planet, it was required to actually go to the shrine and pray. And your IC monitored it. Jane reckoned; this is how James had become so religious. She had been alone in this house for months with no one but the religious statues as her company.

Jane put her formal dress on over her bra and underwear. "Mirror," she said, and a full-length mirror appeared. Jane looked at herself and then took out the hairpin Admiral Jei had given her and put it in her longish brown hair now. But it didn't look quite right. Then she did something she never thought she would ever do. She went into her bathroom and asked, "Mirror, could you do my hair with this hairpin?"

"Yes, Jane," the bathroom mirror's light came on, and soon it was displaying different images of Jane's possible hairstyles. "Please select one of the styles, and I will assist you."

Jane picked a loose braid with the hairpin at the side.

The bathroom mirror sprouted little arms and managed to do Jane's hair perfectly with the hairpin.

Jane surveyed her final Alliance look but at the last minute decided to put on just a little bit of make-up. Not much, but just enough to show that she was still human or rather, if she was honest with herself, that she really wanted Jei to see that she could be feminine and beautiful. And then she thought to herself, *Oh, you are setting yourself up, this is what a crush feels like.* But she couldn't help herself. She had on her best dress, the hairpin, and some makeup.

After she had finished getting ready, she put on her ID necklace and a ring to complete the outfit. As she went down to House Human's shrine, she passed some of her wards in the hallway, and they all complimented her on her appearance. It made her feel good that her efforts weren't in vain. But they complimented her in that way young women who never feel they will get old complement an older woman who has put in the effort. Jane smiled at them and thought, *You just wait. It's not easy to look this good when you're my age.*

Jane entered the small shrine. There were eight statues in the House Human shrine. However, two were the most important to the human women that lived there, and these two goddesses' statues had at least a hundred little candles in front of them, all burning and melting together in little mounds of white wax, the goddess of home and the goddess of fertility.

Jane stood reverently in front of the goddess of fertility and offered her prayer for wearing undergarments and lit the candle. Then she didn't know why. She also randomly asked the goddess's statue, *And should I even be looking for love again? I only have months left before I'm ineligible for marriage.*

Jane contemplated everything in the quiet of the shrine for a few minutes. She didn't know what she was waiting for. "Do I really think she is going to reply? She's just a statue." Jane chided herself out loud for even speaking to a lifeless statue. But even so she still stood there for some time waiting for something to happen. Jane even closed her eyes and then felt different, she couldn't describe it, but as she left the shrine, she felt better. But she didn't dwell on the feeling too much as she wouldn't want to admit to herself that she was beginning to believe in the pantheon of Alliance gods. She was resolutely human and an atheist.

Jane left House Human with Jei's guards, as they appeared out of nowhere, just as they always did, but then she reminded herself that everyone in the Alliance was tracked and of course, they would be watching her movements and be ready to leave when she was. This was the kind of seamless interaction she liked about the Alliance. She didn't even need to greet them or them her. It was all understood. They took the House Rega transport to the Grand City Temple, the ceremony to honor the god of war and Admiral Jei would take place. Jane didn't know what to expect. She had never been to a religious ceremony before if you didn't include marriage ceremonies, and she didn't. She had only read about religious ceremonies in the Day and from second-hand information from Kara.

Jane had never been to the Grand City Temple before, and it was magnificent. It was, of course, a large yellow stone building, with many rooms that held giant statues of all the gods surrounded by lit candles.

There seemed to be priests everywhere now. Usually, one only saw priestesses, but Jane surmised that this was a ceremony for the god of war who was male, so it would make sense there would be more men here today.

Jane found the room she was looking for. She was one of the last to arrive. She found a place to stand at the back of the room. She could see the High Priestess of the Grand Temple and a few other priests she didn't recognize with Admiral Jei at the front of the room at the feet of a massive statue of the god of war. Jei was dressed in what she supposed were ceremonial robes of black and green. Green was the color all the gods wore, and ironically the color slaves were permitted to wear as well. She scanned the other guests or 'witnesses' as they were all called, and just like she thought, she was the only human. She was pleased to see some members of the High Council she knew and liked there, including Kes of House Zu. So, she would have someone to talk to during the reception besides Jei.

The ceremony began only moments after Jane arrived. She braced herself for there to be both blood and pain. These were the two elements she had come to expect from every religious ceremony in the Alliance. They seemed to love to torture themselves. Jane reflected that it must be because they wanted to prove to themselves and others that they really were alive. Humans, of course, expressed this realness in other ways through art and literature. Still, she supposed in the past humans had probably done the same before they had become more sophisticated, creating other forms of expression. The Alliance had never developed any arts, so it held on to these archaic practices of pain and suffering. Jane was at least grateful that this was all happening before the evening meal rather than after it.

Sure enough, after some prayers and lighting some candles, Admiral Jei stripped off his shirt, and two priests began cutting him and filling his blood into a massive silver chalice, which they began to throw around to represent the blood he had spilled all over the galaxy. Jane frowned then and thought, *The blood on this man's hands probably would fill this entire temple.* She wondered suddenly if Jei felt at all remorseful for anything that he had done or for any of the deaths he had caused. After a few minutes of watching the ceremony and thinking about it, she decided that there was no way he would feel any remorse because to do that, he would have to consider that the people he conquered or killed were equal to Alliance people. Jane knew that Jei felt there was only one civilization, the mighty Alliance civilization, and that they were better than all the rest as they had been blessed by the true gods. Everything about the Empire was the best. And that there were limits to what their colonies and vassals could do to emulate them, but that no one, but Alliance people, could truly live the good life and walk in the light of the gods. Still, even from that perspective, the people in the colonies and their vassals were expected to try and always be as close to the Alliance culture as possible, even though they would inevitably fail.

Jane tried to pay attention to what was happening in front of her again, just in case people questioned her about it later. She didn't know if people were going to comment on where the blood was taken from or how much from each place in the reception afterward. One thing she had come to realize about Alliance people is that they could talk about anything, even subjects that humans would never discuss in public. So, she wanted to be prepared. From what Jane could make out, they were taking blood from the sacred areas of the body, the chest, knees, and wrists. Blood was also being taken from other places like his back. Jane didn't know the significance of those other areas, so she marked it as something she could ask if she ended up in a conversation about blood later. After a while, when the chalice was sufficiently full, they handed it to Admiral Jei, who raised it and said more prayers. Jane was transfixed by this. She didn't know what he was going to do with the chalice. She watched as he tilted the chalice filled to the rim with his red blood. Maybe Jane was imagining it, but she thought she could smell its coppery scent in the room. She watched Jei carefully now as she had no idea what he was going to do with his blood. He was a bit shaky for someone so big and strong. He was praying and raising the chalice, and she thought, *Do not drink that or pour it on yourself. I cannot bear it. Please don't be so barbaric.* But she could not deny that another part of her would find that kind of barbarian behavior sexy. Like an archaic warrior returning from battle with the blood of his enemies on him. Jane tried to focus again on the ceremony and not get taken away with sexy fantasies about her and a bloody warrior in a medieval castle.

Admiral Jei held the chalice for many minutes as the prayers continued. He prayed, as well. Thanking the god of war for his gifts throughout his years in the fleet and Jei asked for the god of war for his favor in the coming years. Jei's arms wavered from the loss of blood and from the lack of food. He had been fasting for days before this in preparation to present himself at the temple as a humble man. Finally, when Jei didn't think he could hold the chalice any longer, he handed it back to the High Priestess. He was surprised to catch Jane's eyes at that moment and see her relief. He wondered then if it had been so evident that he might fail and drop the chalice.

He found his second wind then and he urged himself to try harder to impress her further. The High Priestess then poured the blood through the eyes of the massive statue of war. More prayers were said, and candles lit. The room was overwhelmingly rife of the smell of coppery blood, candles, and incense, which smelled more like the petrichor than sweet flowers. More prayers were said, and then finally, after an hour and a half, it was over.

After the ceremony, everyone was directed to a different area of the temple for a reception with food and zota. Jane took a ceramic cup of zota and found Kes.

Kes was more than happy to see Jane, "How are you? I hear you are on the *Kzi* now? What a pity! You were the only one I trusted to keep an eye on Kara, and now who does she have except my son? And with the child to look after too."

Jane smiled sympathetically, "I think it's impossible for anyone to keep an eye on Kara. And, yes, I was transferred."

Kes leaned in closer and said as if it were a secret, "Not by choice, I understand as well."

Jane replied, "It was for the purpose of integration." Jane said the word 'integration' in a conspiratorial sort of way, and both women smiled.

"Oh, these men," Kes remarked. "Although I must say, if I were you and I was forced to integrate at least I could comfort myself knowing that it is at the top level and with one of the most honorable of men in the Empire. Although, who really knows what kind of man he really is? Sometimes he steps outside the lines and tries to push his will on women as if we don't know what's best for the Empire. Still, he has done a better job at leading the fleet than any other man in centuries, I guess that is something.

That's why we are here today honoring him after all. You could do much worse."

Jane was surprised by Kes's frankness. "I've found him to be respectful enough," Jane replied not knowing what to say in the face of such blatant sexism

"And more?" Kes questioned with a knowing look. Kes had absolutely no doubt that something was going on between Jane and Jei. She could think of no other reason she would move to the *Kzi*. And she had his personal guards with her. Of course, they were all worried about the humans after what happened to Doctor James. Still, two superior guards from Alliance Planet Two was over the top unless they were romantically involved.

"No more," Jane answered, but she knew she was blushing, and Alliance people now knew what that meant.

"It's a pity you fair-skinned humans reveal your emotions with that blood that rushes to your cheeks. Otherwise, I might have believed you. Nice hairpin," Kes smiled and then walked away.

Jane watched her go and then looked across the crowded room at Jei. He was talking to a woman she didn't know. And she surprised herself by checking the woman's left wrist and thought, *No, marriage bracelet, who is that?* Before Jane could look at the woman's ranking jewelry though, another member of the High Council began a conversation with her, and she had to turn away from Jei and the mysterious woman.

Admiral Jei had made the High Priestess wait for Jane before beginning the ceremony. He was so pleased when he saw her slip in the back just half a minute late. Not only did she look gorgeous in a formal Alliance dress, but she was finally wearing the hairpin from Juio's that he had given to her weeks before.

Throughout the ceremony, he thought of her. And when he caught her compassionate look for him, he wanted to tell her that none of this hurt, as the honor was more significant than the pain and that the pain was the honor.

After the ceremony, there was nothing that Jei wanted more than to speak to her, but he knew people were already gossiping about them. Whispering about his transferring her and ordering his Second Alliance Planet guards to accompany her. And he knew an Alliance woman of Jane's status would be upset if the gossip columns picked anything up from the reception, so he kept his distance. He consoled himself that there would be a time to speak to her later. Although it was so painful to avoid her. She looked so stunning, and he rarely saw her like this, in women's clothing. Without even thinking, he would find her in the room, and they would make eye contact for a brief second. He wanted so much to speak to her, but he didn't want to ruin his chances of pursuing their relationship further because he was unable to control himself now. *Think of the gossip columns,* he thought, *She will think I'm a fool if I risk her name romantically connected with me here today.*

After the ceremony, Jane returned to House Human and was immediately bombarded by a long line of human women who all wanted advice about one thing or another. Thankfully, she had had a lot of zota at the reception, so she patiently sat down with a glass of wine and listened to them all in the dining room, one by one. Jane almost felt like she was a queen holding court, it was so odd. But she was grateful for the distraction as she had been so crestfallen that Jei had not even spoken to her at the reception at the Grand City Temple. And she had felt like a fool wearing the hairpin he had given to her. She tried to remind herself though, *He gave it to you to be worn. Maybe nothing more? It's fine. You're not a blushing schoolgirl.* But she didn't feel good about it as she felt she might have misunderstood everything and that made her feel confused and embarrassed. And this made her feel even more ridiculous as she felt she was too old to have a man make her feel so uncertain of her actions. Jane felt like she should know better. However, after listening to her wards in House Human, she was reassured that she at least had gained some experience in the years she had lived as she wasn't as silly or naïve as they were.

After Jane finished with the women who had sought her out, she had to send for Babette. She asked one of the surly slaves to find Babette and tell her to come to the dining room. After a lot of back and forth, the slave finally agreed and went to fetch Babette.

Jane watched as Babette entered the dining room, "You could at least look a little ashamed," she said.

Babette replied as she sat down, "But I'm not ashamed. I'm human."

"Yes, you are, but you have agreed to come here and follow the Alliance rules. You can't go around kissing men, especially men, you are not even courting."

"Why would I court someone before kissing them? There is no better way to know you love a man than to kiss him. You know you can have a crush on someone, and then you kiss them and poof," she made a gesture with her hand, "the kiss proves that it was just a crush and it's over."

"Babette, your logic is sound, and this method is good for human men, but it's not appropriate in the Alliance, and House Human cannot continue to pay these fines. You must find another method."

Babette laughed, "Can you suggest one? What is more innocent or telling than a kiss?"

"I don't know, but in the Alliance, kissing is not innocent."

"It should be."

"It's not. You must stop. Think of something else."

Babette had a pout.

Jane felt like such a House Mother then, "I'm sorry, but these are the rules. If you do it again, I will not pay the fine."

"Then what will happen?"

"You will be sent to the High Priestess for physical punishment."

"You wouldn't."

Jane nodded, "You must see that this is their culture, and you signed a contract saying that you would live by their rules, and you must do it or suffer their consequences. House Human is poor, we cannot afford these fines, especially if other women begin to follow suit. Am I making myself clear? No more kissing."

"Yes, very clear," said Babette, but in her heart, she knew she wouldn't stop kissing men. It was the only way to know. Babette got up and walked out of the dining room.

Jane followed and went to her room and quickly got ready for bed. As she lay under the covers in the darkness, her mind wouldn't let Babette's words go, 'There is no better way to know you love a man than to kiss him.' And then her mind jumped to kissing Admiral Jei. She chided herself, *How many times did he look at me today and say nothing? I'm a fool to continue this fantasy.*

Jei was in his Alliance grand home in the Capital City in Residential Ring One. His real home was on Alliance Planet Two. However, he was in the Capital City so much that he had decided years ago to buy a residence here rather than use his quarters assigned to him by rank. It was also convenient because his sons used the house as well. But tonight, he was alone here thinking about Jane. He wished that he could invite her over. He hated the idea of her alone in her room at House Human. He had seen the images from the inside of that building, and it looked like a prison. But he suspected that was because no one really knew how the human women would behave in the Alliance, and there had been serious concerns that they would be too unruly. Hence the building could be easily transformed into a prison. Jei smiled, thinking, *And how we've changed our opinions so quickly*. The only human woman who seemed to be terribly unruly was Captain Kara. But Jei thought Tir was clever keeping her in his fleet and away from the Capital Planet for many reasons, most of all though so that she didn't influence the other human women on the planet. And he liked to think that Jane had already benefitted from being away from Kara. And then his thoughts went back to Jane's appearance that afternoon and how wonderful she looked and behaved. *Just like an Alliance woman*, he thought. His thoughts were interrupted by a chime on is IC.

Jei opened his IC, his son had messaged him,

Father, I never thought I would see you in the gossip columns over a human woman.

Jei frowned and then went to the Capital City Gossip and found the article about him.

Admiral Jei of House Rega received the highest honor at the Grand City Temple earlier today in the presence of the god of war. However, if you have already read the Day, you know that. We are mentioning it because there is a rumor that Admiral Jei and Lieutenant Commander Jane of House Human are secretly courting. At the reception, the couple were stealth and did not speak to one another, but Lieutenant Commander Jane was wearing a hairpin that was rumored to have been a gift from Admiral Jei some weeks ago, before her transfer to the Kzi. *They are both still on the Capital Planet now, so we have our eyes and ears open to watch these two. Write in with what you think. Is this romance all in our heads?*

Jei sighed and hoped that Jane would not be troubled by this article. He had heard a rumor that the humans' ICs were blocked from any news about them unless it was reported in the Day. However, he did not know if that was true or not. He doubted that it would be true for Jane as she needed to keep moral tabs on all the women in her House. Jei looked at his IC and debated with himself whether or not to message her. In the end, he decided that she would be annoyed either way if she saw the article.

Jei messaged Jane,

Are you available to meet me for lunch at Leld in the Promenade Ring tomorrow?

Jane messaged back in real-time, it was disturbing for Jei to see that she was writing but to have not received the message yet. He was sure she was cross at being mentioned in the gossip columns. He wondered if she was in bed, and then his mind ran to her being naked, and he wondered what she would look like without clothing.

Jane was surprised to receive a message from Admiral Jei. At first, she began typing,

Is this an order?

As she was still a little hurt, he didn't speak to her

earlier today. But then she decided that she wasn't that childish, and she was curious what he was going to say after his behavior today. Her heart leapt at the idea that there was a reason behind his ignoring her at the reception. So, she would be civil. But she sure wasn't wearing the hairpin and making a fool out of herself again though so she simply replied,

I will meet you there.

Jei was relieved that she was at least going to meet him. He quickly arranged for a private room at Leld and looked forward to seeing her the next day. He chided himself though, *Maybe I should have just invited her here? We are, after all, allowed to do that as widowers.* But he couldn't change it now, so he finished his cup of zota, rechecked the message to make sure she really said she was going to meet him and then went to bed himself.

He had forgotten that, of course, Vran, his slave artist would have come down to the planet as well and would be sleeping in his bed. Or not sleeping.

He entered his sizeable sleeping chamber, and he was going to tell her 'not tonight', but he was so wound up from the ceremony, and seeing Jane, he couldn't resist Vran's advances.

She was scantily dressed in green and had on a new perfume he assumed she bought during the day. Vran jumped up and began undressing him as soon as he walked into the bedroom. "I'm humbled to be with a man so honored by the god of war." Vran purposely kissed and licked all of his wounds as she exposed his grey naked flesh.

Jei instantly was aroused by Vran's attentions, the pleasure, and the pain she was giving him from his wounds. He let her undress him as she often did while onboard the *Kzi*. And when she had finished, he did the same to her, kissing her on her neck and down to her nipples, biting them gently the way that she liked. Then he moved down her slender grey body kissing everywhere, especially the bottom of her abdomen as he knew she loved that, it gave her the shivers.

"The god of war has also blessed you with being a good lover," Vran said breathlessly as Jei played with his tongue at the bottom of her abdomen, teasing where he might go next, where he had been a thousand times before, but she never got tired of his tongue there.

"Has he?" Jei asked as he suddenly plunged a finger into her sex.

"Oh gods, yes," she said at the welcome intrusion. "Should we be human?"

Jei didn't stop moving his finger but looked down into Vran's green eyes, "What do you mean, slave?"

"Enter me without my coming first?"

Jei withdrew his finger. He didn't answer Vran but then moved his mouth directly on to her clitoris. He knew how to make her come in minutes. He had studied her body for years. Right before she climaxed, he moved away and then said, "Vran is this the punishment you want? To be brought so close and then left unfulfilled?"

"Jei, please, no. I just. Please," she was begging him for release.

Jei looked at Vran and then bent his head to finish his task. Vran came so hard around him, his face was wet with her pleasure. Then he entered her and said consistently with his thrusts, "Humans are Alliance people and have lost the way of the gods. We will not be tempted by their perversions. If you ever ask that of me again, I will have you punished and banished."

Vran loved his desperately hard thrusts. He was so angry, and she loved it when he was as rough as he was now. She would even have bruises tomorrow, but she loved it when he pounded into her with such force and determination. "I'll never ask again. I'm sorry. I was misguided. Thank you."

Jei turned Vran over onto her back and lifted her hips with his hands. He began plunging into her so deep with his throbbing penis, he thought he could never move fast enough. He imagined Jane then, thinking about how he would teach her the sexual Alliance ways and take her away from the wicked ways of human sexuality. He wanted to make Jane come again and again, the way it should be. He finally found his own release inside Vran. He watched as she scooped up his warm sperm from her vagina and licked it seductively in front of him.

"Let me clean your penis with my tongue," Vran said while she was still licking the sperm from her fingers.

Jei nodded.

"Goddess of fertility forgive me for what I'm going to do," Vran said and then licked all around his penis and cleaned all evidence of their sexual encounter with her tongue.

When Vran had finished licking him clean, he went into the bathroom. He looked at himself in the mirror. His hair was grey, and he was older, but he still thought he looked good enough for a woman. *But she is only 39 Earth years old. If she were Alliance, she would probably consider me too old. What am I thinking?*

Vran knew better than to follow Jei into the bathroom. He liked to have his privacy there. However, he was in there for a long time, and she wondered what he was thinking about. She had heard the rumors of his infatuation with the human named, 'Jane'. But she had been with Jei for many years now and knew his infatuation came and went. She doubted this plain human could replace her. Vran had purposely asked for him to take her like a human to weigh out his fantasies with Jane, and she was relieved that he had not wanted to. That there was nothing in their sex tonight out of the ordinary.

Jei waited impatiently in a private room at Leld for Jane. He hadn't felt like this in decades. He liked Jane, an alien, a human, a member of the Lost People, so much, and he didn't want to make a fool of himself and have her deny him because he was decades out of practice for courting.

Finally, the door opened, and Jane was escorted in. Jei noticed immediately she was not wearing the hairpin he gave her and asked himself, *You expected she would be after that article in the gossip columns?*

"Jane, thank the gods for the day."

"They provide for us," she replied, and then the hostess of middling class left them alone. Jane sat down across from Jei at the large but understated yellow stone table. "I've never been here before," she admitted trying to make conversation.

"Then, you have been missing out on the best food the Capital Planet has to offer."

"Not the Empire?" she asked with a smile.

"No, only the Capital Planet. Alliance Planet Two has much better food, in my humble opinion."

"I've never been there and know little about it. Only what Doctor Rea has told me. I don't even know, am I allowed to go there as a woman of the Alliance Capital Planet?"

He smiled, "You're allowed to go as an officer in the fleet, but just don't mention you are a woman when you are there."

Jane smiled back, "Is it interesting enough that I should go through the trouble of getting a disguise or something?"

"I think to alien eyes, I mean to Lost People's eyes," he paused to see if she was offended that he referred to her as an alien, but she didn't react to it. He continued then, "It would seem the same to you as any of the Alliance homeworlds."

"Do you think the differences would be too small for any alien to recognize, just humans or just me in particular?"

"Any alien," he said honestly. "The differences are only slight, but those differences are very important to us on the Second Planet."

"I'm Alliance now I should notice these differences, right?" Jane joked. She was still struggling with standard Alliance culture on the Capital Planet, the last thing she wanted to hear was that there were different variations of this confusing culture on the other Alliance homeworld planets.

"Of course, I misspoke. I'm still getting accustomed to the idea of humans being Alliance people."

"Can you give me an example of a slight cultural difference from the Second Alliance Planet? I'm curious. Doctor Rea has told me some simple things, boring things really about food and architecture already."

Jei smiled, "Our bathing practices are different. We actually schedule them, and we usually don't shower. We prefer ancient baths with friends."

Jane laughed, "What kind of friends?"

"The good kind," Jei replied.

"Are you going home before we leave Alliance space again?"

"No, not this time. But another time I will of course, and if you would like, you should join me and then I can show you these slight cultural differences myself." Jei's mind was imagining her now in his large bathroom at his home on the Second Alliance Planet, the warm stones and her naked with him there.

Jane noticed his demeanor changed and that he was looking at her with lust in his eyes. She didn't trust herself not to follow suit so she simply replied, "I would like that." Then she was quiet. She looked around the fancy private room. It was beautiful and had a line of windows overlooking the Promenade where lots of people were walking. Jane wondered how many UCs this lunch was going to cost her, probably more than a month's salary, she reckoned.

"People are talking about us," Jei said seriously bringing her out of her own thoughts.

"I don't care," Jane lied. She couldn't believe he was jumping to this topic so soon and after he had ignored her yesterday. Maybe he brought her here to tell her that there was never going to be anything between them and that he will do his best to make sure the gossip stops. Her heart was pounding, and in that moment, she knew that Anu had been right, she did love him. She looked into his grey eyes and was waiting for his response. Expecting the worst but hoping for the best.

Jei had not expected that reply. His heart was overjoyed, but her face expression didn't match her words, so he wondered if she meant something different. It annoyed him that she didn't speak Alliance. Translators no matter how perfect were actually never one-hundred percent exact and now trying to speak about matters of the heart he felt like her translator wasn't doing its duty. But then again, he reminded himself, you can have the perfect translation but if you don't understand the culture you will miss its true meaning. "I'm more concerned for you than for myself." He was trying to gauge her demeanor as she listened. *Did she want to take their relationship further?* he wondered. *Or did she not care because she didn't care about the gossip because she didn't care for him? Surely not the latter.*

"Why would you be more concerned for me? Because I'm a woman, human or part of your crew?"

"All, I guess." He paused, then he took in the situation and decided he had to know. He reached across the table with one hand and stroked her cheek. His heart fluttered when she leaned into his touch wordlessly, "And most of all, because I've come to care for you a great deal, Jane from Earth."

Jane felt electricity run through her body. This was a feeling that she thought she had never felt before. Her heart was beating so loud in her ears, she didn't know how to reply to his admission. She was thrilled, but what should they do? There was no set protocol for their situation, her situation. She took a deep breath, closed her eyes, and then asked, "I think about you often. But I don't know, what should we do about this?" She realized after she said it that she might have not sounded sincere about her inexperience but didn't want to say more and ruin the moment. She was breathing fast and if he suggested they leave to go somewhere private she would agree without question.

Jei reluctantly removed his hand as a waiter entered their private room. He asked her a question as if they had been talking the entire time politely. "You've been busy meeting many people these last two days," he commented, knowing full well where she had been and who she had seen as his guards, Gio and Sra, had been reporting back to him details about her conversations and movements.

Jane was surprised by his sudden change of countenance when the waiter walked in but then reminded herself, she didn't want to be in the gossip columns for fines, and obviously neither did he, "Yes, I've had quite a bit to do. One-thousand new human women is a lot." Jane's mind was racing though, and she wondered what kind of fine she would receive for kissing Jei or more now. Almost curious enough to try, and then she thought, *I'm just as terrible as Babette! Is there something in the water on the planet that is making me crazy like a hormonal teenager that I just want to be defiant? And kiss random men?*

"I'm assuming they are settling well, though. I've not read about any scandals."

Not yet, Jane thought thinking of Babette again. "So far, they have been relatively calm compared to some of my old crewmates. But a few are struggling with the culture as it is so different. We don't marry, and I don't think all of them fully understood what it would really be like to live in a culture that had religion and marriage."

"And how do you cope with it?"

Jane smiled, "The best I can."

"But they chose to be here," Jei said. He left off, *And you didn't.*

Jane was charmed. He was the first man to hint at that they were taken by Admiral Tir, and she knew enough now to know it was not by Jei's order either. Tir had been acting entirely on his own. "Yes, but just because you sign up for a job doesn't mean you are not going to have some moments of doubt."

"That's very true. However, I'm sure you are a good role model and they will adjust in no time. Which is good as this endeavor is important for both of our civilizations."

Jane was stunned as this was the second time, he separated humans and Alliance people. She couldn't' help herself and asked, "You don't think we are the Lost People, do you?"

Jei hesitated and then answered honestly, "I don't know. I'm waiting for more evidence. You might be or you might not be."

And everything changed for Jane then. She saw Jei in a completely new light, and she liked it. If he didn't think that they were the Lost People, then he held some kind of respect for her as a human and humanity for just allowing her to serve on his ship and even more so to single her out for lunch almost in a romantic way. "Isn't that blasphemy?"

"Probably," he said casually. "But I'd like to see the High Council fine me for saying it. I've seen enough species in the galaxy to know that although it's unlikely we are genetically the same, it's not an impossibility. And I know my gods. Alliance gods give many signs, I guess because we aren't all paying attention as well as we ought to be," he smiled, "But they have been reticent about humans."

"What about the ancient Alliance records that were written by mortal hands?"

"Oh, you've been snooping around the High Council database?"

"Of course, as Head of House Human, I want to know everything about the relationship between the Alliance and humanity from the very beginning."

"So, you know about all those experiments we did on humans for centuries, and you are still sitting with me here, now. I'm impressed, you are a brave woman."

Jane knew he was referring to the monstrous abductions and medical experiments the Alliance had carried out on humans. In their records, in their defense, they were only checking to see if humans were genetically similar; however, they went to some sick lengths to prove that. "Thankfully, the last abductions on record were a few centuries ago, so I would say you all have gotten it out of your system to confirm we are genetically similar."

Jei wanted to point out that she was also an abduction but that they had become more sophisticated about it because of the Galaxy Court, but he held back. "Have you found anything else you find of interest in the High Council records?"

"No, but I have a question. Why is it that the Empire only feels a need to help humans now when the Alliance also needs help? If you all have always known, we are the Lost People? Why did you leave us to muddle through life the way we have. Humanity has almost destroyed itself hundreds of times and you all were just going to let that happen? Let the Lost People go?"

Jei weighed the question in his mind, trying to decide how much information he should answer with. Of course, there was a man's answer and a woman's answer to this. "We've always watched over humanity. If you ever gain a high enough rank in the fleet, you will have access to those records and our standing orders to always protect humanity when we are able. Do you think it's just luck that you have survived so long without becoming a colony of the Jahay?"

Jane looked at him in disbelief, "Yes."

Jei shook his head, "No. Everyone in the galaxy knows we protect you, except you, I guess. So that is why humanity's only threat has been yourselves and many believe that if you were to commit suicide as civilization then it was your choice."

Jane's mind was spinning with this new information,

and she was trying to remember a time when the Alliance had just destroyed a human ship, but he was right, in her memory, they never had. Severely damaged, yes, but not destroyed. "This is why the Jahay always put human inferior ships on the frontline during the war."

Jei nodded, "I would have thought Captain Kara would have figured that out."

"She might have, but she wouldn't have necessarily told me about it. She keeps a lot to herself."

"That's what worries us all," Jei said more to himself than Jane. Then he changed the subject, "And how do you find life on the *Kzi*?"

"Exciting. Too exciting at times," she said referring to the incident with Nun.

"Hopefully, it will be the right kind of excitement from now on." He wanted to apologize for Lieutenant Nun's behavior, but didn't want to bring that up again, and anyway it was over, she had gotten her justice. It still angered him that one of his own crew would act in such a way, and no one had noticed his serious mental problems before they had progressed to that level. He now had all his doctors on alert for mental changes in the crew. He never wanted something like this to happen to Jane or any other human woman in his fleet again. It was an act of barbarism and an embarrassment. "I must say, I'm impressed with how well you've integrated. I didn't expect you to manage it so quickly."

"What did you expect?"

"For you to be a disruption."

"And I'm not?"

"To no one but me," he said almost under his breath.

Jane looked him straight in the eyes and said nothing but reveled in hearing what she wanted to hear from him. Her heart beat faster and her pupils must have grown larger looking at him across the table. "Am I a good distraction?" she asked, and she wanted to follow it up with, 'Or a bad distraction given you didn't speak to me yesterday? As if you were embarrassed to be distracted by me.' But she left that off because she didn't want to sound desperate or nagging.

Before he could reply, waitstaff entered their private room with food. And just like that, their moment was gone again.

"I took the liberty of ordering our midday meal, I hope you don't mind?" Jei asked.

"I don't mind, I hardly know what to order myself," Jane replied honestly. Alliance food was all so bland it never mattered to her, she thought it all tasted more or less the same.

"These are some new dishes for Leld," Jei explained. "Apparently, one of your wards is thinking of opening a new restaurant, and the chef here was inspired. Now you humans cannot say that we don't try to change."

"I never thought I would hear those words. An Alliance person inspired by a human," she said more sarcastically than she meant to. Jane was actually very proud of Jade and pleased that the esteemed chef of Leld had met with Jade to discuss recipes. Jade had told Jane that she was going to reach out to different chefs, to try to gain momentum so that the High Council would grant her wish of opening a restaurant. Apparently, it was working.

"Jane," Jei said sincerely, "I'm sorry that in some ways, you have only seen the worst of us."

Jane didn't reply, she just watched the different dishes being placed before them and listened to the explanations from the waiter of how they had intermixed new human spices and traditional Alliance ingredients. Suddenly all of this felt so right. She caught Jei's grey eyes and gave him a smile.

Jei urged Jane to try a meat dish with the human vegetable coriander. He had tried this before and thought it must be the food of the gods. It was so delicious.

"It's still somewhat troublesome for me to eat too much meat," Jane said declining the dish. The fact was she still couldn't bear the thought of eating animal flesh.

Jei took a small spoonful of vegetables and put some on her plate. "Then try this first," he said. It was polite in Alliance culture to eat the meat first and then the vegetables, but he was not going to hold her to those standards when they were alone.

Jane took a bite. She knew this Alliance vegetable was like a potato, but usually served as a plain potato, but now the chef had added salt and rosemary to it, and finally, it tasted right, no delicious actually. "It's so good. Almost like home."

Jei smiled. Pleased, he could at least do something right, "I'm glad you like it. We should both consider this our new homestyle food."

"Maybe this is your sign from the gods that we really are the Lost People?" Jane goaded him.

"Oh, Jane, you know so little of our gods. They aren't sublime. They let us know and they've said nothing of humans."

Jane stopped eating and just looked at him in disbelief, "What do you mean? Can you give me an example?"

Jei put down his fork, "Yes, ten years ago, I was visited by the messenger goddess Raga. She told me not to pursue the current mission I was on as it was a trap."

"How did you know she was a god?"

"Because she looked like the statue Raga, and she

came to me on my ship in the middle of the galaxy and then disappeared again."

"What did you do?" Jane was on the edge of her chair. She knew by the way he spoke, he believed this to be true.

"I abandoned the mission."

"Did you ever find out if it really was a trap?"

"Yes, it was. Raga had visited all the other ships at the time, but it was only me, and a few others who had abandoned the plan. I tried to warn some of the other captains, but they called me a religious fool." He took a deep breath, "So you see, the gods are forthcoming with their views."

"Do you think they set the trap to see who was a true follower and who was not?" Jane thought for the first time that maybe the gods were a small group of superior beings who liked to play with the Alliance people. It was beyond her imagination to imagine there was such a real thing as deities, however, in the same way she could not imagine someone as serious and as honest as Jei lying or not being able to distinguish fantasy from reality.

"I don't know. It is a possibility, of course. Are you a believer, Jane?"

Jane hated this question, "Of course I am. I'm an Alliance citizen now. I pray every day."

"You will be. The longer you stay, the more you will see, and then even someone like you that needs strong evidence will be convinced. The gods are real."

"I'd say it will require more than just strong evidence to make me as reverent as others," Jane replied thinking of James and then changed the subject. "Please, if you don't mind, will you tell me about your children?"

Jei smiled, and then they spent the rest of their lunch trying dishes that were a fusion of Alliance and human recipes discussing their families.

After lunch, they took a walk in the busy Promenade Ring, Jei was happy that Jane had agreed to it. In his mind, she was giving him the clear signal that she wanted to begin courting soon as the gossip columns would be writing about this within the hour. He felt especially confident as she did have other obligations with House Human today but took this time to show that she wanted to be seen with him. As they walked, he wondered if he should say the words that marked this as a meeting before courtship.

Jane had never walked on the Promenade Ring with a man before. She knew this was a popular place for couples who were courting to walk as well as friends, but she had only been here once before and she had been alone. Now she felt she was really living an Alliance life. She wondered if Jei had already said the words to signal he wanted to court, and she had missed it. She had been so cross with him about not speaking to her yesterday at the reception she hadn't bothered to refresh her mind on courting protocol.

Jane and Jei walked together and received some looks. Jane assumed it was because he was an important man and Jei assumed it was because Jane was human. It didn't bother either of them.

Jane was on the verge of asking him if this was their meeting before courting when his IC went off.

He didn't apologize but just looked at it.

Jane watched him.

"It's nothing urgent."

"I should go anyway," she said thinking of all she still had to do with House Human.

"Let me walk you to the transport."

"Thank you for thinking of me and allowing me to use your House transport and guards."

"After what happened to Doctor James and what happened on the *Kzi*, I didn't want to take any chances."

Jane had wanted him to say, 'I love you that's why I did this for you.' Not the logical reasons he had just given her. But she knew Alliance people never spoke of love and the best she would ever get is, 'you are my other half'. It was a myth that both Alliance and human people shared however, humans didn't think much of it. "Thank you all the same."

His guards trailed them as he walked her to the transport, "Thank you for joining me for the midday meal, Jane."

Jane looked up into his grey eyes and thought, *Thank me by kissing me you strong alien man.* When he didn't make a move even though she swore her eyes must have been screaming at him to kiss her, she said in what she hoped was a seductive way, "I'm curious. How much of a fine do you reckon we would get for kissing now?"

Very little surprised Jei, but Jane had just blown his mind. Without replying with words, he put both of his hands on either side of her soft, warm face and kissed her. Chastely at first, but then when she stepped close enough to him that their bodies touched, he instinctively moved his hands down to her waist and pulled her strongly against him while allowing his tongue to seek out hers.

Jane had never thought she had wanted a Tarzan, however being in Jei's arms that is exactly what she felt like. He was physically large and strong. He kissed her like a man who had all the strength in the world but was holding back as to not hurt her. It was the most arousing thing she had ever experienced. She wanted nothing more than to drag this man into the transport and let him have his way with her. Jane couldn't describe this feeling, but she wanted him to dominate her. His tongue was strongly exploring her mouth in a way that she imagined, he probably made love, and she loved it. Her hands found his long grey braid in the center of his back, and she grabbed it. As he kissed her neck, she whispered in his ear, "I really want to be fined, a lot."

He continued kissing her, "I also want to be fined." He ran his hands up and down her figure. It was driving him crazy the way she was pulling on his hair. It was so wrong to do so, but so human at the same time. He wanted to show her how to make love like an Alliance woman, but at the same time, take pleasure in the slow education he would give in to her on that particular subject as well.

After many minutes of passionate kissing, Jei slowly and reluctantly backed away, "I think the fine we receive this evening will answer any questions you might have about UCs fined to widowers."

Jane smiled, her body hot with desire for him, "I wish I could watch as they discuss what the fine will be given our circumstances."

He couldn't help it, he caressed her cheek with his thumb, "Your face is flushed pink."

Jane looked down and then back up after a second, "And you know why."

"Yes, I just want to drop everything and invite you home with me now. But we both have other plans."

Jane looked at him in disbelief and thought he must have changed his mind because she could definitely change her plans for sex right now. But she was not going to say that because she didn't want to be told that he really wasn't interested. She hated how contradictory the Alliance was. "I'll think of you when I receive my fines."

"I will pay them."

"No," Jane said, shaking her head, "It was my idea."

Jei laughed, "No, you only tempted me with what I've

been fantasizing about for weeks now. Go with the gods, and I'll see you back onboard the *Kzi* very soon and we will definitely resume this," he touched his finger to his heart.

It was only when Jane was in the transport that she realized she never asked Jei why he'd not spoken to her at the reception. Clearly, by his behavior today, it was not because he was embarrassed by her.

Jane got out her IC and messaged Kara,

Me Jane, Him Tarzan. I'm going to have more fines than any of my wards. I might need to borrow some UCs. I think this is exactly what Doctor Ko meant when he said, 'Be wary of being too positive.'

Jane's IC chimed and she assumed it was Kara replying, but it was Doctor Anu of all people.

I knew that I would enjoy this. And you enjoy it too, Jane.

Jane immediately went to Capital City Gossip but couldn't find anything and was disappointed. Most likely, she was blocked. But then she thought about it and decided she didn't care anyway as what would the article say, that she was walking with Admiral Jei? That they shared a very romantic kiss for all the Empire to see. *We are adults and can do what we want*, she thought defiantly, but she knew that she was being hypocritical as what they did was against the norms of Alliance society. She was glad then that all the humans were blocked from articles about them except for in the Day.

Jei received a message from his son on his way to his

next appointment which he would have happily kept waiting longer if Jane would have wanted to stay with him longer,

Father, what is going on?

Jei smiled and then checked the Capital City Gossip Column without replying to his eldest son, and sure enough, there was an image of Jane and him walking along the Promenade Ring, looking pleased with one another and then a short video of them kissing. He watched the video and was aroused again thinking about the kiss. *My human*, he thought. He cancelled his next appointment and decided to go directly to the Shopping District to buy some known jewelry. On the way, he read the full article,

It is true. You are never too old for love. Admiral Jei of House Rega and Lieutenant Commander Jane, Head of House Human, took a stroll after the maximum amount of time permissible for lunch at the exquisite Leld restaurant, which has recently began creating a few fusion Alliance, and human dishes. Unfortunately, these two are leaving orbit soon, so we won't be able to follow their romance as readily as we would all like on the Capital Planet. Still, already I have, like many of you are probably doing right now, added the Kzi to my list of followed Alliance ships in the galaxy. And we should all petition the military feed to show every interaction on ship between these two. They are scandalously delicious.

5

Officially Lovers

Jei's son Ule joined him at his home for the evening meal. Ule was 160 years old and also still in the fleet and held the rank of admiral. It was rare the two men were able to meet up together, especially on the Capital Planet, so it was a special occasion.

They had a good relationship. Ule respected his father and felt that he had, for the most part, made wise decisions, and even when he hadn't, Ule could see the logic behind the decision made. But now he was baffled by his father's romantic interest in the human woman Jane.

"Father," Ule said after the meal, while they had some zota in front of an open fire in the drawing-room of Jei's Capital City house.

Jei looked at his eldest son, "You've not used this tone for decades, what is it?"

"You know what it is. You've read the gossip columns."

"Ule, your mother began her next life years ago. I want to have a companion again."

"You have Vran."

"Not just a slave artist who is only around as long as

the UCs are. I want someone to smile with again."

"You are the Admiral of the most powerful fleet in the galaxy. You could have anyone. Choose another Alliance woman."

Jei waved his hand at his son, "I wouldn't want to take a young woman. She would say 'yes' only because of my rank. Jane is different."

Ule laughed at the preposterous comment, "Is she not young and using you for your rank? She is 39 Earth years old. What is that really, 35 years old in Alliance years? I think she's used witchcraft on you."

"Ule, I'm only going to say this once, don't ever speak of Jane that way to me ever again. She didn't choose to come here, and she has given up a lot in doing so. She left behind a husband and children on Earth. Can you imagine how that must feel for her? And not that I need to explain myself to you, but I will because I want you to understand. I am the one who initiated our relationship after I met her. And she was very reluctant to be transferred away from her group of humans on the *Zuin*, but again, she complied without complaint. Now she is almost completely integrated into Alliance culture, and I want her. You can almost consider her my wife already. She will live with me on the *Kzi*. This is a new dawn for us. Men will truly rise to equality through human women. Don't spread propaganda against our cause." Jei never thought he would have to threaten his son, but many men didn't want equality, they didn't want to push for this new era in the Alliance. And this was exactly the kind of complacency women had relied on for years, keeping men just happy enough not to ask for more. More power, more equality and more of the good Alliance life.

Ule shook his head at his father, "I think when you come to your senses, you will regret this. There are so many things wrong with Admiral Tir's ideas and I don't see how human women will be a means to an end for us. And what more equality do we really need?"

"This is the problem. You and your kind are too content with the scraps the women throw at us. We are the true force behind the Empire and it's time that we begin to exert our power. Too long have women made conservative decisions, chosen peaceful routes that have only led to drawn out failed peace treaties, which we end up having to die for. We should be ruling the galaxy with more force. Then our colonies and other civilizations would be less likely to rebel or think that they could win a war with us. There would be more peace in the galaxy by ruling with a stronger hand." He sighed seeing that he was getting nowhere with his son, "And human women see men as equals. Jane doesn't look down on me. And Kara is going to give Tir the power he needs to see our cause through to fruition."

"Because she's ignorant of our ways? Is that why he is keeping her away from spending too much time here?"

"No, because she believes men and women are equal. And because of this, Kes of House Zu would have her killed. A simple challenge and it would be done. You know that."

"And it's convenient that Tir only allows her to see what he wants her to see of the Alliance," Ule said sarcastically. Then more seriously, "I've heard rumors that she speaks Alliance and even a rumor that Tir has taught her the men's language. But I can't believe that as she seems to hate everything about the Empire except our warships and weapons. I can't imagine her going through the hassle for something she hates. What interest would she have in ruling except to see Earth become a colony? You know Captain Kara talks about that, right?"

"Yes, I know, but if we must sacrifice one of our oaths to the Lost People so be it. It would be by one of their own anyway." Jei replied, but this did trouble him. Kara's desire for vengeance on humanity. However, if that was to be the price for Tir gaining all the power in the Empire and flipping the dominance of the sexes, then so be it.

Ule didn't want to discuss this anymore with his father. He knew they stood on different sides of the issue. He just hoped that his father would not be executed with Tir when this all fell apart. "Do you mean to have any hybrid children?"

"Are you keen to have a sister?"

Ule couldn't help but laugh at the idea. "It could be a playmate for Hso," Jei's great-great-great-grandson, who only recently had been born.

Jei smiled at the thought, "Well, I don't know if Jane would want another child. I assume she would as a means to see her human children again but it's not something I expect." He didn't even mention her husband as Jei considered him only as a lowly human man and nothing compared to him. And seeing as how Jim, that was his name, Jei had looked it up in the database, had not even tried to rescue Jane, Jei didn't think he could be much of a man. Even more so that he gave up on Jane so easily as well. Jei had gone through all of her records since she joined the *Kzi*, including her personal files. He knew about Jane's personal life and the reason she asked for the forget-me-not procedure.

"You really are taken with her, aren't you?"

"Yes, and I assure you that no witchcraft has been involved," Jei replied honestly.

"You've checked?"

"Of course, I have. I had Tir checked too. Nothing. And I don't think the humans could come up with any technology that would be undetectable to us. And their doctors don't even possess any clairvoyance traits," Jei spoke earnestly to his son.

"I guess I've nothing more to question about it then. I just hope you don't regret this."

"Good. You just have to accept that your father has fallen in love with one of the Lost People. It's high time people began accepting humans into our society. I mean really accept them, not this farce."

"I don't want to hear about your emotions, father," to speak of love made most Alliance people very uncomfortable.

"Sorry. I feel young with the feeling of it," Jei tried to explain his inappropriate admission about how he felt about Jane.

"What's your plan then? You can't have Jane living with you as your wife on the *Kzi*."

"Why not?"

"Because it isn't done, and you know that. Just because humans are on ships, we shouldn't be integrating them together like some kind of a mix between slave artists and Alliance women. They should have never been allowed in the fleet."

"I don't know, I'm rather enjoying it," Jei said with a grin. Just then, his IC went off. The specific chime was from the government, so he looked at it and then laughed.

"Is something the matter?" Ule asked as he also knew it was a message from the government, and he imagined it must be some high-ranking information for only the Admiral as he had not received a message himself.

"It's only the fines for kissing Jane today in front of Leld."

"Gods, I never thought I'd see the day where my father of over two centuries is receiving fines like a junior officer for inappropriate behavior with a young woman. So, Father, what will it be, pay the UCs or visit the High Priestess's punishment rooms?"

"I'm glad you can find some humor in this," Jei smiled at his son.

"I guess I'm just trying to look at the more positive side of it all that when I'm your age, I too will probably still have the stamina to be with a woman of 39 Earth years old, which is young, very young."

Jei just smiled as he paid the fine, and his son frowned at him, hearing the cost, "I, Jei of House Rega, agree to pay the fines of 1,050 UC." Then he hit another button, "I, Jei of House Rega, agree to pay the fines of 1,050 UC for Jane Johnson, House Human." He, of course, paid Jane's fines too before she could pay them. He knew very well that House Human was always borrowing money from House Zu and now probably from House Vo as well just to cover their costs. One thing was for certain, Jei was not going to have Tir inadvertently paying his fines.

Jane heard her IC chime and then looked at it and almost fainted when she saw the amount of UCs the government had fined them. She had assumed that they would be less than the usual price given that she and Jei were older. However, she was wrong. Apparently, the government deemed them worse because they should know better than to set bad examples.

Jane Johnson, House Human, Fines for 2nd day of the 12th week of the year 18906

The Promenade, Leld, kissing Jei, House Rega at 14:03
*Fine: 525 UC per citation.**

The Promenade, Leld, holding Jei, House Rega at 14:03
*Fine: 525 UC per citation.**

Total: 1050 UC

Disputes can only be made publically.
Added charge for geriatric display of affection.

Just as Jane was about to message Kara to admit she needed to borrow some UCs; she received another message:

Jane Johnson, House Human, Fines for 2nd day of the 12th week of the year 18906

Paid in full by Jei, House Rega, 2nd day of the 12th week of the year 18906

Jane was grateful that he paid the fines, but after a moment's reflection felt like she should still pay, so she decided she would somehow pay him back.

Her hand hesitated over her IC. She was debating with herself whether or not she should send Jei a message right now. But she decided against it. She would thank him in person and then try to reimburse him when they were back on the ship.

Jane looked at her IC again and the fine. She reflected on her behavior and actually had no idea what had come over her earlier. Jane wondered if this had something to do with the forget-me-not. She was about to message Doctor John when she saw that he was available for an RVM.

"Jane. It's so good to see you. How are you?" John asked with concern.

"That's why I'm calling. I've not been acting myself; I don't think. I mean, I don't know? Is this really me?"

"Slow down. Tell me in detail what you think is out of the ordinary, and I will tell you if I think this is a problem." John, of course, knew about the kiss on the Promenade. Everyone was talking about it, but he wanted to hear how she perceived things before he deemed this to be entirely out of character and an adverse reaction to the forget-me-not procedure.

"Ever since I was transferred to the Kzi, I have developed feelings for Admiral Jei. They are so strong," she touched her hand over her heart. "I don't know if I've ever felt this way. I can't remember. And I don't know if I would feel this way if I could remember everything." She knew she had tears in her eyes, but she didn't care. She needed to tell him. He was a doctor and a friend. She trusted him.

"Had you ever met the Admiral before the forget-me-not procedure?" John asked gently.

Jane wiped away some stray tears and tried to remember, after a few seconds, she replied, "Yes, I met him at a High Council reception."

"And what did you think of him then? Was there a connection?"

Jane smiled through her tears, "Yes, I believe so. He told me not to cut my hair and gave me a hairpin. But I didn't think much of it at the time because I still had my Jim."

"But do you think you were attracted to him, even just a little when you first met him?" John didn't know how far the forget-me-not actually went in changing a person, not only just in personality but physically altering them. There were conflicting studies. Most believed though that by altering memories no biological changes would take place. However, new studies showed that different pheromones could be favored when one altered memories so much that it changed one's personality. John wondered if that was what has happened here. That Jane would have never been attracted to Admiral Jei, but because so much of her memory had been altered, she was now favoring different pheromones and therefore a completely different kind of man.

"I don't know. I wasn't repulsed by him." Jane thought about her feelings that first night she met Jei, but it was so difficult to remember, she felt so different now. "I don't think I could even consider him liking me at that point because I was in no place to like anyone else. I was still living with the belief that Jim and I would one day be together again or that we would both just be in love with each other across the galaxy forever. I know it sounds so stupid when I say it out loud now, I was a fool. And I still am. I've no doubt you and everyone else know about what happened today. I'm setting a terrible example for the women in House Human and the worst part is that I don't regret it."

"I don't think you're a fool, Jane. As for today, you are human and just like everyone else and you have physical needs and desires. You and Jei like each other, and it's not wrong that you shared a kiss by human standards. Nor really by Alliance standards either, it's not as if a million fines don't go out in the Empire every day. And as much as the Empire wants us all to conform you can't just change your basic cultural core overnight. You're hard-wired to be human because you were raised on Earth. Your fundamental values were set in your childhood. To truly make drastic changes to your core is almost impossible, so don't be so hard on yourself. I think if anything, your behavior with Jei shows to the women of House Human that even you, the illustrious Head of House Human, are open to temptation and that it is difficult to change. As for you and Jim, you shared a lot of your lives together. Then you were forcibly removed from your family, and you and Jim held on for as long as you could to those memories and the commitment to one another. I do believe you would have held on forever, but you are in an alien environment, and so it's not as easy to move on for you. But in Jim's life, things were the same but different. He has been living with a hole in a place there shouldn't be a hole for a while now, if you see what I mean?"

Jane nodded, "But this behavior, what I'm doing with Admiral Jei, do you think it's really me? Is it right? That I would be so reckless?"

"Let's not jump to conclusions. If you were doing this with a man of questionable circumstances and of a young age, I would be very concerned. However, the Admiral is anything but young and doesn't strike me as a man who makes impulsive decisions. Nor does he have anything to gain by showing an interest in a human. I think you can be sure, at least from his side, this is all normal. That he is attracted to you. However, as for you, I can't say. By the time we met, you were already married to Jim with children. I don't know how you ever were single. But given that we've known each other for years, I would guess the way that you are behaving now towards Admiral Jei is your true nature if you see what I mean? You are this person. The forget-me-not has stripped you of a lot of your memories, so it is mostly instinct that is guiding you now."

"That doesn't reassure me," Jane admitted. "My instinct is a bit of a whore."

John smiled, "Jane, it's fine. Is this the only thing in

your behavior that worries you? You've not had any sudden changes in food choice, friends, clothing, etc.?"

"No, just this," Jane said, thinking through everything else.

"Then you have nothing to worry about. There are only a few more months left of the forget-me-not anyway, and then you will be able to put everything into perspective and you'll see this will all be fine."

"How is that going to be? I mean, when I remember everything. Will it be a rush of memories coming back to me?"

"No, it will be very gradual. If you have any issues, like severe headaches, then see Doctor Rea and let me know."

Jane thanked John, and then they ended the RVM. She looked at the blank screen, then closed it and picked up the hairpin from Juio's she'd left on her desk after the reception. She turned it over in her hand and said, "Ironically, I meet you just before the forget-me-not is administered, then I'm wide open for an Alliance man to fill this space in my life. Maybe this is the work of the gods?"

After leaving the Capital Planet, the *Kzi* and the flagship fleet were sent on a purely diplomatic mission on the edge of the galaxy. It would take them ten days to get there. Jane didn't have too much to do as everything was in good order as they had just left space dock. However, the senior officers were busy with the diplomats onboard preparing.

Jane passed Jei a few times in the corridors, but he didn't even acknowledge her as he passed, busy working. She had expected nothing more. However, her heart always leapt when she saw him.

Three days into their journey, she returned to her quarters and was surprised to see a black wooden box on her desk, a bottle of French champagne and a handwritten note.

Jane

I have a new puzzle jug should we play tonight with this human drink?

Jei

Jane knew enough about Alliance culture to know that she needed to reply with a handwritten note herself. However, handwriting had never been very popular on Earth so she could barely write in a straight line. Jane took out the stationary from her desk that she had never used before and the old-fashioned pen. She looked at the paper and decided it was best she wrote the least amount of words as possible. She didn't want Jei to think she was a complete heathen by her terrible handwriting. Alliance people believed one's handwriting was an indication of how blessed they were by the gods. It took Jane a few minutes to write the one word,

Yes.

Then she summoned a squire and he would deliver it directly to Jei. She sighed thinking how strange Alliance culture was. Written messages were seen as heavenly, and whatever that squire had been doing he would now have to drop everything to do her bidding because this was a written message. Jane considered this to be one of the oddest things about their culture.

Jane then opened the black box. It was from Juio's.

Inside was an exquisite silver necklace with three tiers of different length chains, and at the end of each chain was an intricately carved Alliance flower called a 'vil.' She took the heavy necklace out of the box and held it up to herself, then commanded the computer in the room for the full-length mirror to appear.

As she looked at her reflection, she said, "Oh, this won't do at all." Then she put down the necklace and opened her wardrobe. She had only two boring Alliance day dresses with her. One in navy and one in black. She took out the black one and took off her uniform. She also changed her bra and underwear to a black lace pair, just in case things went very well later. Then, she put on the dress, Alliance thigh-high stockings, and then the new necklace and looked at her reflection. "I don't know if I am losing my mind, or I've just been here too long, but I think I look good." She returned to her desk again and found the hairpin and added that to her hair. Then she said, "Computer, capture image and send to Captain Kara."

"Sent to Captain Kara onboard the *Zuin*," the male computer voice replied.

Jane smiled, not knowing what Kara was going to think. But she was pleased when she got an immediate reply.

Jane, I had to look twice to see if that was really you. I would ask if you are settling into life on the Kzi well, but the whole Empire saw that little make out session with you and the old man, and there you were giving your little darlings in House Human trouble. I was waiting for you to come to me for UCs so we could talk about it. Tir said the fines must have been extraordinarily high because you are both geriatrics!

Jane messaged back,

Yes, it was robbery, but you can guess who paid the fine. I will tell you more later. He's coming over now.

Kara replied,

Just so you know, he keeps his slave artist in his quarters. I don't know if that means he is incredibly boring or likes threesomes or whatever, I just wanted to mention it. But I suspect you know already as you're onboard. Who knows? Maybe this is old news and you've been having threesomes for weeks now?

Jane was annoyed by this comment. Of course, she knew very well that Jei kept a slave artist in his quarters, but most of the time, she tried not to think about it. Whenever Jane passed Vran in the corridors, she always reminded herself, *It's her job just like this is my job. He uses her for sex, and she's paid for it. He chooses to spend time with me without paying and for a possible future together. It is different.* But it was difficult to get her heart to listen to the cold logic of her mind. And sometimes her heart wanted to just smack Vran and pull her hair when she passed with her semi-clad perfumed body. The last thing Jane wanted was Kara reminding her of this fact as if she didn't know.

I think he is into orgies. I will let you know.

Jane smiled. She knew that reply would make Kara a little jealous. Jane herself had never, as far as she could remember, ever been with more than one sexual partner at one time, but she was becoming more open to it the longer she stayed in the Alliance, and the more she was surrounded by this sexual freedom. She didn't think she would want to share Jei with many people at once, but then again, if she searched her soul, she did have some fantasies with multiple men. She blushed, even just thinking about it.

Jane wanted a drink to calm herself a little before Jei came over, but she didn't want to ruin her palate before drinking the champagne. It had been a long time since she had had any champagne, and this was not the cheap stuff either. It was nice and from an excellent vineyard. Jane assumed that Jei had bought it from the Earth Store in the Capital City. She smiled, imagining that Frank must be making a fortune now from all the Alliance men wanting to charm human women by buying Earth products that were out of the human women's price range.

While she waited, she opened her Alliance social media account and checked Jei's account for any new purchases of known jewelry. And sure enough, there was a new piece there. It was breathtaking, of course. A large silver necklace with small clear teardrops falling beautifully from the top. She thought to herself, *Don't jump to conclusions.* But she knew from supervising so many young women marrying Alliance men that this was a sign that the men were definitely thinking about marriage. Then she checked if anything else was new on his social media account. For a minute, she was both horrified and excited that he might have posted new nude portraits of himself. And when she didn't find any new ones, she couldn't decide if she was relieved or disappointed. But she couldn't help herself from looking at the nudes from his youth, she reckoned he must have been about 30 years old when they were taken. She wondered how his body had changed or hadn't changed since then. Even with his uniform on, he seemed to be in top physical shape, and everything about him was huge. That was also obvious by the images. She was so aroused looking at them, thinking about his large ridged penis. *Calm down hussy*, she chided herself. But her body refused to listen to her mind and was already making plans to just jump on him and start riding him like a rodeo star.

Jane poked around a bit more on his social media account and then suddenly, as if her wish had been heard and come true, new nudes of Jei appeared. She almost hesitated to open the album of six new nude images of him. She thought, *Of course six.* The number six was a sacred number in the Alliance, although she didn't know why. Jane smiled devilishly and said to herself, "Forget my palate, I need a drink for this," she opened a bottle of red wine and poured herself some in a ceramic cup and then sat back down at her desk to look at the nude images.

She wondered if he was in his quarters and had uploaded them just then and if he could see she was looking at them now? She drank some of her wine and decided that she didn't care. Jane looked at the first image and was surprised to see that this one was not on the bridge of the *Kzi*. Most of nudes men posted were taken at their stations on starships, as ridiculous as that was. Jane had commented before, 'How could you ever imagine them working in the nude?' But as Kara had pointed out, 'Alliance women don't know as they are forbidden to be on ships so maybe that is what they think or like to think when they are alone on the Alliance planets.' Jane was trying to figure out where the first image was taken and decided it must be from his Capital City home. Then she looked back at his body. Older yes, but sexy as all the stars in the galaxy and she would take him. All of him in every way she could. His penis was not erect in the image, but it was still closer to the size of her forearm than her wrist. She could feel her vagina become wet at the thought of him thrusting into her with it. She took a sip of wine and then when to the next picture. He was sitting, naked at his desk in his quarters she assumed. Jane smiled and wondered if Alliance women really liked these kinds of pictures. She of course, liked the first one where he was posing looking sexy, but the ones where the men were working in the nude, she found strange. The next three pictures were the same and then the final picture was of him on the bridge of the *Kzi* in the nude, standing in a stance that she knew well. And it made her want to reach between her legs and pleasure herself right then. She checked the time. He would be here any minute so she thought it would be a bad idea to do that now. *What if he came before I finished?* she questioned herself, but her vagina was almost throbbing after looking at the nude images of him.

Jane did something then she never thought she would do, "Computer, where is Admiral Jei?"

"Admiral Jei is in the conference room," the male computer's voice answered.

Jane thought for a minute and then decided he was probably still in a meeting. She closed her computer and then went to her bed. She put her hand inside her black lace underwear and began caressing her vulva with vertical strokes, but then said to herself, "I don't have time for this." So, she began rubbing her clitoris in circular motions trying to bring herself to orgasm as quickly as possible. She closed her eyes and thought of the new nude pictures Jei had posted of himself. Of him standing on the bridge and then a fantasy of him having sex with her on the bridge. Then she changed the fantasy again, of him having sex with her in front of the crew on the bridge. Of all of them playing with her, stripping her down, marveling over her curves and the hair under her arms and between her legs and then pinning her over a chair and all having sex with her. Jei being the instigator of it all. Ordering the men to do all kinds of things to her while he watched and then took her himself. Jane came so hard with this fantasy she thought she would have to change her underwear again.

When she came to her senses, she went into the bathroom to wash her hands. She looked in the mirror and said, "You naughty woman." And then asked herself seriously, thinking of what John had told her, "Are these your natural instincts then? To be taken in public sexually by a group of men?" She looked at her reflection, looking for who she really was, wondering if this was who she really was or if this was just the forget-me-not playing games with her and the over-sexualized Alliance culture influencing her.

Jei wanted to finish this meeting. He had finally made some time to meet Jane, but the Ambassador was going on and on. They still had eight days left of travel and Jei decided all of this could wait. He wanted to see his Jane now. He stood up and the rest of the men followed suit, a bit surprised, "The gods will show us the way. Thank you, Ambassador, we will resume this meeting tomorrow. I have another meeting I must attend."

Everyone one stood and bowed as Jei left. He walked directly to Jane's quarters. He started to become nervous like a young man again wondering if she liked the necklace and the human drink. Tir had told him about it, and Tir was not the brightest man, so sometimes he could get things completely backward. Jei honestly hoped this was not one of those times.

Jei stopped in front of her door and took a deep breath then chimed.

Jane answered, and she looked so beautiful; he couldn't

help himself. He took her in his arms and just kissed her right there in the corridor for anyone passing to see. She was wearing an Alliance dress and the jewelry he had given her. There was no more apparent sign a woman could give to a man that she was interested in his advances. And she smelled of a woman who wanted to be touched and it encouraged him.

Jane had been surprised to answer the door and be immediately pounced on like a ball of yarn, but she wasn't complaining. His cool mouth set her body on fire. It took her a few seconds to realize that they were still half in the corridor when she noticed crew members passing and pretending to not look at them. "Come in," she said breathlessly, drawing him in.

They kissed for a while longer, and then Jei pulled away, "I've been thinking about you."

"As I have you," she replied, looking up into his grey eyes. He looked like he wanted to eat her, and she definitely wanted to be eaten. She tried to pull him in for another long kiss, but he made it chaste.

"We do have things to discuss," he said gently.

Jane pulled away from his arms then and walked over to her desk with the champagne, "Thank you for this. How did you know?"

"I heard that human women prefer it to wine or zota," Jei was watching Jane's face expression to decide if this was true or if Tir had misunderstood.

She smiled, this was the second time she had heard that and assumed it must be Tir spreading this rumor as Kara loved champagne over all else, "It depends. Unfortunately, I don't think it would work very well in your puzzle jug. It might be best to just drink it in cups, that is if you wouldn't be too disappointed?"

"That works out well as I forgot to even bring the

puzzle jug with me. I was so looking forward to seeing you."

Jane took out two black ceramic cups and began to open the champagne and pour. She was relieved to not have to play with the puzzle jug, she was terrible at trying to figure out which hole to drink from, and she didn't think it was very much fun.

Jei made a toast, "To the first human woman to truly integrate into the Alliance military."

"And in doing so, I've learned frightening truths both about myself and the Alliance," she replied in all seriousness.

"But you've done it with more grace than any of us could have imagined."

She smiled in acknowledgement and they both drank some champagne. Jane closed her eyes and almost cried it tasted like home, Earth and humanity.

"I've never had champagne before, it's nice in a bubbly and refreshing kind of way."

Jane opened her eyes at the sound of his voice and reminded herself, *But I have this here and I want him too.* She steadied her mind and asked, "Have you had much food or drink that was human-made before?"

"No, just the midday meal at Leld the other day," he admitted. "I've never had a reason to try anything made by humans until now."

The way he said that last sentence struck Jane that he meant it as a double meaning, and suddenly she began trying to recall the exact protocol for courting. But she had forgotten to look it up. She wondered if she would recognize the phrase when he said it. *If he said it*, she reminded herself. "I would be more than happy to introduce you to some things," Jane said in what she hoped was a seductive way.

"You can introduce them to me now," he said casually. "I'm curious about a few human women's customs."

"Oh?"

"Yes, I hear human women like to wear undergarments. I've seen your prayer candles in the officers' shrine and often wondered about what they look like."

"Do you think about those candles a lot?"

"Every now and then," he admitted. "It's a gentle reminder that we have a woman onboard."

"Is that a good thing?"

"It's neither. It's a fact and a new fact."

She nodded, gazed into his grey eyes and wondered, *Are we going to have sex or not? What's going on? I thought we were getting somewhere, but now I feel like I'm teaching a cultural class on women's undergarments in the Alliance in accordance with the gods.*

Jei enjoyed the sultry look she was giving him. He knew she had not had a slave artist visit her quarters since she arrived. *She must be desperate for sex*, he thought. He had heard that some of the human women didn't like to pay for sex, and he assumed she must be one of them, that she wanted to torture herself like this. "Please put in an order for whatever you think I should try from Earth, and I will try it for you," he instructed her, not realizing that it would be very expensive for her to pay for the cost of transportation.

"Sure," she replied, having no intention of doing that whatsoever. She would just offer herself again and again. An image of her lifting up her skirt and spreading her labia flitted through her mind then, and she imagined herself saying, 'Try this then.' But then she shooed that thought away.

Jei took Jane's free hand and squeezed it, "I mean it, put a request in for whatever you want."

"What kind of things would you like to try, do you think?" *I think my natural lubrication would taste fantastic with this champagne,* she thought of suggesting and smiled to herself.

Jei ran his hand up her arm, covered by her dress, wishing he could feel more of her soft skin, "I'd love to become more accustomed to some of human women's nocturnal rituals."

Shivers ran up Jane's arm when he ran his fingers up her arm caressing her strongly over her sleeve, "I'm sure you've heard from your cultural source, we sleep in pajamas."

"I've heard that, but I just can't imagine it," he said while his hand moved up to her neck. "When I imagine you asleep at night, it's how the gods intended it, naked. With only the sheets touching this pink flesh with furry areas."

Jane took a sharp intake of breath. His cool hand felt so good on her neck, she closed her eyes and could barely concentrate on the conversation, "I'm sure you've seen those candles for my pajamas at the shrine too."

His hand moved to caress the side of her face, "I have, but I just can't believe in pajamas as they don't interest me as much as your undergarments." Her skin was so warm and soft. He knew that if he continued to touch her, he would not be able to stop, and then they wouldn't talk about what they needed to talk about compromises to escalate their relationship as he wanted it to be. He needed her to come to some understanding of his relationship with Vran.

Jane reached out and put her hand on top of his and closed her eyes, this felt so right. "I feel so naughty doing this with you."

Jei smiled, "This is my ship. My fleet. Haven't you realized yet that the eyes of Alliance women don't reach us here? There are no fines, no prying eyes. This is the men's world you walk in here."

"I have noticed," Jane said seriously. And thought, *And you are the Emperor out here.*

Jei took his hand away, noticing her change in expression, "And this worries you?"

"I'm a woman, after all."

"Not an Alliance woman. Not in the way that would be detrimental."

Jane gave him a look of disbelief, "Isn't that what all of this is about? Humans being the Lost People? And taking Alliance citizenship as we are meant to do to level your demographics issue? How can we not be real Alliance women?" This was something Jane struggled with herself. She was and she wasn't a true Alliance woman and the truth of his words, for she knew them to be true, hurt her because she was forced to live here as a second class citizen with all of this talk of humans being equal but then being treated as less behind closed doors. She hated the hypocrisy of it. Yet she also hated that he acknowledged it as well.

"I've told you before what I think about humans being the Lost People, and I'll not repeat myself because I know you were listening the first time."

"You don't fear me then for being a spy for the Alliance women?"

He laughed, "No. I know you human women have your own agenda, just as the men have theirs and the Alliance women have theirs. Ever since Captain Kara escaped and came back on her own terms, we all know there is a third party to our Alliance race now."

"Why did you allow it then?"

"Why not? Distraction," he said evenly.

"Distraction for what?"

Jei gave her a curious look and actually answered her in the Alliance men's language that her translator could not translate.

Although Jane was a member of the crew, she was still a woman and a human. Sometimes she would walk into a room, and they would be speaking the Alliance male language unidentifiable by her translator, and they wouldn't translate for her. She knew a lot was going on outside the Alliance Empire that she suspected none of the Alliance women knew anything about. However, she wasn't naïve enough to think that they were unaware of men hiding secrets, but only that they just didn't know or care what those secrets were. "I'm glad we can be a distraction," Jane said disapprovingly.

"Human women have brought a lot to our lives here. A distraction to let us live more freely, and might I even suggest more equally." He paused, "By the look on your face, I think 'distraction' might be poorly translated into your language. What about the word 'amusement'? Is that better?"

"I can't decide if that is better or worse. Neither one is very positive." Jane was dismayed when she realized that their romantic moment had just disappeared, and she wanted more than anything to bring it back. She didn't want to talk about politics.

"Although this is a positive thing. Human women have brought much-needed change to the Alliance and something else to turn our attention to. This struggle between Alliance men and women was becoming unbearable."

"I see, and we are the distraction for both, but given the way some of the human women have been treated, I'd say the men appreciate us more." *Come on, bring him back to wanting to kiss you,* she rallied herself into the conversation.

"We were the ones suffering, and we were the ones that

pushed bringing human women here. Alliance women wanted to have multiple husbands as a way to solve the issue."

"Seems logical."

"If you are a woman, how convenient to have five or six husbands all coming in at different times for conjugal visits? But it wasn't an answer to our problem. Our problem rests somewhere in our population."

"What do you think? Is it a virus of some kind?"

"I don't know. I'm not a doctor or a scientist. All I know is that none of our enemies have ever gotten close to our home planets, so I think it must be something we, the men, might be infected with but is undetectable. That is my first instinct."

Jane thought, *Of course, he would want to believe that his number one goal would be to protect the heart of the Empire, and as women were not allowed to leave the planet they were born on, it would be terrible for him to think he had allowed enemies through.* "But we are all screened thoroughly when we return, and Alliance medicine is the best."

"Yes, it is," he agreed. He looked off lost in thought and then smiled at Jane, "Tell me again about women's undergarments. Are you wearing them now?"

Jane finished her champagne, stood up, and held her hand at the curve of her breast, caressing it slowly as she spoke, "I can show you now if you would like?"

"Please," his eyes were transfixed on this small human beauty before him. He had imagined her without clothing, so many times, he longed to see what she would look like. Her alienness and familiar shape all combined.

Jane was inwardly smiling. She couldn't remember the last time she had had this much fun. She was nervous and excited at the same time. The kind of feeling only felt when you were really attracted to someone. She slowly leaned down and grabbed the hem of her floor-length skirt, then she slowly began to lift it up. Past her knees, the top of her stockings, her underwear her waist and finally over her breasts and head. Then she threw the dress to the floor and stood with her hands, slowly caressing her breasts over her black lace bra. She could see by his eyes that he was fascinated, and it gave her more confidence to take this all even more sensually, "This is the undergarment we wear on our breasts as they are bigger than Alliance women's breasts."

"I've heard this, but I must admit I've not paid much attention to other human women."

"Only me?"

"Only you," he confirmed. "And do human men like to kiss women's breasts too?"

"Would you like to do that, Admiral?"

"Gods don't use my title," he said, almost breathlessly.

Jane smiled, obviously, he had never been in a situation like this before, and she finally understood now. This kind of fantasy was something humans played out frequently, but this was something totally new and forbidden in the Alliance. "Admiral," she said as sultrily as she could, "Would you like to see the rest? Would you like to order me to do it?"

Jei had never had a woman speak to him like this before, and he was enjoying every second of this, "Yes, but first, turn around. I want to see all of you in these undergarments."

Jane lifted her hands above her head and slowly spun around. After one twirl, he caught her by the hips and pulled her close to him. He ran his hands up her warm skin from her hips to her breasts. Her scent was overwhelming, she wanted him. It encouraged him to explore her body further. Jei was fascinated by these black undergarments with holes in them. He ran his hands along the fabric covering her breasts and loved how her nipple immediately became erect even through the fabric at his touch. He brought her chest down to his face and sucked on her nipple through the light fabric. It felt so different, but she seemed to like it just as much as he did. He repeated the same on the other nipple, making the fabric wet with his mouth. Her nipples were totally erect through the material, and then he moved his hand in between her legs, "There is something so wrong about your lubrication being caught here rather than spilling down your legs for me."

Jane didn't know what to make of that comment, so she didn't reply, but she didn't need to.

"One of the compromises I will ask of you, if we ever get there tonight, is not to wear underwear, I find great pleasure in licking the thighs of my women before I reach their apex's of pleasure."

"Oh?" Jane said, imagining it and becoming even more aroused. She bent to take off her underwear then, and he smiled. "Just keep kissing my breasts and I guarantee there will be a lot to lick up my thighs."

Jei brought her closer to him. He tried to figure out how to take off her bra but failed. Jane did it herself so that he wouldn't destroy it as he was reaching for his sword. When she had reveled her breasts to him, he took them in his hands and began sucking on them, "I've never seen a woman without pierced nipples. You are going against the Contract human."

Jane couldn't answer him. He was giving her so much pleasure. She closed her eyes and all she could think about was his tongue and where it was going to be next.

Then Jei stood up and put his large hands on either side of her face and kissed her properly. His tongue exploring her hot mouth. She tasted so delicious like the human champagne and herself. "You are divine," he said between kisses. "I'm going to taste every part of you."

Jane was melting. She pushed her naked body against his large clothed body for another kiss. His copious ranking jewelry coolly nipped at her skin as he held her close. She loved that he was still fully clothed, and she was naked. Moving her body against his like a cat that needed attention.

Jane tasted so good, he was kissing her neck now, and his hands were exploring the curve of her hips, but he wanted more. He stood, then he kissed her again and ran his hands successfully from her ribs down to the top of her thighs, admiring the swell of her hips. When his hands rested on her hips, he could only imagine pulling her towards him in a rhythm of sex.

Jane's hands seemed to have a mind of their own and were beginning to quickly undo his collar and pulling his uniform open to expose his grey, muscular chest underneath, and he gasped a little when she caressed his nipple.

Jei had never imagined this evening going this fast At best, he had hoped for some kisses like before, but he reasoned through his lust filled mind that they were both adults and knew precisely what they were doing. And maybe the sooner they did this, the better. He stopped kissing her then and looked directly into her eyes, just to be sure, "Jane, I wanted to agree on a compromise first, but we can do that after if you trust me? I must admit I have only one thing on my mind now and it's licking your furry clitoris followed by thrusting my hard penis into your wet vagina."

Okay Tarzan you can do whatever you want to me, thought Jane because some things through translation just sounded terrible. She also wanted to say, 'We don't need a compromise to have sex,' but she knew this was just a part of Alliance culture, so she said, "Yes, afterwards, I trust you. I want to have sex with you now too."

"You are so intoxicating, Jane," he commented as he touched her breasts again. Then he bent down to suck on one nipple while he turned the other in his fingers.

Jane sucked in her breath. His rings were cold against her skin and it was another reminder of how important he was in the Alliance. In the galaxy. And he was with her. She began removing his clothing again.

"I've never seen a woman with as big breasts as you have, they are magnificent."

Jane didn't think she had big breasts, well not compared to most human women anyway, she was average, but no one would ever describe her with large breasts. However, compared to Alliance women, she supposed she was very curvy. Jei had been the first Alliance man beside a slave artist she had ever been with and the first man to comment on her lack of piercings. She wondered if he was turned off by this, but with the pleasure he was bringing her, she couldn't dwell on that thought long.

"I would still give you this as part of our personal compromises," he said, still holding on to both of her nipples, squeezing them as he spoke. "But if we were to marry, I would want these pierced."

Jane leaned her head back, "I can't think when you are doing that. Talk to me later about compromises. Now I want something different."

"Should I stop?" he asked, still squeezing and rubbing her nipples with his thumbs and forefingers.

Jane shook her head, "No, don't stop." She could hardly speak. His fingers felt so good. She loved the difference between one nipple being exposed to the cold air and his fingers and the other warm and titillated in his mouth.

Jei began sucking on her nipple again, and she undid his thick silver braid with her hands, so his hair cascaded freely down his back, kissing his head and neck as she did so.

Jei moved one of his hands between her legs, "You're so hot and wet." She even jumped a little when he caressed in between her upper thigh and vagina. "And I think it's been a while, or is it my touch that is making you so ready Jane?"

"It's both," Jane knew that everyone in the Alliance Empire was having sex all the time, if not with their marital spouses, then with slave artists. And she knew people on ship had talked about her abstaining from sex, Doctor Rea had even mentioned it to her as unhealthy and had offered his services, which she had quickly declined.

Jane began removing his clothes in earnest now. First his shirt, she just left all of his ranking jewelry on as it was kind of hot that she was sleeping with the Admiral of the Alliance Fleet, one of the most powerful men in the galaxy. When she pulled down his trousers, she kissed all the way up and down his hairless and powerful legs. And then she licked his testicles, and he made a sound of pleasure, so she put her hand delicately on his thick ridged cock and began stroking it. When he didn't stop her, she put it in her mouth, and after about ten minutes, she brought him to climax into her mouth. She didn't know why she wanted to do it. She knew it went against the law in the Empire unless she was married and pregnant, but she just wanted to do it. Just like she had wanted to kiss him in front of Leld. Apparently, when it came to Jei, she loved breaking all the Alliance rules.

"You are so very naughty human," he said, picking her up as if she weighed nothing and taking her to the bed. He sat down and held her in his arms. He ran his hand lightly over her bottom, and then without a word, he flipped her over and pinned her to his lap.

"What are you doing?"

"Punishing you for sucking on my penis like that. It goes against the gods."

Jane had never been hit in her life, and she didn't want him to do this, she didn't think. She put her hands up to cover herself. He was a big strong man. She didn't want him to strike her, not even in a sexual way. And she wasn't too sure if he would hold back either, in her limited exposure to Alliance culture, she noticed a strong theme of pain. Something she wanted no part of.

"Jane, you are only making it worse for yourself. You had your pleasure now receive your pain. Put your hands down and count." Jei didn't know why he wanted to do this so much. Maybe because she was a part of his crew and in some ways, he would have punished one of them with a slight physical punishment. But he knew that wasn't necessarily it, but he didn't want to dwell on it now, he wanted to enjoy this. Her being bent over him like this. A woman bent to his will for the first time for punishment. He was aroused again just thinking about what he was going to do to this human.

Jei slapped her butt cheeks so hard she winced and bit her lip not to cry out. She couldn't believe she was allowing this. *Why aren't I fighting back?* She knew though that a part of her wanted this. It was the same part of her that had wanted to suck his penis until he orgasmed in her mouth. She knew it was wrong and that made her think it was sexy. Just like him smacking her rear was wrong, but she wanted it. She wanted this pain in a strange way from him.

"If you forget to count, then that strike doesn't count," Jei said sternly.

Jei hit her again, equally as hard. He watched her pink

skin turn red with where his hand struck her. *Gods, why does she make me want to do this, and why am I completely aroused by it? Is it the sight of a human woman's body that makes me want to dominate her? She hasn't even come yet.* But he was aroused by that too and consoled himself by reminding himself, *No, she broke the rules first. I must teach her Alliance ways, and then I will expect her to behave by them.*

"One. Two. Three. Four. Five. Six." Jane couldn't believe that not only she was allowing this to happen, as he was not holding her tightly, and she was sure if she said 'no' he would stop, but she was also enjoying it. Her body was close to coming at the thought of what they were doing and his hand, sometimes so close to the entrance to her vagina. She loved the thought of what would come next.

And she had to admit, she liked letting him just take control. She had never not had control over her entire life. In the Alliance, she had a lot of responsibilities, and she should be punishing Jei as he was a man. However, she realized now that, of course, he wanted control of her. And had she thought about it a couple minutes longer, she would have realized that he wanted complete control of the Empire. That Alliance men and women couldn't share power, to be equals, and that is why they had the contracts, and that at any opportunity, one sex would overtake the other. However, she felt so aroused she didn't think that far, she just enjoyed him dominating her as such a new and exciting experience.

After Jei spanked her, he began rubbing her swollen backside and kissing her lower back and thighs.

She could feel his cock stiffen again under her stomach.

"Now, stand up and show me your red bottom, you naughty human woman."

Jane stood just a couple paces away from him as he sat on the edge of her bed, desire heavy in his eyes. She turned around and then bent down to the floor on her way back up, her fingers ran along the sides of her legs to her hips. With her back still turned to him, she slid her hands all over her red bottom, which seemed to make him even more aroused. "Is this what you wanted to see? My wickedly red bottom?" She thought *This is definitely the champagne talking.*

"Yes, now turn around and show me your furry sex human."

Jane almost laughed at the mention of her 'fur' again. She wasn't going to correct him. It was hot in a weird alien kind of way. She slowly turned around, her hands covering her sex, and she looked down as if she were embarrassed, which she wasn't at all, but for the show. She wondered if she had always been like this, thinking momentarily about what John had said about her relying solely on her instincts now.

"Move your hands," he commanded.

Jane loved the way he ordered her to remove her hands, covering her sex. She wanted him to order her around some more. She slowly pulled her hands away and looked up at him, looking into his grey eyes, "Do you like my fur? It's so wet with my desire, do you want to touch it in earnest. I want you to run your tongue up and down my thighs like you promised. You've made me so wet; it's dripping down my legs. My sex is begging for your tongue to caress it. Admiral, I want you to make me come like you make Alliance women come."

"Come here," he commanded her again. "Stand in front of me." He ran a hand from her knee to her sex. Then he took his fingers away and licked the wetness from them. You taste as good as you look, and I can't wait to taste every centimeter of you. He began kissing her abdomen and stomach then. He loved the look of her naked body. He ran his fingers down the curve of her hips and said without looking up at her, "This beautiful body has brought new life into the galaxy. There is nothing closer to the gods than mothers. You are so blessed."

Jane had never been fat, but she had been pregnant three times, and her body revealed that, and she had always been a little self-conscious about her stomach that after the third child didn't bounce back. And she had become even more self-conscious about it when they were both naked as his body was gorgeous even for his age, so big and strong.

Jei ran his hands over her abdomen and then said, "A true woman's body."

At that moment, she understood a new thing about the Alliance. Something that had been repeated to her over and over again but that she had not quite grasped until now, they embraced inevitable natural change in themselves and in their bodies. Even more so, they embraced the inevitable aging in ways that humans were still unable to do. And they embraced the women's body as it was meant to change. As she stood in front of him, she didn't think she had ever felt as beautiful as she felt at that moment. She couldn't describe it. She didn't think any man had ever made her feel the way he was making her feel now, and this made her want him anymore.

Jei was gently holding her hips, kissing her abdomen and whispering softly to her, how lovely she was. He loved the way her hot flesh felt against his lips and the taste of her skin. He ran his forefinger along her vulva to her anus and then just barely crept a finger along her labia, just brushing her clitoris so lightly she moved instinctively closer.

"Open your folds, I want to see if your inner labia matches your lips and nipples," he didn't admit this had been something he had thought about a lot since he started to think about her without clothing. It had all begun when he saw the prayer candles for her human clothing at the shrine.

Jane almost hesitated at the direct translation. It made this all feel so very naughty, and she smiled a little thinking, *Yes, Alliance translators might be the best for everything else, but not for these more intimate moments.* She obeyed him though and watched his face, full of lust and desire, as he looked at her spread herself for him. She moved her finger along to caress herself, and he grabbed her hand.

"Make no mistake, Jane, this is mine now. You don't get to touch it. If you want to orgasm, you ask me to do it for you."

Jane thought, *Well, this is different.* "Please touch me and make me come, Admiral. Do what you promised to do. Lick me and make he come."

It was too much that she called him 'Admiral' again, too pleasing. Jei remained seated but picked her up by her thighs and then leaned back on the bed with her wet vagina on his face the entire time, holding her as if she weighed nothing. While balancing her above him he licked and sucked on her clitoris. He knew she was so close to coming. She was very wet and ready for it.

Jane was so overwhelmed with his show of strength that alone was enough to almost make her come, but then his tongue was licking and his mouth sucking all along her vulva and then finally her clitoris. She was writhing on him in minutes while he held her in place with two hands firmly on her red bottom. After she had come, he flipped her onto her back on the bed and began sucking on her breasts again. Her hands were on his back and in his hair.

She had never felt so sexy in her entire life. He was looking at her like she was the only woman in the galaxy, and she loved it. After a few minutes, Jei positioned his thick ridged penis at her vagina opening and made eye contact with her before he slowly began entering her.

Jei was unprepared for how hot, tight and wet her vagina would be. He had just come in her mouth, but he might come again. He was no young man, but it had been a long time since he had had sex with someone, he actually cared about rather than just a slave artist. They desired each other, and he hadn't realized how much he had missed this connection until now. He was looking into her beautiful blue eyes and was so full of the need to take her.

When his penis was fully in her vagina, he began to move slowly in and out. He could feel the tip meeting her cervix and wondered if this hurt her. He had never been with a woman with such a small vagina. Jei looked down at her and put his hands on her shoulders. And as she looked to be enjoying herself, he thrusted faster and faster.

She closed her eyes and then said breathlessly, "I'm going to come again, I can't help it. It feels so good. Don't stop. Don't change. Just keep doing that."

He felt her come again, and it took all his strength not to come himself again. However, after that, he was able to fully release his energy into this. He picked up speed at her commands.

"Please, harder, much harder Jei," as he was pounding into her little form.

He could feel her coming again and again, and then finally, when he was taking her from behind, his hands pulling her short brown hair back roughly, he found his release again.

As they lay in each other's arms, he said, "I've not felt like that in decades," he admitted to Jane.

Jane smiled as she absently caressed his chest. "I don't think I've ever felt this way," she admitted but then didn't know how much was the forget-me-not procedure.

Jei didn't want her to think about the memories she had put on hold. All he wanted her to think about was now and their future. "We must talk about compromises now," he said casually as his hand held one of her breasts, playing with her pink nipple.

"What compromises do you want?" Jane asked, wondering what she would have to sacrifice to not have her nipples pierced. She assumed he wanted to court for marriage. She began trying to remember what was in the handbook Madame Bai had given her when they first arrived. She knew the protocols of course as she had to keep track of her wards, but she didn't know the exact phrase to begin because she never imagined she herself would be courted. And she had been so interested in looking at his nude images she had forgotten of study the handbook.

Jei surprised her then and got up and took up his trousers from the floor and pulled out two bracelets.

"Those aren't marriage bracelets, are they?"

"No, you said you never wanted to marry when we were in orbit around Leta. These are lovers' bracelets."

Jane looked at him in disbelief and thought, *This is what you get with Alliance people*, and then decided that it didn't matter she wanted to be with him and if he wanted to be lovers or whatever, as long as it was legal that would be fine. "What's a lovers' bracelet? How does it work?"

"They're for people like us, widowers who might not want to get married."

Jane didn't know why, but she was somewhat disappointed that he didn't want to marry her. It was fine when she thought it was just because she had said that, but now she realized it might be from his part too. "How do people view individuals in a lovers' pact, if I can call it that, in society? I've my reputation as Head of House Human to think about."

Jei looked at her while he considered her question, he had never had to articulate this before, "It's about the same as if we were courting. We'll be linked, but we have the advantage that we can stay with each other as if we were married without incurring fines."

"Is there a time limit? Do we have to marry afterward?"

"No, to both questions. We can do this as we please," he held out a bracelet to her. "Would you allow me to put this on you? Would you consent to be my lover?"

Jane gave him her left wrist quickly and freely, "Yes, of course."

Jei put the bracelet on her and then his on himself, "Now, kiss me again so they'll become activated." He joined her on the bed for another sensual kiss, and the bracelets tightened on both of their wrists.

Jane looked at hers to investigate it. It was very similar to a marriage bracelet, both of their names were on them, but instead of only having one House, his house listed, both of their houses were listed. Jane decided she was definitely going to have to send Madame Bai a message to ask about them just to be sure she wasn't missing anything. She had learned very early on that Alliance people loved to leave out details so that they weren't precisely lying but not exactly telling the truth either.

Jei watched Jane investigate the lovers' bracelet, "Are you worried about something?"

Jane didn't look at him but continued to investigate the bracelet, "I've never seen one of these, nor ever heard of it. I'm just curious."

"You're the only human eligible for this kind of arrangement, so it's not something I think your cultural teacher would have covered. And you're still young enough to marry legitimately."

"There's so much Madame Bai never covered," Jane said dramatically. "But I've never been married before," Jane said concerned then that she could not partake in this lovers' bracelet ritual.

"Well, not by human laws no, but by ours you have. You know that."

She shrugged her shoulders. Wondering briefly if she should still consider herself married as the father of her children is still living.

Jei put his hand on her face and turned her head gently to look at him, "This is the right choice for us. I want to be with you, and you want to be with me. This way, no one will say anything, and we remain in our own quarters and our own lives, except for when we want each other."

A thought just occurred to Jane then, and she sat up and looked at him, "Vran, is she going to remain in your quarters?"

Jei sat up then and looked at Jane, confused, "Yes, why wouldn't she?"

Jane tried to take off the bracelet then but couldn't get it off.

Jei put a hand over hers, "We must decide to take it off together at the same time. Otherwise, it is like a marriage bracelet. You cannot remove it. I don't understand what Vran has to do with this."

"I'm not going to wear a lovers' bracelet and be connected to you all the while your favorite slave artist lives in your quarters on the same ship I'm serving on."

"Why not?"

Jane looked at him, disbelievingly, "Because I'm not."

"I'm Alliance, I don't believe in monogamy, it is unhealthy."

"Well, I don't believe in sharing anyone who's not a slave artist."

"What's the difference?"

"Get this off," Jane said, trying to take hers off again.

"No."

"Yes," she pushed against his massive form, futile as it was. "I don't want this."

He grabbed her by the shoulders and said, "Explain human."

Jane took a deep breath and counted to ten in her head, "I've only been in one emotional relationship in my life. It's not just sex with you. I can't emotionally share you, even though it might be just sex for you with Vran, I can't know that for sure, so I can't allow it. It will break me. You're not off in the galaxy. We're on the same ship. I can't share you like that. If you want a relationship with me then you must get rid of her."

Jei listened to her words and tried to understand, "It's only sex with Vran. I promise. I could never think of her as I do you. You've had sex with slave artists yourself. You know it is different."

"That's not good enough, Jei," Jane said quietly and touched her heart with one finger.

"You really would forgo our future enjoyment because of jealousy over a slave artist?" He looked at his adorable human and caressed her short hair. She was so young, and he found it endearing this jealousy streak he had not expected it from Jane.

"Yes," she said decidedly.

"If I change my situation with Vran, will you pierce your nipples?" Jei, of course, was going to move Vran to the slave artists' quarters, if it meant keeping Jane, and no doubt Vran would switch ships the first chance she got, but he wanted to compromise for the best he could get from Jane, and of course there was still so much she didn't understand about Alliance culture so he would use that to his advantage.

"No."

"Will you remove the fur from your body?"

"Will you remove Vran and not have sex with her or any other slave artists while we wear these bracelets on your ship?"

"You must remove all of the fur from your body and not cut your hair," he touched her head, "here ever again." He looked at her seriously and added, "And we will share slave artists together. I'm too set in my ways to practice monogamy Jane."

Jane looked at him and wondered if she could agree to that. She had her fantasies of course, but fantasies were fantasies and what he was talking about was real. Real orgies. The lie she had already told Kara. "You want to share slave artists with me?"

"I want to enjoy slave artists with you," Jei corrected her.

"I don't understand how that makes it any different."

Jei thought for a minute and then tried to articulate this cultural practice. "I want to see someone else give you pleasure because it's a different kind of arousal for me."

The way he said that made Jane aroused again. The idea that he would watch while another man or women licked her clitoris was exciting. "You promise that if I agree to these things you will remove Vran from your quarters and not have sex with any slave artists without me?"

"Yes, I will give you this compromise." He couldn't help himself; he pinched her nipple. "And I want your complete loyalty to me at least once a week."

Jane knew when he said 'loyalty' that he was talking about doing whatever he said once a week, it was foreplay for people of the maximum class. However, Jane didn't want it to be formal. She just wanted him to naturally dominate her privately, but she didn't want to have to tell him that. She didn't think she could she felt embarrassed about desiring it, "No, our relationship will be as it develops with no prescriptions."

Jei was a bit annoyed, he had fantasized about having her in specific ways that could only be on loyalty days, but then he reminded himself that she had just given herself to him in almost a loyalty regard, so he would think about all of that later. "I want full access to the lovers' bracelets."

Jane had no idea what he was talking about now. She knew that marriage bracelets were connected with one's DNA but little else. "What do you mean?"

Jei smiled, "Why don't you let me demonstrate over the next couple of days?"

Jane was too curious to say 'no,' "If I find I don't like it?"

"We can negotiate something else." Jei looked at her young body again, "And one more thing, of course, I'm not on any kind of birth control."

"If you are worried about pregnancy, don't be. I'm almost 40 years old, and human women aren't as healthy as Alliance women."

"But if you were to become pregnant, I would insist that we marry so that the child would not be without a House."

Jane was confident that she wouldn't become pregnant she was too old. She nodded, "We don't even need to think about it. I am too old."

Jei wasn't an expert on women's fertility. It was something Alliance men were not taught as part of the

Contract. He of course knew that women's fertility dropped naturally by the age of 50 in Alliance women, but he knew nothing about human women. He had no idea if Jane could still have children, but he assumed that she would have no reason to lie and that this would line up with why she was given the opportunity not to marry when she arrived in the Alliance Empire. Because what would be the point of making her marry if there would be no children. "I just wanted to let you know the situation if that were to happen."

Jane nodded and asked, "Will you stay here with me tonight? "She realized that maybe even more than the sex, she wanted to be close to someone in her bed all night. And the fact he was so big and strong didn't hurt that fantasy either.

"Yes," he said and then moved her closer to him, so he could hold her close. He took in her scent now intermixed with his and realized that he had not slept with a woman or held her like this since his wife. Vran never allowed him to hold her as they slept. Jei reveled in the closeness of Jane and kissed the top of Jane's head and thought, *This feels so right. We just need to work out a million details that make a couple settled.*

Jane closed her eyes, feeling secure in Jei's embrace. She shooed away all the negative thoughts her mind was trying to throw at her as she drifted off to sleep. *Just listen to my instincts,* she told her herself thinking about what John had told her and her body was telling her this was perfect.

Except she still held on to her small disappointment that he didn't want to marry her, and she couldn't shake it.

6

A New Status

In the middle of the night, Jane pleasantly woke up to Jei rubbing her breasts from behind and gently kissing her neck. She responded by turning towards him and kissing him.

"I can't keep my hands from you. It feels so good to touch you," he said between kisses.

Jane loved his touch in the darkness and his words. She felt really close to someone and this feeling was filling a space in her heart which she had convinced herself she could do without. Even with her memories dimmed from the forget-me-not, she recognized this. Now she realized that doing without this intimacy was only living a half-life and she had been missing out on all the sensual pleasures of life. And for what? Because she was afraid of using an alien? There was no way she was going to get pregnant now. Her periods were completely erratic, and she assumed she was too old, and her body had shut down that part of her life. If she would have been on Earth, of course, she would never truly be too old. However, Alliance scientists refused to use any medical technology in reproduction as their religion told them that reproduction was governed by the gods alone. All she was forfeiting was the pleasure of someone close who wanted to be there. Someone she wasn't paying. And she could feel the difference.

Jei's hands ran up and down her body, reveling in her warm and soft flesh. He wanted to take her from behind. He gently flipped her back to the way she was and put a hand on her clitoris, expertly learning her body.

"Your hands feel so good," she commented.

"I must still be doing something wrong if you're able to speak," Jei said and then began kissing behind her ear and trying a slighting different tactic with his fingers on her clitoris. A different rhythm of rubbing and tapping. He could sense her body responding more and asked, "And now?" When she didn't respond he said, "Exactly." It wasn't long before she climaxed and then he entered her hot and wet vagina from behind.

Jane had never experienced such lovemaking her life, she didn't think so anyway. It was hard to know with the forget-me-not, but she didn't think so. Jei was now entering her from behind, but so gently and softly, it was keeping her body on this nice edge of heightened arousal but still away from completely orgasming again, although the promise was definitely there.

Jei enjoyed the feel of Jane's body and was pleased with her reactions to him. Of course, he was a competent lover. He was over 200 years old. Alliance men studied how to be good in bed as it was a means to an end for them. It was considered rape to have sex with a woman who had not climaxed first. So, the longer it took to bring a woman pleasure, the longer they would have to wait for their own pleasure. Jei had never questioned this logic. Women's anatomy was purposely designed this way that is why their clitoris was not close enough to their vagina to orgasm from the act of sex alone. He loved the feeling of knowing a woman's body so well he could bring her to orgasm in minutes.

Jei had met some human men before when he was young. He had just become an officer and it was the first time he had been near the Solar System, where Earth was. He was shocked that they believed that women didn't need to orgasm before sex and that sometimes that was not always possible. Even at that time, Jei was unsure whether or not humans were the Lost People, but it was a fact that they were genetically the same, so Jei and the other men were disgusted that these men would take women in such a way. Disgusted that they took very little pleasure in pleasuring a woman and as such had no skills to pass on. One of Jei's commanding officers had made the comment that without women, there would be no humanity and therefore women were to be treasured. This was the idea on which the Alliance Empire was built. But the human men laughed and talked about equality. Jei and the other officers were disgusted and from that moment on they knew why the Alliance kept their distance from the heathens on Earth. And why if they destroyed themselves it would be better for the galaxy. They had lost sight of the natural order of things and were perverse.

Jei himself had been opposed to taking human women into the Alliance based on this one encounter. He had been annoyed with Tir for pushing it when he captured the Dakota. However, when he heard the rumors about Tir's wife not being able to keep her hands from him. Something occurred to him, that maybe human women needed and wanted to be liberated from beastly human men. And when he met Jane that thought became a fact for him. And everything that Tir had been whispering in his ear about maybe men having a turn at ruling the Empire became true.

A small voice inside of him said that this was going against the gods, but he pushed that thought away. He already loved Jane. He wanted to be with her, and he would have her. This broken but strong woman who finally had her chance to find true happiness with an Alliance man. To experience life how it was meant to be. Not with some terrible human man in the squalor and backwardness of Earth.

Throughout the night, they had had sex a few more times. When it was time to get up in the morning, Jane said, "Let's not have breakfast."

Jei kissed her head and then got out of bed, "I wish that we could." He picked her up in his strong arms suddenly and carried her with him to the shower. "Computer change temperature for Jei," he commanded the bathroom computer.

"Temperature changed to 18C," the male computer voice said.

Jane began to squirm, "I'm not getting in. It's too cold."

He held her tighter, "It'll only be cold in the beginning, and then you'll get used to it. Cold showers are good for your health."

"But this won't be cold for you?" she protested.

"No, but if it's warm for you, it will burn me. The cold is good for you. You will feel refreshed and I want to spend as much time next to your naked body as possible. Come on, cold shower time human." Jei took her in the shower with him, and she screamed, and he laughed. After he was sure she was reasonably settled, he put her down to wash her hair. "Let me take care of you now since you are taking a cold shower for me."

Jane didn't run out of the shower like she thought she would. She just stood there frozen, letting the cold-water rush over them. She liked him touching her though and concentrated on that and not the cold water. Soon she was numb to it and was just reveling in his touch. She didn't know if she imagined it or not, but it felt like the cold water was making her more sensitive to every area he caressed with soapy hands or soft kisses.

When they were both clean, they got out of the shower and were dried by cool air. Then they walked out the bathroom, Jane saw clothing laid out for them on the bed.

"What's this? Who's been here?"

"My squire," Jei said as if it were the most natural thing in the world. "He knows what I need and does it."

"Why did he bring this dress? Whose is it?"

"Don't be silly. It's yours. I bought it for you. You will need it." He touched her hair, "I bought many things for you that I will give to you as you need them."

Jane was in shock. She didn't think that anyone had ever given her so many presents. But she knew this was a core element of Alliance culture, the gift-giving, especially between men and women. She held up the formal Alliance dress. It had dark blue clouds that moved subtly over it. She was no expert on Alliance fabric or fashions, but she could still feel that this dress was definitely of better quality than her other formal dress given to her by Madame Bai. "But where will I wear it onboard? Now, who is being silly?"

He smiled at her, "You'll wear it now. There is a morning meal reception with the Ambassador and the other diplomats."

"I can't attend that. What would people say? I'm just an engineer?"

"No, you are my lover. This is somewhere between wife

and courting. You'll attend in this capacity. There's nothing strange about it. It's just a morning meal. And besides, the Ambassador has already expressed an interest in meeting you."

"Why would he want to meet me?"

Jei gave her a look, "Because you're human, and she's curious."

Jane stood there and looked at the dress, "When did you have time to buy this? And how did you know my measurements?"

"I bought it and many other things for you after we had the midday meal at Leld. I knew your measurements because they are in your file, Lieutenant." He was already dressed now but came up behind her and wrapped his arms around her. "Will you wear it and come with me?"

Jane leaned back into his uniform and ranking jewelry gently piercing her back. She put her hands on his, "Yes, but I'll feel strange about it."

"Why?"

"I don't know the term 'lovers' makes me feel like we are doing something wrong."

"Nonsense. And people have suspected it for a while now, these bracelets," he held up his wrist, "just legitimizes our relationship."

"Legitimizes us to have sex. Ridiculous," Jane said.

Jei picked her up, began kissing her. He moved so that her back was against the wall. He held her with one arm while his other hand found her clitoris. "Tell me," he breathed into her ear, "don't you want this to be legitimate?"

His fingers felt so good she could hardly answer, "I don't know. I guess, yes."

He began rubbing faster, "Yes?"

"Yes, don't stop."

He increased his speed, and she was so close to coming. It was all so intense, her being naked and vulnerable, held up against the cold wall while he was dressed in his formal uniform, making her come.

"Human," he said.

His breath on her ear gave her shivers. She couldn't answer she was so close.

He kissed her ear and neck, "This is how it should be Jane. I touch you and you can't speak from the pleasure." She came, but he didn't stop until she had ridden out all of her pleasure, every last tremor. Then he held her in his arms and said, "I think we both want this legitimized. Now put on your dress and don't clean yourself. I want you to remember why your thighs are wet and sticky."

"Aren't we going to finish?" She really wanted his penis inside of her again, it was so big, and the feeling of the ridges were addictive. It brought a numbness to her opening that was so sensual she craved it.

"No, it took too long to make you climax. It's my own fault for not knowing your body well enough. Tonight, I promise I will study it more." He set her down and picked up the dress and handed it to her.

Jane ignored him and went to her wardrobe. She took out some Alliance stockings, underwear, and a bra. She held eye contact with Jei as she put these things on.

"Remember what I said about the underwear?" he asked seriously.

She did remember. She was aroused again, just thinking about him licking her thighs clean, so she took the underwear off and put it back in her wardrobe. Then she put on the formal dress, her jewelry, and then they left for breakfast.

As they walked through the corridors, everyone stopped and bowed to Jei. Jane was surprised that none of them seemed surprised to see her in such a fashion. Standing next to him in a formal dress and not in her uniform. Even when they passed her friend Doctor Rea, he simply bowed to Jei as he always would.

Jane said to Jei when they were alone in a corridor, "Does no one find our new relationship status odd? I find it odd."

"Odd that no one finds it odd or odd that we are together?"

"Don't play with me, you know what I mean."

"I do. As I said, everyone on this ship has been suspecting this for weeks, my crew isn't stupid, and neither am I. I know their minds. So why should they be surprised that something they thought was going to happen happened? When you know, it is going to snow, and it snows, are you surprised?" he asked rhetorically.

"I guess humans are just a bit more dramatic about things," she smiled a little, thinking about the snow reference. She wasn't going to mention that humans did even remark about the weather or something of interest even if they knew it was going to happen, just like snow.

Soon they reached the formal reception room. It was grand for a starship, and only the flagship *Kzi* had one. It was a room located at the top of the ship where the battle shielding could be retracted to reveal only space. Jane, of course, had never been in this room. She had only heard rumors about it, and when she walked in, she was in awe of it and the technology that enabled it. It felt the same as the first time she went swimming in the ocean and looked out on the vastness of it. She felt so small and insignificant but curious to go explore at the same time.

Jei looked at Jane, "It's impressive, isn't it? To think we can do this and still travel as fast as we do is both a technological and I hesitate to say, artistic accomplishment."

Jane didn't stop looking up, "I would say, after living in the Alliance now, you aren't completely devoid of artistic accomplishments as you like to proclaim to the galaxy, you just don't always value or identify art as art. However, there is, of course, room for improvement."

Jei took her hand, "Another time I'll bring you back here, just the two of us, so we can look up and be amazed at this Alliance art. Unfortunately, we must socialize now. Let me introduce you to the ambassador who has been asking to meet you."

Jei led Jane over to a group of men and introduced her. The last man she was introduced to was surprisingly young.

"Jane, this is Ambassador Wol. He has been so looking forward to meeting you."

Everyone around them dispersed then, and Jane was left alone with the Ambassador. She looked at him and was surprised when she felt sure that he was actually a she.

Wol gave Jane a minute to collect herself. She was used to this when people first met her. It didn't bother her at all. After a suitable amount of time, she said, "Jane, how do you find your new life in the Alliance?"

"I find it exhilarating," and that was no lie.

"I must apologize, as I am sure you have heard before. I'm sorry for Admiral Tir's rough handling of you all. Sometimes, Tir especially, can be impulsive and mistakes are made."

Jane had heard this before, of course, she had. This was their way of saying, 'I'm sorry you were taken, we didn't want any women who already were mothers with families being brought here.' "Only the gods know our destinies," Jane replied. This was the Alliance way of saying, 'It's fine, and I don't want to talk about it.'

"Indeed, they do," Wol replied. She had heard so

much about Jane. She was excited to meet her now. Wol felt it was right that Jane and the Admiral had formed a genuine and public bond as lovers. This would make Jane even more respected throughout the Empire. "And how are the new 1,000 settling into life in the Capital City?"

"Well enough," Jane said, more comfortable talking about women other than herself. "They're young, and with that comes a bit of rambunctiousness, but otherwise, everything is falling into place."

"I've heard of a woman named Babette who is randomly kissing men she's not even courting."

Jane had to resist rolling her eyes at the young ambassador. "As I said, these women are young. Babette will fall into line or be sent to the High Priestess's punishment rooms. It's difficult for her to imagine finding her other half without physical contact first."

"I'm surprised she hasn't been sent there yet, as it's no secret House Human has very little UCs. And after your geriatric kiss, you must be without any UCs for any of the other women's fines."

Jane actually blushed because of the word 'geriatric' not for the mention of House Human being poor or for the kiss itself, "Yes, strange that."

"Where does House Human find the money to pay all these fines? It is a mystery."

"As you might have guessed, there are those who feel sympathy for House Human and are generous enough to cover some of these growing pains' costs."

"House Zu? House Vo?"

"Oh, you can guess well enough Ambassador," Jane replied as a young squire came and brought them tea. Jane thought this was an excellent time to change the subject, and she wondered if the Ambassador was going to be offended, but she had to ask. "Ambassador, excuse me, but are you a woman dressed as a man?"

"I am a woman dressed as an Ambassador just as you are a woman dressed as an Alliance engineer when you are working."

"Sorry, I just..." Jane stumbled, realizing how ridiculous her question had been and something she would have never asked on Earth just because of clothing. "I've become so accustomed to the rigidness of Alliance society and the clothing as identification, I didn't think about it that way. I also thought that women couldn't leave the planets they were born on, so you see I was confused."

"Oh, that galactic myth," Wol said, smiling. "Of course, there's something in the Contract about women not leaving the planets they were born on, but that's not for the reasons that most people in the galaxy assume it is. And if you look closely, there are further compromises afterward, and it's something of a grey area now. However, most women don't want to break convention as they are happy with the opportunities on the planets they were born. And in my personal opinion, too content and this has become a bit of an issue. That is why I'm so keen to meet you."

Jane ignored her praise but was suspicious of why she thought this was an issue, "Why don't more women leave, do you think?"

"Why would we risk our lives when the men are more than willing? True women are stronger. All the endurance tests showed that, in the beginning, as you probably know, that it was only women sent out on space exploration as it was thought men were not mentally or physically strong enough. However, after enough time men were added to the crews and if you look carefully at history, especially around the 500 years, or so the Lost People became lost on

Earth, you will see that men and women were the most equal that they had ever been in Alliance history."

"What happened to that equality?"

"It made a lot of people uncomfortable. There was a movement to take power away from men, but it needed to be strategically done, so we gave them the stars and convinced women it was pointless to see the galaxy as the Alliance was the best and at the heart of everything worth living for. But the issue now is that the Alliance is the most powerful in the galaxy and we've trusted the men to do our biding unsupervised."

Jane was entranced with this new information and surprised that even the Ambassador spoke as if men were inferior and she was there to keep an eye on their actions. Jane wondered then if she spoke the men's language and what her objectives really were.

Wol added, "Didn't it ever occur to you to wonder how humans could be the Lost People if there were only men on ships?"

"I'm embarrassed to say I hadn't questioned it. But in my defense, I've been busy settling in and helping others of my house to settle as well."

Wol frowned, "Yes, I understand. But now you know and remember that in everything you do. Do you understand what I'm saying?"

Jane looked into Wol's green eyes and knew she was telling her something meaningful, and to even prove the point further, she touched her cheek with two fingers. Jane knew this explicitly meant something, but she couldn't remember what. "I will remember," she replied confidently although she didn't know what she was supposed to know. She knew she couldn't ask any of the men on the ship though. Still seeing the searching look in Wol's eyes, she knew she was missing this message, but there was nothing she could do about it. Of course, they were being watched and listened to. Jane then said, "I'd love to talk to you more about human culture if you would be interested. You know how to find me, perhaps before we reach our destination?"

"Perhaps," Wol said. "In the meantime, I'll recommend some reading for you. You should have clearance as you are Head of House Human if you wouldn't be offended by the suggestion?"

"Not at all. I've found this brief conversation alone enlightening."

"Good, you should. You're in a tricky situation and how tricky I don't even think you've begun to realize."

"What do you mean?"

Wol smiled, "Oh, Admiral, Jane and I were just discussing how interesting it was to be women among men in the men's world."

Admiral Jei came to stand right next to Jane. She wondered how long he had been there and what Wol meant by her other comment. Unfortunately, she wouldn't know now. Jane suddenly wondered if she were right in accepting Jei's offer to be his lover or if this had been a mistake. However, when she looked at him, she wanted him and wanted to be with him, no matter what the consequences as she couldn't imagine any dire penalties because of the arrangement.

As Jane was leaving the morning reception, Wol said the most cryptic thing to her though which left Jane uneasy, "When the forget-me-not wears off, don't give up on this new you. Alliance Jane of the Lost People, Head of House Human and lover of the illustrious Admiral Jei. We need this Jane more than the other one pinning for a human."

Jane was stunned, "I don't have a choice, do I?"

Wol frowned, "We always have choices in the Alliance,

Jane. Especially as a woman. Don't ever forget that is always an option for you."

Jane was escorted away by Jei then. She didn't mention Wol's last comment as she didn't want to think about how she would feel when the forget-me-not wore off. Right now, she just wanted to enjoy the pleasure and contentment she felt in her life.

Jei left Jane in her quarters. She had to go on duty.

"Will you come to my quarters tonight for the evening meal? I want to prove to you that Vran is gone," Jei said seriously.

Jane frowned at the mention of his slave artist's name, "Yes, I'll want to see it for myself."

"Then why are you frowning?"

"It makes me jealous to even think that you have to remove a woman from your quarters to make room for me."

Jei shook his head in disbelief and then kissed her forehead. She was so young and so human, "Most women would feel as if they had won a battle. You should be smiling."

"I'm not most Alliance women Jei. I'm human, and it makes me uncomfortable." If he would have been human, she would have added, 'Make sure you've changed the sheets as well.'

"Because you worry about Vran?"

"No, yes, I mean, there are so many things you don't understand about how this makes me feel I cannot articulate them all now. I'm not even going to try. I'll just be happy that she is gone. I'll see you tonight."

Jei left her then thinking, *Humans are the most delightful little creatures. Sometimes so caring and other times, so vicious.* He knew the second part from the records of humanity. One of the reasons that the Lost People were abandoned was that it was thought that they had gone mad. All the experiments done on humans were not only to see if they were genetically Alliance but to see if they could be saved from their insanity. Their lust for violence. At that time, it was thought that they were incurable. There was even talk of exterminating them. However, it was decided to let the gods see to humanities fate. Jei thought it was good that Jane was still barred from seeing those records. No one needed the humans asking about what might be added to their food or water.

After Jane had come off of duty, she had just enough time to go back to her quarters and change her clothing. She put on the dress he had given her that morning with the jewelry and some makeup. She had decided during the day, when her new lovers' bracelet caught her eye during the day, that she was, in fact, celebrating that Vran was vacating what was to be her territory now. So, she wanted to look her best.

As Jane walked to Jei's quarters, she was surprised to see that other crew members bowed to her in the corridors. This made her uncomfortable. She and Jei weren't married, and she didn't want to gain rank through him. Jane was her own person, and she wanted to be treated according to what she had earned herself, but she knew keenly it would only insult them to tell them not to bow, so she graciously accepted this new position as best as she could.

Jei's squire answered his door and lead Jane to his private dining room.

Jei dismissed his squire while walking towards Jane and then ran a finger over her lips, "You're so exotic, so alluring, with that face paint" and he took her in his arms and kissed her passionately. "And just now, all I want is that lovely dress off."

"Good because I'm not hungry either," Jane said in between kisses.

Jei simply picked her up then and carried her into his large bedroom. He set her feet down on the floor and quickly undressed her, pleased to see that she was not wearing underwear under her Alliance dress as she should be. He covered her body in kisses and then laid her on the side of the bed so that he could access her sex easily. He ran a finger over her, vulva, "Have you been a good human woman? Your thighs are covered again with your desire."

Jane looked up into his grey eyes with desire and thought, *Yes, this is precisely what I want. Maybe this is the second chapter in my life, my Alliance life?* "I've been thinking about what we did last night and this morning, all day," she said. "Wondering if this lovers' bracelet is right?" Her heart was pounding. He was looking at her intensely, but she couldn't focus on anything but the desire in his eyes and the erotic feeling of his finger moving up and down her vulva.

"How could my touch and being publically connected to me not feel right? Doesn't this feel, right? Didn't my tongue on your sex feel right last night? Maybe you just need more convincing. Do you want me to lick your thighs clean? Do you want me to suck on you until you come again?"

She closed her eyes and answered him, breathlessly, "Yes."

"Good. I wouldn't want to have to punish you for really questioning your change in status." He pinched her labia, and she squirmed a bit. "Tell me," he was rubbing her vulva again, "what was your favorite part of last night?"

She closed her eyes and licked her lips, "When you spanked me."

Jei was so turned on by this human woman he didn't know if he was ever going to be able to concentrate on work again, he had been thinking about her all day too. "I enjoyed that too. I especially like how ready for sex it makes you. Would you like me to spank you again?"

"Yes," she said, breathlessly excited by this idea.

"But you must tell me what you've done to deserve such a punishment?"

Jane's mind was hazy with lust, she thought questioning whether or not their relationship, the lovers' bracelets would have been enough for punishment. Obviously, he wanted something sexy, "I masturbated before you came over last night."

Jei was surprised by this admission, "That does deserve punishment that you couldn't even wait an hour. Would you like your punishment now, Jane?"

"Yes, what?"

Her mind was blank, *Would he want to be called Admiral now?* She didn't think so.

"Yes, Admiral," she hazarded.

"No, try again," he knew he was testing her knowledge of Alliance culture now, but he wanted to gauge what she had and hadn't experienced in these regards.

"Yes, Master?"

"You are not a slave. You call me 'Primary' in this situation," he said sternly.

"Yes, Primary," Jane's mind was reeling, *What was a Primary?* She would have to look this up in the database. But she soon forgot as he had stripped off his clothing now and had her over his lap rubbing her bottom. She thought, *Soon, he is going to do it, and I can let go of everything completely*. "One. Two. Three. Four. Five," and *Yes, touch me there*, she thought as his fingers explored her wet vagina.

Jei had never had this kind of a relationship with a woman before. He had never wanted to dominate his wife in this sexual way. What surprised him, even more, was that Jane seemed to want this herself as well. He wondered about human sexual practices then and whether or not they had really been properly studied. When she called him 'Primary,' his desire flared, and he thought of nothing but her and what he wanted to do to her.

After he spanked her, he rubbed her bottom gently and then moved his fingers so lightly around her vulva, playing with the dark brown fur there. She was so wet, and he knew it wouldn't take too much to make her come, but he wanted to make her wait.

Jane wondered what he was doing now. He was way too gentle, and it was driving her a bit batty. Her rear was on fire, and her vagina dripping, all she wanted now was for him to have sex with her and make her come. After a few minutes, she asked, "Primary, I want you inside of me."

Jei smiled, although she couldn't see it, moved his hand away, and said, "No, we can end this now and actually have the evening meal if you would like? There's still time to eat."

"No."

"No, what?"

"No, Primary," she answered, wondering how she was going to get what she wanted. Her mind was a blur of lust, though, only focused on one thing.

"Here we do this at my pace," he told her, flipping her over and holding her like a baby in his great arms. Then he bent down and kissed her. His loose, grey hair surrounding her face.

Jane had never felt like this before in her life. Complete

surrender and comfort. This complete leap of faith into a man's arms. Jei was an alien, strong, and unknown. She didn't know if he might accidentally kill her or really hurt her, and instinctively, she felt that this was the edge she had been searching for all of her life.

Jane put her arms around his neck, pulled herself up and pushed him back on the bed. It wasn't long before she was straddling him and was trying to position herself to slide his large ridged penis into her wet sex . However, before she could complete the action, he stilled her quickly with his large hands on her hips, so tightly, she would definitely have bruises there tomorrow. "Primary, please," she begged.

Jei loved the look of her all curves and breasts, like perfect, pert fruits and her small, hot, wet human sex covered with fur hovering above his cock. It was all so primal. And most of all, he loved that she was begging for it. A woman begging. This was better than any loyalty day, this was the way she liked it too, he could see that in her eyes. And even more so, the way he liked it. "I'll let you down if you tell me one thing."

"Anything," she replied breathlessly, trying to squirm down anyway.

"Are you going to come immediately when you move your vagina all the way down around my penis?"

"I don't know," she replied, then hastily added, "Primary."

He moved her off of him and had her on her back in seconds. Then he put a hand between her legs and began rubbing her clitoris in light circular motions as he kissed her neck, ears, and breasts. In between kisses, he said, "You know in the Alliance, you can't enter a woman until she's come first, to do so is rape."

Jane just closed her eyes; his fingers were moving so

expertly it was not long at all before she was writhing beneath him. Then just as quickly, he rolled onto his back and pulled her back on top of him and said, "Now Jane, impale yourself."

Jane would have laughed at that translation. However, she wanted him so much now she just replied, "With pleasure Primary," and sunk herself onto his thick cock, and it felt just as enjoyable as it had the night before. His hands were on her hips, that were now already a bit sore, and it made her even feel sexier. She began to move back and forth slow then fast, working herself up again. Her clitoris was almost numb with all the friction, but in a way that held the promise of another orgasm so she couldn't stop. And the ridges on his penis felt so perfect. She couldn't help but wonder then, *Are we the Lost People? This feels too right for us not to be.*

Jei watched Jane ride him and couldn't believe how sexy she was. He watched her and thought, *This is a real woman. This is no slave artist. She has the marks of a woman who has brought life into the world. She has the confidence of a woman who has been married, but the insecurity to know when she is with someone new, adorably fumbling at first.*

Before Jane could bring herself to climax again, he quickly flipped her over and began entering her from the side and then she truly came again. She had been unprepared for his sudden move, but it only took two strokes of him gently entering her as she lay on her side with her legs up for him to bring her to climax again, "Primary," she said softly.

When Jei heard that, he felt the primal urge to pound into her harder. And he took her ankles with one hand. He quickly hoisted her up as he crushed into her with such force she was moaning with such pleasure, he was completely overtaken with lust. After he came into her, they lay next to each other and after some minutes he was somewhat himself again.

Jei held Jane's naked body next to his and said, "I want to do this every day, but not miss any more mealtimes."

Jane smiled and brushed some of his long grey hair back with her hand, "I agree. I'm starving now. It's going to be a long night."

He began playing with one of her nipples, "Oh, I am sure we will find ways to occupy ourselves throughout the night with a little sustenance here and there."

The next day, Jane was in the mess hall, eating lunch with her friend Doctor Rea when she began to feel a tingling sensation in her clitoris. It became so intense she needed to excuse herself from lunch, but as Doctor Rea was a telepath, he messaged her after she had left,

It's the lovers' bracelet. It can manipulate sensations in your body. You should do the same back to him. Mealtimes are a typical time to do this if you can't be together. No doubt he was actually trying to call you to him.

Jane read Rea's message after she had had an orgasm alone in her room without even touching herself and questioned out loud, "But how do I do that back to him?"

How can I control it? You must teach me how to work the bracelet.

Rea received Jane's message and laughed,

There are certain limitations to friendship. You must ask the

Admiral, but I'd be surprised if he'll tell you without something in return. It's an old Alliance trick.

When Jane did not respond, he added,

And just so we are clear, Alliance people think this is romantic and fun.

Jane sighed and said to herself, "I definitely wouldn't say this is romantic or fun until I can work it too." She looked at the bracelet and wondered who she could ask. She opened an RVM to Madame Bai as she could see that Madame Bai was available on her messaging account.

"Jane, just the person I wanted to speak to. You must be becoming telepathic."

Jane gave her a small smile, "Hardly, I've a question for you, but it's nothing important. What do you want to speak to me about?"

"It's about Babette."

Jane braced herself for the worst, wondering what that little minx had done now, "Yes?"

"She met a man at her punishment with the High Priestess."

"A priest?"

"No, another sinner."

Jane shook her head, "They put the sinners together? That doesn't sound like a good idea."

Madame Bai defended the practice, "Usually people that are there for punishments are so ashamed that they don't speak to one another."

"But instead Babette found a kindred spirit, great," Jane supplied and couldn't keep the sarcasm from her voice.

"It's worse than that."

"Tell me," Jane said seriously and was genuinely concerned now.

"This young man has no House," Madame Bai said the words solemnly.

"What does that mean? His parents were from different classes or what?"

"No, it's not quite that bad. He was born a slave and is now trying to become a part of the maximum class."

"Can people do that?"

"Of course, sometimes even the gods make mistakes, so there is a small amount of fluidity in the class system. It's rare though and until he is accepted back into the House, he was born into as maximum class, he is Houseless."

"How long will it take for him to be a part of his House again?"

"No one knows, years if at all. So, you see, it's completely inappropriate for Babette to see him now, she must wait."

"I see. Is she trying to court him?"

"No, he's forbidden from making her an offer. But they went for a walk in the Promenade, and I know they communicate through messages and VMs frequently."

Jane frowned, it was a violation of Babette's privacy that Madame Bai and her assistances watched the women in House Human like this, but apparently, it had to be done. "What would you recommend I do?" Jane asked. She had the power to take away Babette's right to private communications and assign her a chaperone for wherever she went. However, Jane didn't want to do that unless Babette had really stepped over the line. As far as she could work out now, she was only flirting with it. Maybe she likes him enough to wait for him and that's why they communicate often. *What's a little message here and there?* Jane thought trying to be positive and give Babette the benefit of the doubt.

"Jane, I think it would be very beneficial if you talked to her about this and why it's so problematic. I've tried to reach her with logic, but I think she might need a human touch to make her understand the full gravity of the situation."

"Let's just say she hypothetically married him, what would be the consequences?" Jane wanted to know what the worst would be before she talked to Babette.

Madame Bai took a sharp intake of breath, "Hypothetically, he would never be invited back into his House, their futures would be in jeopardy as it's difficult to employ people without a House, they could behave in anyway without any repercussions and any children from the union would also be Houseless. House Human would also be socially marred. Theoretically, you could petition the High Council for her to be allowed to remain in House Human, but any children they had would still be Houseless even if you were successful."

"I see, there would be no way to annul a marriage? What about that two-week annulment period?"

"No, as they couldn't marry in the normal way there is no annulment allowed. You as Head of House Human could kill them to bring some honor back to your house."

"Um, no," Jane couldn't help but think of Nun and how it felt to kill him and never wanted to do that to anyone else, especially not a human woman in her care. "Okay, I will speak to her. Thank you for bringing this to my attention."

Madame Bai nodded, "Now, was there something you wanted to speak to me about?"

Jane felt embarrassed then and didn't want to say what

she was really calling about, "If I did decide to marry, would it have to be before my 40th birthday?"

Madame Bai looked at Jane quizzically, "It's a bit of a grey area you know that as you have a husband and children from before in a way. But technically, yes that would be ideal. Tell me, I've heard rumors about you and the Admiral." Madame Bai had also seen the kiss, but she didn't want to bring that up directly.

"Yes, the problem is I don't know if he wants to marry," she couldn't help it now. She hadn't told anyone, and she was bursting to tell another woman of her situation, especially someone like Madame Bai who could offer more insight than another human woman.

"Has he bought new known jewelry?"

"Yes."

"New images of himself to show off his physic and strength?"

"If that's what you want to call it," Jane said ironically, "Yes."

"Has he given you any jewelry?"

Jane held up her left wrist, "This and some jewelry from Juio's."

Madame Bai leaned into her screen, "A lovers' bracelet. Why in all the galaxy would you agree to that?"

"I told him weeks ago I would never marry, and he took it literally."

"You said that?"

"Yes, I didn't think it meant anything at the time. We were in a group and I thought he was asking casually."

"When someone asks you something you always answer with your true intention, just to leave your options open," Madame Bai was perplexed why Jane would not want to marry the Admiral of the Fleet, one of the Alliance's most powerful men, and even if she didn't, she should want to and lie. And as he already had children, grandchildren and more, it would be a comfortable arrangement. "Is it because he is from the Second Alliance Planet?"

"No, that has nothing to do with it." Jane wondered then if she should look into some of the Second Alliance Planet's customs just to make sure everything was about the same as on the Capital Alliance Planet. She had a suspicion, though, that there would be some strange differences which Madame Bai was probably referring to now and more than just a sash of purple on uniforms.

"Did you say you didn't want to get married because of the family you left behind on Earth?"

Jane nodded.

"Jane, as I have told all of you who volunteered from the *Dakota* during the war, you must let them go. Let your Alliance life in. You are doing such a good job so far."

"I will never say 'goodbye' to them," she touched a finger over her heart, but as she did that, she did want Jei to want to marry her. It was confusing, but she didn't want to show her inner conflict to Madame Bai.

"Then, your heart will always be clouded by their memories," Madame Bai said sadly. She sympathized with Jane. In her mind, Admiral Tir should have sent her back with the male crew when they were taken. But he was too infatuated with Kara to consider any of the other women's circumstances and obviously, Kara not realizing at the time that she would have been able to make a case of Jane to return, didn't.

Jane nodded, and then after a second, asked, "Now, how do I make the lovers' bracelet work?"

"I'm not of maximum class, so I've never experienced one myself, but I've heard you make it work by touching yourself in similar ways and focusing on the other person while you do it."

Jane looked at her in disbelief, "Excuse me?"

"I know, maximum class people have some strange practices. You're beginning to know better than even I do, these days. It is also rumored that after a year or so of wearing them, the wearers become more aware of each other's emotions."

"Is there anything else I should know about these bracelets? Are they socially acceptable? I mean, am I putting House Human in a scandalous position by accepting this?"

"Oh no, not at all. It's socially acceptable, however, more so for the Admiral than you because he is so much older than you. You really should just marry."

"Easier said than done," Jane said.

Madame Bai stiffened, "You need to overcome your racism." She knew full well that half of Jane's issue was missing her family and the other half was her racism against Alliance people.

Jane didn't defend herself, "I never asked for this life, and you know it was wrong, Admiral Tir taking me as well."

"The gods willed this destiny for you. Your Alliance life is a gift, and now you must live it. Take your own advice that you give to the other human women and accept this new life. If you have given up on your human husband enough to become Admiral Jei's lover, then why not his wife? Why not have a child and then see your own human children again?"

Jane felt sick at the thought, "Because I can't."

"I don't understand you, Jane. We didn't make these rules to put you off from being with Alliance men, quite the contrary."

Jane shook her head, "I can't explain this anymore. I'll always love my human family, and my heart isn't big enough for more. I can't break my heart off into sections and still love."

"Are you sure there's no room to love an Alliance family as well? You must love the Admiral very much?" When she saw Jane's look of surprise, she explained her statement, "Normally, you know I would never speak of love directly, but I know humans well enough now to know that not only do you not feel awkward speaking about your experiences with love but that you actually seek out occasions to do it. And when you do so, it's easier for me to understand how you think about situations with Alliance men troubling you. Tell me about how you feel. I'm only trying to help."

"I had Doctor John administer the forget-me-not a while ago to get past my love for my human family. My partner Jim found another woman, my best friend actually, and I couldn't get through my days because of the heartache. It was after that that I began developing a romantic interest in the Admiral. I fear that when the forget-me-not wears off, I'll feel the same and not feel anything for the Admiral at all."

Madame Bai took in this new information and explained, "You can extend the forget-me-not for the rest of your life here on the Capital Planet. Doctor James can do it for you."

Jane thanked her for that bit of information and thought, *But I wouldn't want James anywhere near my mind for fear of what she would find out about what Doctor Anu and I have done.* "Thank you for letting me know. But I think after this reprieve, I'll want to face things head-on."

"And that's why you don't want to marry?"

"I think so," Jane admitted, "But I'm under the impression he doesn't want to marry either, but then he said if we had a child, he would want to marry, but that is exactly the opposite of what I would want to do."

Madame Bai was utterly confused now, "But why? That should be an excellent reason to marry and we aren't talking about any low-level officer either. He's the Admiral of the Fleet. Most women would just say 'yes' without any thought."

"Because I would feel like it would be the ultimate betrayal because I know I could not resist seeing my human family again, and I'd have used the Admiral and his baby to see my human family."

"And you don't think after all that, even after the forget-me-not wears off, you will have any love for the Admiral or a child between you two?"

"I can't imagine it," Jane said honestly and knew it was wrong to say to Madame Bai, as it was offensive to say that even a child that was half hers, she could never love as much as her own human children.

"I'm no doctor, but the forget-me-not doesn't change who you really are."

"I don't know, I don't think this is who I really am."

Madame Bai had nothing left to say to Jane, "Walk with the gods, Jane, and let them guide you."

"May the gods light your path," Jane replied and then ended the conversation.

Weeks passed and Jane and Jei's relationship continued just as hotly as it began. Most nights she spent in his quarters, and she had fallen into such a comfortable rhythm with Jei she could not imagine how life would have been before him. Jane loved almost everything about Jei, and she had decided over the weeks that he really was the embodiment of everything good that the Empire represented; strength, loyalty, and compassion. In the galaxy, the Alliance had many colonies, and Jane had witnessed firsthand, the strict measure in which issues were resolved. She was surprised that the Alliance had such a hands-off attitude with most of the colonies.

Jei had explained it to her like this, "We cannot civilize the galaxy with brute military force, we must conquer them and then provide for them a better life than they had before. Most of this comes in the form of technology but sometimes protection too. We don't force our religion or culture on colonists unless they are so feral, they need that guidance too."

"And humanity? We aren't a colony."

"No, but a trading partner. And so, we do look after humans, as we always have. We are genetically the same, we have always checked in and kept you safe."

"Even when we joined the Jahay and were at war with the Alliance?" Jane felt he was hiding something in his answers that she felt that if she knew him better, she would be able to guess what it was.

"Jane, human starships are no match for ours. And we would have never truly gone to war with humans. Didn't you think it was odd we always did our best to disable and not destroy human ships? When we had no trouble at all destroying the Jahay ships?"

"Yes."

"Now you have your answer, and the rest of the galaxy knew that already. That's why the Jahay wanted Earth to be an ally. They knew we wouldn't destroy human ships. It was a tactical advantage."

Jane was reminded of the legend about Cambyses capturing Pelusium and asked, "Is this written down somewhere for all to see in the galaxy? At the GU? How is it this isn't common knowledge among humans?"

"It doesn't have to be. Look at Alliance and humans, we are almost the same, except we are all grey and you are many colors. It's natural for us to want to protect you. Everyone can see that."

"We don't need the Alliance's protection," Jane said quietly.

Jei answered sternly, "Humanity has almost destroyed itself more than a few times, and none of those times came as surprises. Humanity knew it was coming and then waited until the last minute to save yourselves."

"Would the Alliance have stepped in if we hadn't? Would you have saved us or have watched us burn and simply documented it?"

He shrugged his shoulders, "I'm sure we would have watched you burn in the long past, but now, and in the last centuries, of course not." He didn't want to lie to Jane about this, but he didn't want to tell her everything either. It wasn't a pretty history between the Alliance and humanity.

"Are you saying the Alliance interfered before we had space capabilities?"

"It's a possibility. I don't have access to those records. Alliance men weren't allowed to keep records then."

Jane was shocked, "We'll get back to the Alliance's interference in humanity in a minute, what's this that men weren't allowed to keep records?"

"Men were not allowed to read and write well enough to keep records for a very long time. Everything was orally reported and written down by women," Jei said matter-of-factly. He didn't mention the secret writing language that had evolved between men for their own records.

Jane remembered then what Ambassador Wol had said

to her about the brief period in history when Alliance men and women served together, "And even now, you cannot access those records?"

"Not without asking for permission and explaining that it pertains to an upcoming mission. But even that is no assurance that I'd be granted access."

"Can I access the records?" Jane was looking at him very seriously then and her mind was racing. She was beginning to put the pieces together and comprehend for the first time this power struggle between Alliance men and women was so much more than just a cute game over the centuries with the Contracts, courting and all. There was actually a full-out battle going on. And Jane realized what Ambassador Wol's words meant then about her being in the middle of it and not even realizing it. And her mind rushed then with images of Doctor Anu and what she had done. How Jane was actually simultaneously helping both the men and the women's sides. Her stomach felt heavy then as she knew she wasn't skilled enough at these alien political games to last long in this position. Dru was almost killed for just liking a man. What would happen to her? *No wonder Jei had his guards with me,* she thought.

"I don't know. You should be able to as a High Council member, as a woman and Head of House Human. But because you are human, you might be banned from it. It doesn't matter. Let's live in the here and now."

Jane looked at her massive Alliance lover and ran her fingers through his long silver hair, "I can't believe you are so nonchalant about all of this."

"This is not new information for me," he explained quietly. "This is the way it has always been."

"The other day, I was listening to some of the men in engineering talk, and when I asked them what they were saying or to teach me some of the men's language, they said they couldn't as a direct order from you."

"That's right. It's not for you alone but for all women. Although you are human, you are still a woman."

"What about a human man?"

"Point out a human man, who is Alliance?" Jei asked, ironically.

"What about the boys who will be born to human women?"

"I'll not be Admiral by the time they come of age, so that will be another admiral's choice. Jane, why are you questioning me about all of this? What difference do our opinions make on what was or what the greater populations at large believe about humans or who has access to what information?"

She shrugged, "Your opinion means a lot in the Empire actually, and personally, I want to know."

He brought her close to him into his strong embrace, "My opinion is next to nothing inside the Empire."

"But everything outside of it."

"People fear the Alliance Fleet, but we are fair."

"No one ever wants to get too close to a predator, not knowing when they will strike. Nor does everyone want to be a part of the Empire."

"True, but hear me," he kissed her chastely, "No matter what the Alliance's overall stance is, I respect you, human woman. I respect your culture, and you respect mine. You abide by all my culture's conventions on the *Kzi* obediently. That's all that really matters to me. I know you don't like to hear this, but I'm not Tir, I don't care about humanity at large. No more than you care about the Alliance really. Or am I wrong?"

"You're not wrong," Jane admitted, and wanted to add, 'But I think your telling me half-truths. I just can't figure out what they are.' But of course, she didn't say that. "Do you think I'm in much danger on the Capital Planet now that we are lovers?"

"Possibly."

Jane wanted to gauge if he knew anything about her relationship with Doctor Anu, "Why now more than before?"

Jei seemed impatient with the question, "You know why."

"I want to hear you say it."

"I won't," he said decidedly.

Jane ran her hand through his hair and thought, *This is another one of those Alliance things. How can I get him to talk about what I want him to say?* "If we were to marry, would I live on the Capital Planet?"

"No, I'd want you here with me."

Jane smiled but that didn't help her get the answer she wanted, "I'd like that." Then she hedged her bets and went for it, "I'm concerned about my new 1,000 women."

"What's the matter?"

"I'm worried some of their memories of their time in quarantine will resurface and they will be traumatized by what happened there."

"I doubt it. Our doctors are very good," he said casually.

"You don't suspect anything out of the ordinary took place then? They were there for a long time."

Jei sat up and looked directly into Jane's eyes. He couldn't tell if she were baiting him for what he knew or if she was truly on the outside and Doctor Anu had wiped her memory too. He had to think quickly. "It was odd the women were kept for so long. What did Doctor Anu say about it when you questioned her?"

"Only that she was being thorough."

Of course, Jei and many others suspected foul play, but they had no proof, just a couple human traders' words which was nothing to go on. However, Ket's wife James was still privately trying to figure out what was done to those human women. "Then I wouldn't think too much about it. Unless it becomes a problem," he said and lay back down.

Jane was relieved he didn't seem to think it was anything she was responsible for or if he did, he was a great liar. She lay down and went to sleep with her hands in his hair as she liked to do and told herself she was safe with him.

Jane woke up in the morning to Jei kissing her. She was still half asleep and murmured, "You're so cold."

Jei stopped suddenly and moved away from her in the bed, "Jane, are you awake?"

She opened her eyes, "Yes," she said pleasantly. Then she realized she was dreaming she was at home and he was Jim. They both knew it. She felt ashamed. "I'm sorry. It was only a dream."

Jei couldn't fault her for her dreams, but he would wait for her to come to him now.

Jane took in his unreadable expression and decided to quickly move over to him. She tossed herself so fast, he had to grab her, so she didn't fall off the edge of the bed.

Jei laughed, "There now, let's not be hasty." His tone was light, but he was concerned. The forget-me-not was wearing off, and although he had never used it himself, he knew that it was a confusing time. Now Jane would have to deal with both realities she had created for herself. Her past human life and now her true Alliance life.

Jane straddled Jei's naked body, "Thanks, falling off the

bed wouldn't be the best way to start the morning." Then she leaned down and kissed him, "But this is good."

Jei put his large hands on either side of her head and looked up at this little human with so much going on in her mind right now, "It's a nice way to wake up." He searched her blue eyes, looking for anything that would let him know what she was thinking.

"You're looking at me as if I've something more to say," Jane commented, not liking his inquisitive look.

"No," he lied.

"Will you make love to me, Jei?" She purposely used his name to assure him that she wanted him.

Jei was too old to be passive-aggressive. She was offering herself to him, and he wanted her as he always wanted his Jane. He had become so accustomed to having her around to fulfill not only his carnal needs but also his emotional and intellectual needs as well, he didn't want to jeopardize what little time they might have left if she decided she could not be with an Alliance man after the forget-me-not completely wore off. He put his hands on her breasts and began caressing them the way he knew she liked. Not long after, he had her on her back and was bringing her pleasure before he found his own.

Afterward, he said to her, "I'm only going to mention this once as your health in this regard is your business, but you should speak to Doctor Rea about the forget-me-not wearing off. It can be a difficult time."

Jane was surprised that he mentioned this. They had never talked about her having the forget-me-not. She didn't mind that he knew, but it was a discussion she really didn't want to have.

"Jane, you are part of my crew. Of course, I knew from when you came onboard."

"And you're not worried?"

"That you still love the father of your three human children?" he shook his head, "No, I would be worried if you didn't still love him in one way or another. The only thing I'm worried about is you. About you becoming overwhelmed and confused with these two parallel versions of yourself that you've created." He left out, 'And I'm scared of losing the best thing that has happened to me since my wife died.'

"I do feel a little confused," Jane admitted. "But I know, Jim has moved on and I must too, that's why I took the forget-me-not, to begin with, so that I could move on too. And I have moved on, I met you, and I like this," she motioned between them. "But now the old feelings are creeping back in and overlapping with my new feelings for you, and it's, well, confusing."

He gave her a sympathetic look, "See Doctor Rea. If you need time away, a break from us, just ask."

She was horrified then, "Do you want a break?" It was the last thing she wanted.

"No, but I don't want to push this. I feel like we are good together, but if you're not ready to move past your human man, you would only come to resent our relationship."

Jane looked at him now and caught a glimpse of their age difference. He was about 170 years older than she was. She usually didn't feel it, but at times like these, she felt like a child. That he knew what she was thinking before she did and could predict likely outcomes before she even thought of the questions. "I'll see the Doctor."

"Good," Jei said.

They got out of bed and Jei had a shower alone, then got dressed. "I'm sorry we can't have the morning meal together today."

"It's fine," Jane said touched that he was worried about her.

"But please be here for lunch, otherwise," he touched his lover's bracelet with a knowing look. Whenever she accidently missed lunch with him because she was finishing up something in engineering, he made her orgasm wherever she was on the ship. She had never done the same to him though.

Jane replied honestly, "Sometimes I love that you make me orgasm while I'm surrounded by your men in engineering. I think you must do it on purpose to torture all of us for what you have, and they don't."

"Could be," Jei replied and then left his quarters. His guards followed him as he walked towards the bridge, and his squire soon caught up, rattling off everything that needed to be done that morning. However, Jei's mind was still focused on Jane. The look on her face. He was worried she was going to leave him when the forget-me-not completely wore off, and what he was going to do about it.

Jane walked into sickbay before going on duty. The sickbay was quiet, and she found her friend Doctor Rea in his circular glass office.

He looked up as she walked in, "Yes, I was wondering when you were going to drop by."

"Please, at least pretend not to be reading my mind," she said, slightly irritated.

"I wasn't reading your mind. I know the forget-me-not has begun to wear off. It's in your records."

"Oh," she said.

"Please, let's go see how this all looks," he gestured for her to come into sickbay, but instead of using one of the standard medical beds, he led her to the back. A private area reserved for the Admiral and Imperial ranking citizens.

She stopped, "Where are we going?"

Doctor Rea stopped as well and touched her lovers' bracelet, "This puts you at the same rank as if you were the Admiral's wife." Then he turned back around and began walking again.

Jane followed him into the private room and laid down on the luxurious medical bed.

Doctor Rea began pulling up 3D computer images all around them, comparing brain scans. Then he looked into Jane's eyes and said, "I need to dispel the last of the barriers, or else they will linger for months and create even more confusion. The only way to do this is to enter your mind and your memories, do you agree?"

"Do I have a choice?"

"Yes, you can let them linger and cause yourself even more grief, but I wouldn't recommend it."

"Go on then," Jane said and closed her eyes. She felt Rea's cool hands on hers, and then like a narrator flipping through memories, he began bringing them forward and clearing away the cobwebs. After fifteen minutes, she opened her eyes again and declared, "I feel terrible."

Doctor Rea gave her a sympathetic look, "Take the rest of the day off. That's an order. Go to your quarters, don't meet anyone, don't send any VMs or messages, and try to sleep. If you are too restless, do some exercise or pray. But above all else, do not speak to anyone but me for the rest of the day."

"The last thing I want to do is to be alone right now," she admitted. She desperately wanted to VM Jim, but from Jei's naked embrace, it was all very confusing.

Rea caught her last thought and said, "And that is

exactly why you need to be alone. Your emotions will settle in about a day. If not, come and see me again."

Jane nodded and left sickbay. She spent the rest of the day alone in her quarters. Some hours she was happy and others, she was sick with guilt and crying.

Doctor Rea walked into Admiral Jei's ready room off the bridge and waited to be acknowledged.

Jei dismissed his squire and then said, "Tell me about Jane's health."

"She still has very strong feelings for her human husband. He is the only other man she has really been with besides you. She cares for you deeply too. When the forget-me-not began to wear off, it merged these feelings and memories." It was forbidden for him to tell the Admiral these things. Still, Doctor Rea was loyal to Jei and also believed that Jane herself would tell him this if she could articulate it, but at the moment, it was doubtful she could articulate any of her emotions surrounding the two men in her life very well.

"I assumed as much," Jei responded, thinking of what had happened that morning in bed. Her comment about his cold touch.

"I've sorted her memories and emotions as well as I could. It will take a day, but then she will be fully aware of everything. During this time, she should be isolated, and I've blocked her communications."

"Did you tell her you blocked them?" Jei asked, amused.

"Of course not, I just told her not to contact anyone. If I had told her I had blocked them, you know she would be in here demanding they be unblocked. Humans are the worst patients."

"Yes," Jei agreed. "Any advice for me?"

"Let her know your feelings regarding the human man and children. She carries a lot of unnecessary guilt that she feels she is lying to you and betraying them by enjoying your intimacy. Despite my best efforts, this was difficult for me to understand or overturn in her mind. She is quite stubborn."

Jei nodded, "Humans have odd ideas about loyalty and sexual relationships. I don't understand it myself, and I don't know if I ever will. It's driven by the individual's emotions almost entirely without much regard to the bigger picture. It's a strange way to see one's place in the galaxy."

"The Lost People indeed," remarked Rea. "Let the gods guide Jane on her true path."

"The gods will shine their light for her to follow," Jei said and dismissed the doctor with his hand.

7

Fantasies Fulfilled

A week later, Jei walked into his quarters and his heart beat faster when he saw Jane there in an Alliance dress. She was at his desk writing a message. A few weeks ago, this would have been a common occurrence but since the forget-me-not was no more, he reveled in every second that she behaved as she had done previously.

Jei came up behind Jane, put his arms around her and kissed the top of her head, "It makes me happy to see you here like this."

Jane looked up at him, "It feels better to be here than in my quarters."

That wasn't the reply he was necessarily looking for, "Finish what you are doing and then let's talk. That is if you want?"

Jane nodded and Jei went into the other room. He sat on a sofa and waited.

Jane finished her message to Kara,

K,

The forget-me-not is no longer affecting me. I'm with Jei and I love him, but at the same time I still love Jim. I feel like I'm betraying them both. I don't know what to do. They are such different men that a part of me cannot believe that I could be with such different men, but then I remind myself I am almost a completely different person in the Alliance, so maybe this is just natural. I am adrift with my emotions and miss someone who has known me from before to anchor me now. Please write back with any advice.

J

Jane was just about to get up from the desk when Kara RVMed her. Jane hesitated answering as Jei would be able to hear their entire conversation from the next room, but then she reckoned that speaking to Kara was more important than Jei listening in. Nothing would be discussed that he didn't know or guess anyway.

"Jane, what's the matter with you?"

Jane winced, she had forgotten how direct Kara could be when she really just needed a kind word, "Well, I'm suffering from coming off this Alliance treatment, that is what's the matter with me. Have some sympathy."

"I'm calling, aren't I?"

Jane put her hands up, "You are."

"Sorry, Tir is driving me batty. He doesn't want me doing anything even though this baby is not due for some weeks. Ridiculous. This is what happens when men know nothing about these things."

Jane smiled, it was good to have all of her memories back, "Jim used to fuss over me the same way. They don't understand. Try not to listen."

"Easy for you to say. Now, let's talk about you. Why are you still thinking about Jim? Have you spoken to him since he told you he was moving in with your best friend?"

Jane shook her head, "No I still don't know what to say. I know he wants me to forgive him. Or rather them, but I can't. Is that wrong of me?"

"Why should you be the bigger person? They've done something that makes you feel terrible and they know that. Why should you give them your forgiveness when you don't feel like it just to make them feel better?"

"Because I didn't leave, I was forced to go and so they were forced into this situation and I didn't even try to escape."

"Have you thought about escape?" Kara asked almost in disbelief.

Jane was quiet.

Kara looked into the screen directly and said, "Of course you haven't why would you? We are all so happy here. And you are happy with Jei. I see your clothing. And why shouldn't you be? But just because you are happy with Jei doesn't mean that you need to forgive Jim or Sandra." Kara realized then that Jei or his squire was probably in earshot of their conversation.

"Thanks, I needed to hear that."

"Good. I'm glad. Now let's talk about something exciting. Tell me what Jei is like as a lover?"

Jane laughed, "Do you want a play-by-play or what?"

Kara smiled, "No you can generalize. But start from the beginning."

"Well, I initiated a lot. You know there are no male slave artists truly interested in women on the *Kzi*. I mean, the slave artists here would have come to me for UCs, but you know that just feels so wrong when the man you know is thinking about another man… "

"I've never let that bother me, but go on…"

"As the whole Alliance knows, I kissed Jei outside Leld or rather asked him to kiss me, I don't remember but he's really perfected his kissing. He kisses as a preview to how he performs."

"He's over 200 years old, it would be frightening if he hadn't perfected his kissing and lovemaking skills. And how about his tongue on your clit? I imagine he can make you come just by saying he is going to do it."

"Well, now that you mention it, it's something like that."

"I knew it. Gods, I should have gone with an older man if I had been given the choice."

"I thought you and Tir had a healthy sex life?"

"Oh, you know we do, but he gets so jealous and protective of me sometimes, I feel like I am missing out on this whole Alliance world of orgies and fun sex games. And when I'm pregnant Tir doesn't want to do anything fun. I bought some whips and I wanted him to tie me up and play some really kinky games, but he refused. What man refuses that?"

"I don't know Kara. I once put only a bow on myself and was waiting for Jim in bed and he didn't want to have sex. It happens."

"I bet you if you asked the Admiral to do it, he wouldn't hesitate would he?"

Jane didn't answer.

"Oh gods, you've already done that."

"Well not exactly. And not the bow," Jane admitted.

"And you've probably had orgies too. I'm so jealous."

"No, no orgies."

"Why not? Live this Alliance life, forget Jim. That's all in the past."

"I don't know," Jane said, "I just can't imagine…" she trialed off.

"Jane listen to me. Jim has moved on with your best friend and maybe I'm the only one who is going to tell you this, but they were probably sleeping with each other for years before now. Don't waste another second thinking about him. If I could find the evidence for you to prove that to you, I would. But unfortunately, humans aren't nearly the stalkers that Alliance people are so it would be impossible to prove, but trust me, you don't suddenly hook up with your wife's best friend after a year. Even you aren't that naïve."

Some tears escaped Jane's eyes because she knew in her heart this was true. There were some signs, but she dismissed them because she wanted to. She didn't want to believe the two people closest to her would betray her in such a way, "I don't want to hear it."

"No one ever wants to hear that they've been lied to. Look Jane, it's no reflection on you. These things happen."

"Not to me Kara. I'm not like you. I wanted a moral life and I worked hard for it. I wanted the man, the children, and the happily ever after."

"No, you didn't. That's another lie that you've told yourself just because you didn't want to disappoint your parents and friends. You've always wanted adventure and to live on the edge. You didn't hesitate to sign up for the fleet or the war. And since you took the forget-me-not you've been your true self. You like being with Jei and you like this barbaric Alliance life. Why is it so difficult for you to accept that?" Kara knew she was pushing hard now but she felt like this was probably the best thing she could do for Jane right now. And that even if Jane was offended, she would forgive her in a few months.

"I don't think you really know me," Jane said all the while wondering if Kara was right.

Kara laughed, "Oh Jane. I know you. I know you so well that I'm sending you UCs for the sole purpose of an orgy right now. Gods, this will prove to you that you are no "happily ever after" little girl. None of us are, except maybe my precious daughter James living with her precious Ket." Kara began touching her IC. "I've just transferred you 5000 UCs for the sole purpose of getting those slave artists around and having an orgy for me. I want all the details. I'm going now. Do it, it's an order. Kara out."

The screen went blank and Jane just looked at it dumbfounded. Her IC chimed to let her know that she had received the money, but Kara had been clever enough to lock it for everything but slave artists. When Jane composed herself, she went into the other room where she had no doubt Jei had been listening.

Without any preamble Jei asked, "Do you think she's right?"

"About what?"

"That an orgy would make you feel more settled?"

Jane sat down and looked at Jei, a million things went through her mind then and she couldn't answer the question.

Jei got out his IC.

"What are you doing?" Jane asked slightly concerned.

"Do you really want to know, or do you want it to be a surprise?"

Jane went completely still. She had no idea what an Alliance surprise might be, but she decided she needed to know, "Tell me."

Jei looked at Jane considering, "Five male slave artists are coming here, and we are all going to have sex with you. Together. I think Kara is right. This will help."

"No. What? No, Jei."

"You heard me; six Alliance penises are going into that human vagina in about an hour. I know you are getting wet just thinking about it, Jane."

Jei was right but she was a little scared too. She had never been with more than one man. And six alien men she didn't know what to do, "I've never done this kind of thing before." Jane stood up and went to get a cup of zota in the other room, "I need a drink."

"Don't have too much. I want you to remember every detail."

Jane drank a cup of zota and by the time she had finished, five handsome and scantily dressed slave artists had arrived and were talking with Jei in the next room.

Jane felt frozen she didn't know what to do so she just stood there listening, but they were speaking in the men's language so she couldn't understand. Suddenly she heard her name called to join them. She didn't want to. She was scared.

"Jane, it'll only be worse if you don't come out now," Jei bellowed.

Jane took a deep breath and thought, *Maybe it's good to live out one's fantasies at least once.* She walked out into the drawing room and saw the five slave artists and Jei all looking at her.

"Here she is our feral human. She needs to be taught our Alliance ways," Jei said to the slave artists who looked at her as if she were candy to a child. "Jane, these men and I are going to make you submit to our ways, are you ready?"

"Yes," Jane said quietly.

"Yes, what?"

"Yes, Primary."

"Come here," Jei commanded.

Jane obeyed and walked over to stop in front of Jei and the men. He spoke to them in the men's language and it was unsettling to her that she couldn't understand, then he said to her, "Raise up your hands."

When she hesitated, he reminded her, "Jane, these are slave artists and you are with me. Everything that happens here is only between us and the gods. Now raise up your hands."

She obeyed him.

The men disrobed her all at once. Then they tied her hands at her wrists. They surrounded her, touching her as if they had never seen a human woman before. They were purposely speaking in the men's language to keep her ignorant of their plans as they circled her and pointed. It made her uncomfortable and almost scared, but at the same time very excited. They were all still clothed as she stood there bound and naked.

"Centuries ago, Alliance men would catch human women and keep them onboard their ships as pets. Then the men would play with them. Would you liked to be played with human?" Jei asked her.

Jane couldn't believe she was doing this, but she had to admit she was aroused by the thought of these muscular grey men doing what they liked with her. One began to pet her vulva like a human would a cat, but another struck her bottom for her not answering Jei she assumed.

"Speak human," he commanded.

"Yes, Primary, use me like a pet," she answered.

"So feral that I have no doubt that once you orgasm once for us, you'll not stop. Human women are like that. Like sexual animals. Or that's what I've heard and I'm looking forward to testing out this theory." Jei said and then switched to the men's language.

Jane looked at them all, their erect penises visible through their clothing and the lust in their eyes as they talked in a language she couldn't understand. She imagined them then, all taking her, and she was becoming very aroused at the thought of being their pet and plaything for the next couple of hours. Then the men began touching her breasts, licking and nipping at them all at once. She felt like there were hands everywhere.

"Keep your eyes open human. Watch how we use you."

Jane kept her eyes open but didn't answer and then she was struck on the bottom again but this time with something hard and cold. She turned around to see Jei with his short sword, mad desire in his eyes. She wondered if hers reflected the same. She still didn't answer him, she wanted him to punish her.

He struck her again.

Then he commanded the men, but she didn't know exactly what he said. Then he told her, "Bend over pet, I need to teach you to answer me."

She did as she was told but still didn't answer him. It was difficult to hold her balance without her hands to steady her. She was sure he was going to hit her with some force, and she wanted it. They were talking for so long as she stood bent over. She didn't know what they were saying but she thought they were probably talking about the hair surrounding her sex. Alliance men were fascinated by it.

Jei then used his hand and began spanking Jane, "Is this what you wanted naughty human?

"Yes, Primary," she couldn't help but answer as this was actually what she really wanted. She was counting every stroke and he was talking all the while. She couldn't understand what he was saying but she suspected it was very naughty and that just made all the more aroused.

Jei loved that it had only taken Jane a few minutes to completely throw herself into this submissive role. When he had heard Kara suggest it, he guessed that between the two of them, they couldn't be wrong about Jane. And he also believed that she needed this to prove to herself she was really going to live her best life here with him. Keeping the slave artists interested was a different matter altogether. They were so used to men, and preferred men, he was having to talk a lot of things up so that they didn't lose interest. That's why he was using the men's language because he didn't want Jane to lose interest either. Nothing was a bigger turn off than having to be talked up to slave artists.

After Jei finished spanking her and her bottom was bright red. He rubbed his hand between her legs to feel the wetness there and then said something to the men in their language. They came forward then and began using their tongues all over her body. After a few minutes, she was covered in male saliva that made her all the colder in the Alliance temperature room. Her nipples were wet, cold and hard, begging for more attention and her sex was dripping trying to temp anything into it. She made eye contact with Jei then who had moved back to watch. Jane couldn't read his face beyond the desire and that even made her more aroused.

Jane almost felt like this was happening to someone else but not to her, the pleasure and sensations she got from the idea that she was allowing this to happen and from all the men touching her at once was almost too much. She even stood with her legs further apart so that the five men could gain access to her nether regions with their tongues and fingers. They were all speaking in the men's language now, sometimes laughing and she wondered if they were laughing at her. But she didn't care they were giving her so much satisfaction she didn't care if they thought she was a whore, maybe she was, but she was so stimulated now she thought she might have sex with the whole crew if it would make her feel as good as she felt now.

And Jane definitely felt better in this moment with all these men sexing her up and Jei watching her. She loved this role play; she being kept as an Alliance man's pet as in ancient times that he suggested . His pet, no doubt in his mind and now he was giving her to his crew to watch in curiosity how she would behave. Hoping no doubt, she would be as feral as he thought humans would be. Jane had no problem getting into this now. She moved her pelvis up and down against one man's mouth on her clitoris which caused the man who was sticking his tongue in her anus to put his strong hands on her hips to steady her.

"Jane, besides me, has any man ever put his tongue in your anus before?" Jei asked. Although Jane was a more than adequate lover there was a lot that had been new to her. He suspected that this was because her human man was a terrible lover and that there were no slave artists on Earth to perfect the art of sex.

"No, Primary," she answered breathlessly.

"Then I suppose no man has ever put his penis there either?"

"No Primary," Jane answered nervously as she did not expect this. She wasn't Kara. She didn't know what that would feel like and she was afraid that it would hurt. And hurt a lot.

"We are all going to take a turn in your virgin anus, and you will scream with pleasure like any human pet."

Jane didn't think she should answer that but when Jei came around and struck her bottom with the side of his sword again she said, "Yes, Primary." Then one of the men in front of her sucked her clitoris so hard she orgasmed hard from all the attention she was getting from all of the men.

"Good human. That's it. Climax for us. Get all nice and wet for our Alliance penises. Now on your knees."

She went down to her knees her hands still tied, her

body cold from the dampness everywhere from their saliva to her own lubrication running down her legs.

Jei and the men spoke in the men's language. They all disrobed and then stood in a line. Jei spoke then, "You know what you need to do."

Jane looked at him astonished. This was against the gods. He had punished her before for doing it.

"Do it human. I know more than you. You are my pet. I take care of you and you take care of them because I am ordering you to do it. I know human women like this."

The first man put his penis in front of Jane's face, and she opened her mouth. She wanted to use her hands but they were still tied up so she did the best she could to position herself to take the large penis into her mouth without using her teeth or gagging. It wasn't easy. But once she got into a rhythm and she thought about the situation she was turned on, especially knowing how naughty this was for them too.

Suddenly the man whose penis was inside her mouth spoke in the men's language. Then, he put his hands on her head and directed her back away from him. He hadn't come. The next four men all did the same then it was Jei's turn and her vagina was wet again with anticipation of taking his penis in her mouth in front of the other men. She thought to herself, *Gods, I really love being a slut, don't I?*

Jei didn't hesitate to put his hands in her hair, pull it and direct her to his massive penis. His was definitely the largest and she could hardly fit her mouth around it. He mixed up his words between the men's language and standard Alliance so she could hear him. He made sure to talk dirty to her about her being his 'sexy human pet' that he could 'feed with orgies.' This was too much for Jane she put her tied wrists between her legs and made herself come while she sucked his penis.

His words and her own excitement made Jane suck harder and harder, she wanted to make him come so hard and she knew she almost did until he pulled away at the last minute. He patted her on the head and said, "Not yet little pet. Now stand with your legs apart." He tapped the insides of her wet thighs.

"Yes, Primary."

Jei spoke in the men's language and they all surrounded her again, penises fully erect and hungry. They closed in on her and took turns touching the entrance to her vagina and rubbing her pubic hair. They were talking about her amongst themselves.

"You are so wet even when you give us pleasure. It's no wonder that human men feel the need to dominate you. Come pet, it's time for us to find our pleasure too."

"Yes, Primary."

Another man took her by the wrists, and they all led her into the bedroom where she was bent over the edge of the large bed. They left her like this for a few minutes while they spoke unintelligibly amongst themselves. Sometimes they tapped her bottom and it made her jump.

"I'm just putting some oil into this virgin anus. It will be me who is the first," Jei said.

Jane wanted to protest. She wanted them all in her vagina. Her sex and mind were aching for them to all take her that way and she seriously did not think that Jei's penis could fit her virgin anus

"What's that little pet?" Jei wanted her to say what she desired in hopes that being more of a participant in this would allow her to realize this is what she liked and that she was suited to being in the Alliance and with him more than anything else in the galaxy.

"Please, in my vagina first, Primary."

"You want it in here?" he asked as he stuck two fingers into her hot vagina.

Jane moaned if felt so good, "Yes."

"What will you do for that pleasure?"

Jane's mind was racing, she couldn't think of anything except all of these men filling her. "I don't know Primary."

"Think."

Jane moved her hips closer to him, hoping he would put his fingers inside of her again. When she moved back, she could feel his erect penis against the side of her bottom and she instinctively moved and wiggled to try to get it in her vagina.

Jei grabbed Jane's hips and said, "You really are a naughty pet aren't you. You've already orgasmed twice but you still want more. Give me something and then we will give you what you want."

Jane couldn't think of anything and then it occurred to her, "You can pierce one of my nipples if you all promise to take turns putting your penises in my vagina." Jane could hardly believe she had said that, any of it. A part of her wondered who she was right now and the other part of her said, *You know this has always been one of your fantasies.*

Jei gave the men some instructions and they returned from the bathroom with a piercing tool and a starter bar. Jei had had it for weeks hoping Jane would agree to piercing her nipples. And the thought of just piercing one was good enough for today. "Stand up," he said and took the little device from the slave. He held it up in front of her and said, "I'm going to choose my favorite breast. Do you know which one that is little human?"

Jane honestly didn't know, "No, Primary."

He grabbed her right breast and bounced it in his hand a little, "It's this one. Look at it, so large and pert. Perfect for sucking but lacking the most important adornment."

He held her breast tightly then and said, "This has a numbing effect to it, so it won't hurt. I can take that off if you want?"

"No, Primary."

Jei positioned the piercing tool and shot a little starter bar through her right nipple. Then he stood back and looked at his handiwork. "Very good little pet. When it's fully healed, I'll give you jewelry for it and lead you around by it."

Jane looked down at her nipple and thought, *And now I've done something that even Kara wouldn't agree to.* But this thought too made her vagina gush with need. This and the thought that all of these men were going to take turns plunging in and out of her. She was absolutely aching for them.

Suddenly, Jei put his hands on her shoulders and gave her a look that she adored, he blinked once slowly at her. Then he said, "Move back and lie on the bed. With your legs up."

Jane obeyed. She was excited.

Jei came to stand in front of her. He was stroking her vulva. The other men stood behind him watching. They came closer and began caressing her breasts and vulva as well.

She felt that she had cool Alliance hands everywhere.

"What do you want?"

"I want you all to put your penises in me, Primary."

"All of us?"

"Yes, all of you Primary."

"My feral little human," Jei said and tapped her clitoris. He barked orders then at the men and three lined up in front of her aching sex.

Jane was disappointed that Jei moved to the side but then a very good looking and young slave artist took his place. And she became entranced watching him strike his long-ridged penis in front of her.

The slave artist looked down at the hair covering Jane's sex and said, "Just like a little animal." He rubbed her sex a little bit and she made a pleasurable sound and closed her eyes. He continued rubbing. It had been years since he had been with a woman and never a human.

Jane responded by arching her hips up. It all felt too good, the men were caressing and licking her breasts and now teasing her as well.

The slave artist took his large penis and positioned it at her small wet entrance. He looked up as his real lover sucking the human's newly pierced nipple and imagined him as he plunged into the woman.

They all took turns in Jane's vagina. All making comments about what a feral human she was. Finally, it was Jei's turn and she wanted to feel his familiar penis in her. But to her dismay, he flipped her over and said, "Now it's my turn to fill your virgin anus. This might hurt at first."

Jane was so disappointed, and she was thinking about his words as she felt his finger and oil fill her anus.

He smacked her bottom.

"Yes, Primary."

Jei began moving his large finger in a circular motion and in and out of her anus. "Jane, you need to relax and enjoy this."

"Yes, Primary," but the truth was she was anything but relaxed. She already felt stretched by his fingers.

Jei began talking to the other men and they surrounded her again. One began kissing her on the mouth, with his teeth nibbling at her. Another was fondling her breasts and the others were on their knees, one licking her clitoris and the other fingering her vagina. Then with Jei's finger in her anus she let all the attention and pleasure overwhelm her. She was almost ready to come again by the time he slowly entered her with his enormous ridged penis, it was a sweet pleasure mixed with pain that she was sure she would regret later.

"That's a good human pet. Take it all the way in," Jei said and then he slowly began to move in and out of her anus while the other men pleasured her everywhere else.

It was almost too much, all the new sensations of being treated in such a degrading manner but being aroused by it at the same time. Feeling afraid but at the same time trusting Jei completely to know nothing would go too far.

Jei came inside of her anus and then moved back to watch the come and oil spill out. He slapped her bottom and spoke to the slave artists. Everyone switched positions but this time one man laid down on the bed and Jane was positioned over him and another man behind her and then the others in front of her. One man entered her vagina, the other her anus and then the others were kissing and nibbling on her nipples. She really was in ecstasy then. So many sensations that it almost felt like an out of body experience. She felt so naughty but loved it and loved that Jei was watching all these men take her she lost count of how many times she was coming.

Finally, when all of the men had come inside her one way or another they left and Jei picked her up and they both got into the shower together.

"Do you feel truly Alliance now Jane?"

"I do," she said honestly. "So wickedly so, Primary."

Jei gently smacked her bottom and then commenced his daily routine of washing her as if she really was his pet.

Jane realized as he was washing her hair that this had been one of his fantasies just as much as it had been hers. She smiled at the thought and just relaxed as he bathed her. And she remembered what Kara had said about Alliance men wanting to care for their wives all the time and thought, *I'll have to tell Kara it's probably all part of this human pet fantasy they have.* And then a darker thought ran through Jane's mind, 200 years ago, if I were on an Alliance ship I probably would have been taken and used as a pet. She tried to shoo that thought away, but she couldn't and then she was reminded of the brutality of this culture and questioned what she was becoming. She was ashamed of herself suddenly.

After the shower they dressed. Jei wanted his evening meal of course, but Jane made an excuse and wanted to return to her quarters.

"I don't want you to go," Jei said. He was concerned for her. "What has made you so upset?"

Jane looked at this man, trying so hard to please her according to his culture and had she not let the forget-me-not wear off, he still would be so pleasing to her. But now, with her right mind and memories, she was confused and upset. "I can't explain it to you. It's a human thing."

"No, it's not. This is a Jane thing and I'll not just letting you walk away from me without a better explanation."

Jane looked up into his grey eyes and longed for him to be someone else. She didn't know what to do then so she just bolted from his quarters. She ran through the corridors of the ship, but not wanting to go to her quarters either so she ran to the shrine. When she saw that she was the only one in there, she locked the door behind her and sat in the center of the shrine with the statues of the Alliance gods with their short hair and green clothing all looking at her with only the quiet and the smell of incense and burning candles. After a few minutes, Jane put her knees up and her head on her knees and began to cry. She asked the gods through her tears, "Why have you done this to me?

Wasn't it enough torture to take me away from my family? But now this? I hate you. I wish you were real so I would have something more than the vague Empire to hate."

Jei closed the shrine's surveillance off to the military stream so that they would not be able to see Jane losing her mind in the shrine. He went to stand outside the door. He would stand there all night if he had to, waiting for her.

Thankfully, after an hour she emerged. He looked at her. "Do you feel better now?"

Jane was surprised to see Jei waiting there for her. She was relieved in some ways. "I want to say sorry, but," she began but he stopped her with his hand.

"No, Jane. You don't need to apologize. I should have backed off. Now if you want to come with me, you may. I always like holding you when I sleep, but if you want to return to your own quarters, I understand that too. I'll escort you there."

"I want to go with you."

This made Jei's heart sing, but he merely took her elbow and they walked back to his quarters in silence. When they reached his quarters he asked, "Do you want something to eat?"

"I've missed the evening meal haven't' I?"

"Yes, but you can eat if you want."

Jane shook her head, "I don't want to do anything else wrong today."

Jei took Jane in his arms, "You've done nothing wrong." He touched her forehead, "You're making this all up in here."

Tears welled up in her eyes, "I don't know how to stop it. I just want one life and now I have two and one I can't ever have again."

"Let's get married, have a family and then you will have both," Jei said gently. "You'll be able to see your human family. I know you want that more than anything. It's natural to want that."

Jane shook her head, "I can't. I can't." She began to sob.

"Jane," he took her chin in his hand and directed her gaze to him. He felt so sorry for her that she was so sad, but he was confident that time would work this out. "Listen to me, I'm only going to say this once. I'm the Admiral of the Alliance Fleet. I'm over 200 years old. I'm not jealous or intimated by any human man who you used to have a relationship with. In fact, I think he's a fool not pining away forever for you or trying to rescue you. I can share your love with him and with your human children. You don't need to choose between us."

"My heart is one. What you are asking me to do is to break it in half. I can't do that, not even for you." She cried and he held her. "I want to love you with my whole heart. That's the way I love Jei. Not half here or half there, I'm not an Alliance person."

Jei stroked her hair and listened to her. He didn't know what to say. More than anything he wanted to resolve this issue so that they could go back to being happy. He wondered then if he should tell her that she was pregnant. Doctor Rea had told him as her urine alerted the Doctor to it immediately but the he didn't think she should be told given the condition she was in. Jei also knew that she wouldn't necessarily suspect because she always said her period was untrustworthy and liked to play hide and seek. As he stroked her hair, he considered her reactions, but in the end decided now was probably not a good time. However, any Alliance women would have been alerted to the fact that she was pregnant by the fact that she was sucking on men's penises and offered food outside of designated eating times. But this was just another stark reminder to Jei how human and ignorant Jane was of so much of his culture. "I want you to love me however you can. Why don't we begin there?"

Jane nodded, "I think I just want to go to sleep now."

Jei led her into the bedroom that had all been cleaned now and asked her, "Do you want to sleep with your night clothing? I can send my squire to fetch it from your quarters."

Jane thought it was very sweet of him to ask, "No I want to be next to you, skin to skin. It'll make me feel better. I just want you to hold me as I fall asleep."

Jei was not tired at all, but he took off his clothes and got into bed with Jane. He held her close to him as he always did. He kissed the top of her head and held her tight. He didn't want to talk unless she did.

After several minutes of silence, she asked, "What if I can't be the woman you want me to be? The woman I was a few weeks ago."

"ZZsss," he said trying to calm these thoughts. "This is just an aftershock from the forget-me-not, the doctors on the *Zuin* were fools giving it to you in the first place. You're still that woman. You just remember more now, but the forget-me-not doesn't change you, it just brings different parts of you forward."

"But what if I'm not?" Jane really believed that her memories changed her. She remembered how free and easy she felt before when she was under the influence of the forget-me-not. Jim and Sandra's relationship hadn't bothered her, but now, it was as if weights were chained to her body and everything, she did was a struggle. "Maybe I can have the memories permanently erased."

"No, don't do that. You'll get through this. Just close your eyes now and sleep. Tomorrow go see Doctor Rea."

"I was going to."

"Good."

After a few minutes of silence Jane said, "I think the sex was too much."

Jei smiled, but she couldn't see it. "I hope we didn't hurt you?" She didn't make any sounds of displeasure that he could remember.

"Not at the time, but it was that pleasure and pain sensation that you know later is going to be all pain."

"Should we call Doctor Rea here now?"

Jane considered this, but they were already in bed having this quiet and reflective moment together, but before she could say, 'no, it's fine,' Jei had already summoned him.

In minutes, Doctor Rea came into the bedroom and asked, "What's the emergency?"

Jane blushed and Doctor Rea knew from reading her mind what the problem was.

"I'm actually relieved you can read my mind and I don't have to verbalize this," Jane admitted.

Doctor Rea nodded and said professionally, "Please come over here. This shouldn't be a problem. It happens to a lot of people."

Jane walked over in front of the doctor naked and he investigated the problem with some of his portable medical devices. After some lasers and she didn't even know what kind of devices he directed into her anus, she felt better.

"I'd also like to heal some of those bruises if you don't mind, I'm a doctor I just can't walk away looking at those on your pale skin."

Jane looked down and noticed that she did have bruises all over her body. She didn't remember anything in particular hurting but then again, it was a crazy afternoon. "Sure," she said casually making eye contact with Jei across the room. He didn't even look the slightest bit guilty for the bruises. "You bruised your pet," she said baiting him.

"Now I'm having her healed."

Jane gave him a smile and he smiled back.

Doctor Rea finished then nodded to Jei and bowed to them both and left.

Jei crossed the room quickly, picked Jane up and carried her back to bed. "Now I am going to kiss away all of these bad thoughts. I'll make you forget how you could have ever loved a human man. And I promise you Jane, if your people were to try and take you back somehow as I know they did with Kara, I wouldn't be as diplomatic as Tir. I'd kill to get you back. You remember that when you think about your heart."

The Alliance part of Jane was wooed by this hypothetical act of love and she tried to tell the human Jane to be quiet and love this strong violent man as this was her new life. After they slowly and gently made love, she drifted off to sleep thinking about Jei rescuing her as if they were in an old adventure story.

For the next weeks, Jane and Jei were in a constant state of flux. Sometimes everything was normal and wonderful, other times Jane felt terrible, as if she we a traitor to humanity and her family. However, she still wasn't ready to talk to Jim or Sandra. She talked to her children just as regularly as she always did and put on a brave face. She told herself that her children were almost adults now and didn't need her, when she felt guilty about her new life with Jei. But that only half-worked.

One day she came off duty and then accepted Doctor Rea's invitation to play a strategy game, so she was later than usual returning to Jei's quarters. But in the Alliance, most things were taken for granted such as mealtimes. One was always expected to have the evening meal with their family. And for Jane that meant Jei. But she was having so much fun with Rea she lost track of the time and had to walk quickly to Jei's quarters as to not to miss the evening meal. It wasn't because he would be angry, but it was just she didn't want to keep him waiting as she knew he wouldn't begin without her as eating alone in the Alliance was considered unlucky.

Jane walked past Jei's guards with a nod, into his quarters and then into the private dining room. She stopped short then when she heard music. She had not heard music in over a year. The Alliance didn't have music. She stood there in awe and listened,

When I am laid, am laid in earth, may my wrongs create
No trouble, no trouble in, in thy breast
When I am laid, am laid in earth, may my wrongs create
No trouble, no trouble in, in thy breast
Remember me, remember me, but ah
Forget my fate Remember me, but ah
Forget my fate
Remember me, remember me, but ah
Forget my fate
Remember me, but ah
Forget my fate

It was Dido's Lament is the aria "When I am laid in earth" from the opera Dido and Aeneas by Henry Purcell. It was her favorite song. She walked into the dining room and looked at Jei with surprise. He was patiently waiting for her. "Do you hear the music? Or am I losing my mind?"

He smiled, "I'm glad you hear it. I went to a lot of trouble to get it."

She went over and kissed him while she listened to the rest of the song. She decided she would have the computer play it over and over again all night. "I hope you like it too. I'm going to play it a lot."

Jei didn't understand how this gift could be more rewarding than jewelry to Jane. She couldn't show this off to anyone and it was for no one but her. He didn't mind the human music, but he couldn't say this was something he would long to hear either. He hoped that this gift would lead her to the realization that she was pregnant. He was surprised now that she had not noticed herself. Doctor Rea had told him that it was best she discovers it than they tell her, but Jei didn't think that was a good idea. He had seen how powerful denial could be in men and assumed it could be two-fold in women. Meaning that he knew if Jane willed herself to believe something, no matter how many facts there were to the contrary she would stick to it until she would be forced to do otherwise.

"How did you know I liked this song out of the trillions of Earth songs?" Jane asked.

"I had to contact Tir and have him pull the files from the *Dakota*. Then find what you liked the best. To be honest, I was looking for your taste in clothing or jewelry."

"Human women don't really have clear set preferences that would be noticeable for men to easily buy as Alliance women do."

"I realized that but then I noticed every crew member had a lot of entertainment and that some music was played again and again. So, I assumed you would like to hear this again."

"That doesn't sound too troubling," Jane commented.

"No, the troubling part was Tir. He charged me a fortune to look through the *Dakota's* files."

Jane stilled then, "You didn't listen to my personal logs or read my messages, did you?"

"No, of course not. I wouldn't want you doing that to me, so I would never do that to you. Plus, what would be the point? Circumstances have changed. If you listened to my messages to my former wife would you feel jealous?"

"No."

"Exactly. That life you had is your own and I didn't know you then. My sole purpose was to find something to make you happy. Now let's eat before the evening meal is finished and we miss it."

They both sat down and ate the food. Jane had the song on repeat. "Did you get any other music?"

Jei laughed, "Not with Tir being so annoying and reminding me you weren't allowed to have it yet."

"I forgot," Jane replied, and she was so lost in thought thinking about her old life she didn't even think about the significance of the music or his comment ending in the word, 'yet'.

Jei sighed and thought while he looked at Jane, I will give her three more weeks and then I will just tell her because we will have to marry, or this child will be Houseless.

8

Problems inside House Human

Jane was just finishing her lunch with Jei when she received an automated message about House Human from the High Council. She said before looking at it, "I hope it's not another fine. These women, I tell you." However, she paled when she read the message,

Please be informed Babette Lynn Thomas of House Human is pregnant and unmarried.

Followed by an even more disturbing message,

Babette Lynn Thomas of House Human is now a member of no House as of 8th day of the 10th week of the year 18906 as she married Lieutenant Mir of no House.

"What is it, Jane?" Jei asked noticing that she looked very upset suddenly.

She read out the messages to him as they were alone in his private dining room, "What do I do?"

"You must hide the fact that she is pregnant."

Then as if Dru knew they were waiting for her message it arrived,

Jane, we have a problem. I am working on covering this up. However, I can only do so much. I have spoken to Zol, my husband's mother, she can be trusted, and she believes that we can solve this, but you must return to represent House Human.

Jane stood up then and said, "Permission to return to the Capital Planet."

Jei looked at her, "No. You don't need to be there. This woman got herself into trouble, and Mir is a smart man, he will figure it out." Mir had been Jei's last squire. He didn't want Jane involved with this situation. Mir was one of the gods and if he had married a human who was not his chosen mate the gods would be angry and begin punishing all those around him. And even worse if Mir was supposed to marry the true goddess of peace, Sif, who became his incarnate bride every time the Empire is in great peril and married Babette instead, there would be real trouble. Jei suspected if that was the case, Jane would be the first they would punish. And she was pregnant and still didn't know it. He didn't want her leaving the *Kzi*. Not with her current mindset or physical condition.

Jane went over and sat on his lap, "Are you really going to make me ask twice?"

Jei didn't reply but kissed her.

"I must go Jei. You know as a Head of House; you can't keep me here."

"Oh, you know that do you?" he half joked.

"You know I do. Now I must go but I'll return as soon

as I can sort this out. And of course, I'll miss you every day."

Jei had to agree, but he would make all the arrangements to make sure she was safe while she was on the Capital Planet.

The next morning Jane took a transport to catch another ship on its way back to the Capital Planet. The first night in her guest quarters onboard the Beta ship *Ilo*, she opened her traveling bag and found a small black box with a written note. She would recognize Jei's meticulous handwriting anywhere,

Please wear this on the planet.

She opened the box. Inside was beautiful ring with a dark purple stone held in place by silver geometric patterns. She smiled and put it on her finger and thought it looked beautiful, but then the guilt of cheating on Jim overwhelmed her and she took the ring off and put it back in the box. Left with her own thoughts and away from Jei, she felt like she had multiple personalities without him to anchor her. One was human and a devoted partner with human children, and the other was an Alliance woman who had a thing for sex games.

Jane just stared at the box, trying to remind herself, Jim and I are no longer together. *This isn't cheating. He's with Sandra now.* However, that thought brought on a whole other wave of emotions and she just laid down on her single bed and cried herself to sleep.

The week's travel it took to reach the Capital Planet

were uneventful except for her own thoughts. Jane kept to herself a lot and a couple times even had a slave bring her food to her cabin and watch her eat, as it was forbidden to eat alone. She knew this also meant that the slave could not eat her meal, but Jane was just too preoccupied with her own thoughts to make small talk with anyone else and so made the slave suffer by going hungry for her own comfort. And as she was human and had just come from the flagship, a lot of the men of the *Ilo* were curious and wanted to make small talk, which she only condescended to do a few times.

When Jane arrived at Space Port One, she was only half-surprised to be met by the same guards, Gio and Sra, with the purple trim on their uniforms and purple stones in their ID necklaces to signify they were from the Second Alliance Planet.

"Lieutenant Commander Jane of House Human, we are your guards sent by Admiral Jei of House Rega. We are here to protect you and will do your bidding until you return to the *Kzi*."

Jane didn't think she needed them but then she remembered the attack on James and thought that maybe Jei was right in assigning her guards. It occurred to her then that Jei might have women pining for him that would be jealous now that he had announced her as his lover. That had been what had happened to James. Also, she knew that Kara had death threats from anonymous Alliance women too for being married to Tir. Jane thought, *Yes, maybe this is a good precaution.* "Thank you. Let the gods' be blessed. Today I must go to the Capital City Hospital and then to House Human."

"Gods be blessed," Gio replied and then the other just looked at him uncomfortably. "We were told you would be staying at the Admiral's official Capital Planet residence in Ring One."

"No, I'll stay at House Human," she said casually trying not to make a big deal about it.

The other guard stepped closer to her and showed her a quick contract on his IC,

Gio of House Rega will protect Jane Johnson with his life for her duration on the Capital Planet and will be given full jurisdiction on her place of residence in her best interests making full use of the House Rega's financial and physical holdings.

Jane read the contract. She knew that there was no way that Officer Gio would let her sleep at House Human now. Although it was in Ring Four, it was not considered as bad as a location as the Immigrant Ring. And even though it was protected with a forcefield and their own guards, it was nothing to the protection of some of the most powerful families' compounds in the higher-ranking rings of the city.

"Fine," Jane said thinking it would be strange to stay in Jei's house without him, but not wanting to have this fight. She had neither the time nor the energy.

From Space Port One, they all took a House Rega transport down to the Capital City. Jane walked into the City Hospital and headed up to the Imperial floor, Jei's guards trailing her. Once there she was met by other guards. "I'm here to see Doctor Drusilla James, I mean Doctor James, of House Vo."

The Imperial Guards nodded to her and she was allowed onto the floor and found James's office with the guards trailing her. When she arrived, James wasn't there, but a passing nurse told her to wait and that James would probably be right back, so Jane sat down in one of the chairs in the office and waited. While she did, she was surprised that James actually had the old-fashioned wedding picture of herself and her husband on her desk. Jane picked it up to investigate it. It had been her and Kara's idea to reintroduce the practice as it seemed the only thing worthwhile from the custom of Earth marriages. James had worn a dress form Earth and make up which made the wedding look like a real love match. For a second, it made Jane feel guilty about what she and Anu were doing, but then she reminded herself that she was doing this because James might have had a better life that she had chosen for herself on Earth if the Alliance had not taken them.

Jane thought about her own situation then and was sad, she would have never entered into a relationship with Jei had she not taken the forget-me-not drug and had they not been captured she would have never had to leave Jim. But somewhere in the back of her mind a voice reminded her, *No, you would have been killed if you had not been taken prisoner during the war. And is this life not more exciting? Haven't I come to love Jei just as much as Jim?* But that last thought made the guilt even worse because, if she were honest with herself, her Alliance life was much more exciting and maybe better than her human life. And this was the bare fact she didn't want to face, that maybe she preferred her Alliance life as depraved as her human family and friends would think it was.

Dru walked towards her office and was surprised to see two guards from Alliance Planet Two outside. She passed them without a word and entered, "Jane?"

Jane stood up, "James, sorry I just thought I would drop by. I hope you have a minute?"

"Yes, of course," she gestured for Jane to sit again. "How are things?"

"You know better than I do. Oh, this thing with Babette," Jane said sullenly.

Dru had felt a wave of guilt and shame from Jane as she entered. She knew it was about her life on the *Kzi*, "We can talk about Babette in a minute. How are you? It must be unique being the only woman on the *Kzi*. There were rumors of an attempted rape some months ago," she said quietly.

"It was taken care of quickly," Jane said authoritatively not wanting to talk to James about the details of that.

Dru sensed everything from the forget-me-not, the relationship with Jei and what Jim had done to her as well as the attempted rape. Then the goddess of home began showing her the whole situation with Jim and urged her to tell Jane information she needed to hear, "Jane you shouldn't feel guilty. Jim always wanted Sandra."

"What did you say?"

"You heard me."

"How could you know something like that?"

"The goddess of home blesses me with certain knowledge. You should forget about him, forget about your other children and live your new life here now. Trust in the Alliance gods they want us here. We are the Lost People. And don't ever forget, our own people sold us." Dru was repeating what had been said to her over and over again when she struggled with the differences in the Alliance culture.

"You'll never know what it is like to have a human partner or children therefore you cannot begin to understand the heartbreak," Jane said that just to hurt James. She hadn't liked what she had just said about Jim and Sandra, even though she knew what James had said to be true. She knew that James was telepathic and who knew what else, she had other worldly talents and now with her religious fervor she might have even tapped into some strange Alliance mystics, giving her more power. Jane looked at her and thought, *I'd definitely accuse you of being a witch in Salem if you go against me.*

"Your racism towards Alliance people or the hybrid child growing inside of you does you no good. This is your life now. It's childish of you to hold on to something that will never be, nor should you even want to. You are only making yourself weak by not recognizing your new future and embracing it."

"I hope you never have to say goodbye to your husband or children," Jane said wanting to end this conversation because she realized she was being childish.

"Praise be to the gods that I'm safe on the Capital Planet. The safest place in the galaxy. I can make an order that you might stay too, it would override even Admiral Jei's command. But I'm hesitant to do that as then everyone would know about the illegitimate child. But Jane, I can feel your confusion, you need help recognizing your true path, let me help you."

Jane only focused on half of what she said, "Thank you for the offer, but I'll work thought this." She was worried that James would look into her thoughts and know what she and Doctor Anu had done and she didn't know how James would react to that. She wanted to change the subject, "What does Babette's child have to do with this?"

Dru broke protocol again and did a quick sweep of Jane's mind. She didn't know she was pregnant. She didn't think she could become pregnant. Dru looked into Jane's eyes deciding whether or not to repeat it. "Jane, you are pregnant. One child. A daughter. A hybrid."

Jane shook her head, "You are mistaken James."

Dru got up from her desk, came around, touched Jane's abdomen and looked at Jane, "I can hear it's little humming. That's what their thoughts sound like in the beginning."

Jane paled and at that moment she knew that James was right. She had felt different, but she thought it had everything to do with the forget-me-not and her guilt. It had not occurred to her that she could become pregnant. "This isn't right," Jane put her head in her hands.

Dru was probing her thoughts then trying to figure out why she and Doctor Anu kept the 1,000 human women on Space Port One for so long but it was futile, without touching Jane and her permission, she couldn't reach those memories as Jane was so upset about this.

Jane looked up and said to James, "Don't tell anyone. I must tell Jei first."

"I can't do that," Dru said. "You know that. I must log it here."

"James, seriously? What about the solidary among human women?"

"I don't understand why you would want to keep this a secret? There's no reason. Jei clearly likes you and would marry you. You are already publically lovers, so this is something to rejoice. And once the baby is born you can see your human family again. Isn't that what you want more than anything?"

Jane waved her hand away.

"Jane," she said sternly, "It goes against the gods to kill it. I don't know how deep your racism goes but I will kill you if you do it."

Jane smiled like a mad woman, "What a ridiculous duel that would be, two human women terrible with swords trying to kill each other in the arena. Don't jump to conclusions James. I'm not going to kill it. You've been on this planet too long only with Alliance people, you are literally one of them now with your religion and all."

"You left me here," Dru suddenly accused Jane. "I was all alone and none of you cared. Why should I protect you now?"

Jane looked at the younger woman and tried to explain, "Drusilla, stop. I'm sorry. I wanted you to have a better life than what you would have had with us. I felt terrible when I found out how isolating it was for you to be alone in House Human. I didn't know what Ket's ban meant for you or the racism you faced in the Capital City. You didn't mention it either. But you were my responsibility and I failed you." Jane then stood up to give James a hug which she accepted. "I am sorry."

Dru finally felt some peace with what had happened over the last year. She had been hurt by Jane's reaction to her memories of how she escaped the Exterior. She would never forget her look of disgust, but Jane of course didn't remember that. The goddess of home had erased all of their memories, so no one remembered it. But she still put most of the blame of her unhappiness on Jane, whether it was right or not she didn't know, and she knew it stemmed from that look of disgust.

Dru accepted Jane's embrace. And then said something in the moment she wanted Jane to hear, "You know I'm from the Exterior." Dru wanted Jane to be touching her while she said it. To feel her thoughts about it. "I escaped. I traded my virginal body to the border guards, and they used me like a common whore, but I walked out."

Jane listened to Dru's words and had a feeling of déjà vu. She hugged Dru closer and thought of her own daughter who was about the same age and said, "I'm so sorry that that happened. Do you want to talk about it?"

Dru leaned back and looked at Jane's face, it was the

same look, full of disgust but now she knew her thoughts, and was shocked that her look of disgust came from the disgust she felt by the men being so depraved to use such a young girl. Whether she was offering herself or not it was wrong. Dru leaned back into Jane's hug again and for the first time in a long time felt that things were becoming right again. She hadn't been wrong about Jane. She'd only been wrong about the face expression. "I don't need to talk about it. I've talked about it enough with Alliance doctors. I just wanted to tell you."

Jane stroked Dru's hair gently, braided in an Alliance style as if she were her own daughter, "Thank you for trusting me with this information. I can't imagine either would be easy to admit. I did suspect that you came from the Exterior from the picture I heard about in your drawing room."

"And what did you think?"

"I thought it all made sense. And I was happy that you left if that's what you wanted and now you have Ket and a nice life here. James, you should be whoever you want to be. We can't change our childhoods or where we were born, but once that time is over, we can change everything. And that's the best part about childhoods for most people, they end."

Dru looked into Jane's eyes and said, "Thank you. I don't know why but I needed to hear this from you, but I did." Dru was being honest and she had read Jane's thoughts as she had done a million times before. Jane had never meant her harm and Dru didn't know how she could have become so depressed and confused she could have ever doubted this woman's intentions.

Jane nodded, "I should have come to your marriage ceremony, even if it would have been just to see you off.

I'm sorry. I've made so many mistakes. I'm not a very good Head of House."

Dru smiled a little, "It's not as if you were born into the role as most Alliance Head of Houses are. I think you are doing just fine. I mean it's only really Babette now. One out of a thousand women isn't bad."

Jane gently let James go and then sat down, "It's only because your name isn't attached to all of these women you can say it's not too bad. Now tell me about Babette."

Dru told Jane everything she knew about Babette.

Jane was surprised that Dru was so supportive of Babette's choice, but decided it must have something to do with her newfound religious fever she had developed lately.

When it was time, they left together to go to House Human to see Babette and Madame Bai to discuss what to do.

Babette was the last to arrive in the Classroom where they were having this meeting.

Jane couldn't help herself and asked before the young woman could even sit down, "Babette, what were you thinking?"

Babette looked at Jane a bit sheepishly, "I love him."

"Where did you even meet a man, who is without rank and without a House?"

"At the temple?"

"In prayer?"

"Of a kind."

"What?" Jane was exasperated. She wanted to throttle Babette for bringing so much trouble to House Human. They didn't need this attention, and she didn't want James so close to all of this either.

"When you sent me to the High Priestess for punishment. That's when I met Mir. He was also there for punishment. It was love at first sight."

"Love at first sight," Jane mocked her. "You met him in the High Priestess's punishment room, and you thought he was a good man? A great man, as you secretly married him. How's that even possible?"

"He organized it," Babette said plainly, and before she could explain, Jane began raising her voice again.

"Of course, he organized it. A man like that would know where to do these things," Jane said bitterly.

Babette looked down at the table.

"And what can we do now?" Jane asked Dru and Madame Bai. "How do we annul this?"

"Why would we want to?" Madame Bai asked. "Unfortunately, they married early, but this isn't such a terrible situation."

Jane was thunderstruck, "Am I the only one who sees how terrible this is for House Human? A woman married to a man with no House and pregnant. Now she is Houseless."

Madame Bai answered her, "You need to speak to the maximum family of House Rog. They may invite him back in. Maybe if Babette were to come with you…" she trailed off.

Jane looked at Babette, and they both said, "No," at the same time.

Dru chimed in then, "Jane, you can petition the High Council for Babette to remain in House Human. Take the blame for her being so taken in with her love for Mir. Don't say that explicitly, of course, but you know what to say to convey that. I think they would grant this small thing to Babette and to you."

"I think the High Council would think they would be setting a precedent for this kind of behavior," she sighed.

"Babbs, do you and Mir have any plans? Have you spoken to him?"

Madame Bai answered before Babette could, "What can he do? We must resolve this here and now. He is a man. He will do what we decide."

All the human women looked at Madame Bai with a bit of disgust. This was the kind of inequality that made them all uncomfortable.

"He's the father of these children and an Alliance man," explained Dru. "He probably has some kind of plan and we must take that into account."

"I've sent him a message, but the *Fira* is across the galaxy. I've not heard back." Sometimes the gravitational wave technology could be delayed. It was rare but did happen.

"Yes, I've not heard from Kara, either," Jane said.

"Why did you tell her?" Madame Bai asked sharply.

"Because she's human and would want to know. She has a vested interest in House Human."

"She is not of House Human," Dru said.

"Neither are you," Jane pointed out.

"At least I was until very recently. And I've been on planet more days than you and know what is going on here a lot better than you. That is why you invited me to sit at this table now."

"Fine," said Jane. "Look, James, I'm sorry. I'm just so frustrated. All these archaic laws. And a completely unsuitable young man for Babette. I just can't believe it."

"He's not unsuitable," Babette said emotionally standing up trying to leave. "And I wish you would all stop talking about him like it's the worst thing ever. We love each other," she saw Madame Bai cringing. "Love is not a dirty word. Humans can say it all the time. And listen, I will repeat it, I love him. And he loves me. And you know what's even more, he just asked me to marry him, and I did it without any agreements. No contracts, no nothing. I just followed my heart."

"Sit down," Jane said, her head in her hands. "Don't tell anyone that you married that way."

Dru couldn't help but smile at her friend and mouth the words, 'Good job.'

Madame Bai said brightly to Babette, "You will go to House Rog and say he used magic to seduce you into acting so irrationally and beg to be allowed into their House."

"Magic?" Jane asked.

And the whole table was quiet looking at her.

Babette didn't want to say anything. She could still hardly say or believe what Mir claimed to be. Still saying the word 'husband' was strange, let alone the reincarnate god of peace. It was all so bizarre. And every time she said it, she felt peculiar.

Dru knew Jane already suspected many things of her that her ordinary little mind didn't like, so she was not going to add this one to the list, to be remembered as the one who used her unworldly sense to know what Mir was.

"What's going on?" Jane asked again. "Is he a magician or something?"

"He is the god of peace," Madame Bai stated as plainly as saying, 'the sky is blue'.

"Excuse me?" Jane laughed.

"He's the reincarnate god of peace. He has married his other half, Babette, but just too soon. She should have resisted." Madame Bai looked at Babette and said sternly, "I expected you to have resisted."

Babette shrugged, "I love him."

Madame Bai shook her head, "I hope he tames this savageness in you." She left off saying, 'And that you aren't killed by the other gods for not being his true chosen wife.' Madame Bai wanted to believe the god of peace would not make a mistake in this, but witchcraft in the past, interference from mortals and other gods had led him astray before and if that was the case now, it was going to be a rough century. As the god of peace's children would either bring peace or damnation to the Empire.

Jane held up both of her hands, "What are you talking about? There is no such thing as reincarnation."

"Yes, there is. Check the records. He's the same again, and again and again, for millions of years, thousands of them are documented. He even looks the same," explained Madame Bai as if she was teaching one of her classes.

"Even if this is true, how can Babette be his true other half? She is human."

"You are the Lost People. Obviously," Madame Bai said as if Jane was a fool.

"Obviously," Jane repeated back sarcastically. Then she looked at Babette, "Did you know this, or did he tell you this to seduce you?"

"He didn't seduce me. I wanted to marry him from the moment I met him."

"In the punishment rooms?"

"It doesn't matter where we met. It could have been anywhere," Babette said, exasperated.

"And it really was, anywhere," replied Dru with a smile.

"So, let me get this straight, he is a god reincarnate but finds himself in this low position without a House and met Babette in the punishment rooms for the same transgressions. How can a god be so reckless with his morals and why wouldn't all the Houses be lining up to invite him in?"

"No one is allowed to give him any special privileges. He must live a mortal life." Madame Bai explained, "And as for his morals, he is mortal and suspectable to the flesh as any young man is."

Jane shook her head trying to understand all of this, "But does he possess some magic then, like a god?" Jane was going into unknown territory now; she rarely read the myths and knew very little about what the gods were supposed to be capable of.

"He is rumored to have all the powers of a god, yes. But rarely does he use them. In the thousands of years, he has been documented, it's less than ten times he has used his godlike power. He is here to be mortal to help us."

Jane just looked at Madame Bai in disbelief, "I'm sorry, this is very difficult for me to believe. Babette is he the god of … I'm sorry, what?"

"The god of peace," Babette said and felt a shiver go up her spine.

"And you've seen this?"

"Yes," Babette replied.

"Before or after you married him?"

"Right before. He had to reveal himself to me or the disciples in the Underworld wouldn't let us in to marry."

"And you didn't think at that time that maybe you shouldn't marry him?" Jane was looking directly into her young and innocent blue eyes. "You didn't think, 'Wait, maybe this is all too much to get involved with a man you met in the High Priestess's punishment rooms? Who claims to be an important god in this extremely religious culture and on top of it, has no House and your marriage would be a sin and leave you in a lowly human position without anywhere to go? Did you consider any of that as you stood at the gates to the Underworld?" Jane had a moment to reflect, *Add that to the list of things I never thought I would have to say in my life.*

"No, why? It's still Mir. I love him."

"Really? Bear with me because I'm just looking at this from an outsider's point of view and this is what I see, an extremely racist and restricted population on the verge of a civil war due to many issues but at the forefront is the introduction of human women to their society. This problem was further aggravated by Kara marrying Admiral Tir and then next by Kara, murdering one of their own."

"It wasn't murder, it was a legal duel," Dru interrupted.

Babette frowned.

Jane continued, "And now, not only have you sneaked off to marry a man who you shouldn't have, but he is one of their beloved gods reincarnate. How do you think this looks to those people who want to see all of us returned to Earth or just plain dead? You have certainly added more wood to an already burning fire."

"Maybe it's the god's will to bring peace through this marriage to prove that humans are the Lost People?" Madame Bai suggested. She was not going to let Jane know there was also speculation of witchcraft and that the humans would be accused of it if Babette was not truly his other half.

"And monogamy," Dru added.

Madame Bai gave her a disdainful look, "No, you are the one misguided there James."

Dru asked Babette, "What did Mir say about your marriage? Your obligations?"

"I told you we didn't ask any questions; we didn't make a contract. We just love each other. It was all so natural. I didn't even think about a contract nor did we talk about the future."

"Well, that is completely obvious," Jane said exasperated.

"He must have hinted though," Dru pushed gently.

Babette looked at her blankly, "Do you mean whether or not I would be faithful to him?" She remembered then his words on the Promenade when he had given her the necklace, "Yes, he said he wouldn't share as he was of the slave class, so I didn't need to worry about that."

"See?" Dru said accusatorily to Madame Bai. "He intends to bring monogamy back as the true way."

"He's doing no such thing. The god of peace always practices monogamy. He is always born of the slave class." Madame Bai shot back. "They all wear binding necklaces to keep it so. But they all live on the planet together, so it makes sense they have no need for slave artists."

Jane looked at Madame Bai in disbelief, "Even though, slave artists, as the name suggests come from the slave class? And you don't feel that this infringes on the purity of the slave class?"

"Or the maximum class or middling class?" Dru asked.

Madame Bai frowned, "You ladies still have so much to learn. I know there hasn't been much time but just remember this for now, as I think it might bring some clarity to the situation. Those of the maximum class are seen as the weakest, that is why they are given the least amount of tasks."

"To rule?" Jane asked and couldn't keep the humor out of her voice, it sounded so absurd.

"Yes, they rule us. But it's not as if they make crazy laws that we all don't agree with. And the slave class is our foundation. Our secure connection to the gods, they watch over us all. They are purity. And the slave artists bring that to the ships and maximum class on the planet."

"I disagree," Dru interjected. "It is blasphemy that the High Council made slave artists lawful, but just because it is a law does not mean that this is the will of the gods or moral."

"Wait," Jane raised her hand not wanting to listen to James and Madame Bai argue.

Madame Bai was pleased Jane was stopping this. She didn't want to have to explain anything about middling class and confuse them further.

"Let's get back to the matter at hand, which is Babette marrying Mir and what consequences that has for all of us. Now Babette, what do you have to say?" Jane asked.

But James answered, "Mir is not a slave anymore. He's of maximum class. He has married a woman of maximum class to prove a point."

Jane clapped her hands like she did when her children were young and arguing, "Stop. Now listen. I will go and speak to the maximum family of House Rog. If that fails, I will address the High Council, and if that fails, I will figure out where people without any House go and how they survive. We won't abandon you, Babbs. Oh, stop crying."

"I'm not crying," Babette said as she was wiping tears from her eyes.

"This will turn out," said Madame Bai. "I only wish you would have waited."

Dru said impatiently to Babette, "Give me your hand."

"Why?" Babette asked recoiling away from the table at the suggestion.

"I'm just going to calm you."

"I don't want you reading my mind again."

Jane looked at Dru, "James, why were you reading her mind?"

Dru looked at Jane, "Is there a secret you are keeping from me, Jane?"

Jane looked at Babette, trying to discern if she remembered the time, almost half a year, that the human women were 'ill' on Space Port One Hospital. She saw nothing in Babette's face that would suggest she remembered anything, but she didn't know how well Alliance mind replacing or erasing worked or if James would be able to find those memories. However, if she resisted James now, she would know for sure that she was hiding something. The last thing Jane wanted was James snooping around what she sanctioned Doctor Anu to do. "Babbs, give James your hand, she will make you feel better, nothing more." Jane looked at James, "Right?"

James nodded.

Babette hesitantly extended her hand, and from the moment Dru's touched hers, she felt calm and relaxed. It was amazing. Until a shocking headache came through like a thunderstorm, "Stop, it worked but now, my head hurts." She took her hand away, "Don't touch me like that again."

Dru looked at Babette and was surprised by her reaction. No one had ever reacted to her that way. She looked at Babette and tried to work this out, but she couldn't think of anything she had done that would give Babette a headache except her own mind, "Don't get yourself so worked up. You've no control over this. It is your destiny. Don't let Jane or Madame Bai fool you. You couldn't' have resisted. Any more than you can resist now. Go and rest, Babette, that is a doctor's order."

Babette nodded and gratefully left the room. She didn't feel that any of them understood and she couldn't explain it or rather she didn't feel the need to explain it to them. She loved Mir and that was all.

Jane and Madame Bai got up to leave too.

Dru said, "Jane wait, we must talk privately."

"Unfortunately, I have a lot to do, as you know. Let's talk later," she lied as she walked out with Madame Bai. Jane did not want to be alone with James again. She suspected that James knew about what had happened to Babette and the rest of the 1,000 women now, and she didn't want to have to explain it. Especially not to James. She had become increasingly devout to the Alliance religion since she married Ket and everyone, meaning all the other human women, except for Babette and Kara, were becoming frightened of her for it.

Dru watched Jane go and replied, "We will find a time soon."

Jane arranged to meet with the maximum family of House Rog. They were very polite to her and very fond of Mir but would not invite him and Babette into their House. When Jane had asked why they had told her straightforwardly that Rez, the woman who had been killed by Kara in the women's duel had been a distant relation, and if they accepted a human into their House, there would be turmoil. They assured Jane that Mir knew this before he married. Jane had not been too shocked by the blatant racism. She replied by saying that she hoped their House could survive without the help of the Lost People and then left.

Next, she went to the High Council, which was much more forgiving of the situation. Jane chided herself for not taking James's advice first, then she would not have wasted her time at House Rog. The High Council deliberated Jane's request to allow Babette to remain in House Human for only an hour. However, their conditions were not favorable. Mir must find a House to accept them both within the month, or they would both be forever Houseless and their children without a class.

Jane had no choice but to take the offer. She knew that

she could not publically ask for more. She was just about ready to VM Kes of House Zu and ask her which Houses were most likely to receive Mir and Babette when she received a message from Kara.

Jane was surprised as the fleet had been out of touch for days. She quickly messaged Kara back, explaining the whole situation hoping she would have a solution.

Jane left House Human and the guards took her to Jei's Capital City residence. As they set down, she noticed that just like the imperial homes, it was in a compound. She asked Gio, "I thought House Rega was on Alliance Planet Two?"

"It is, but we also have a pied-a-terre here."

Jane followed Gio's lead towards the largest house in the compound, that was at least 5,000 square meters of geometric windows and yellow stone and commented, "This is what you call a pied-a-terre?"

"Planet Two is less densely populated and would have been the Capital Planet had we only been just a little stronger in the Battle for Dominance." Gio left out saying, 'House Rega is the Imperial House of the Second Alliance Planet, hence the purple. And probably most importantly the House had almost fallen into ruin until Admiral Jei gained it all back, so the Admiral is not only respected for his position in the Alliance Fleet but also for what he has personally done for his home planet and House.'

When they entered the large house all the slaves were standing to attention. They also all had purple somewhere on their green uniforms. Jane greeted them and they began to ask her questions about being a human, many of them rude. And they were upset that human food had been delivered to them. They didn't want to touch it, but they would do it minimally for her. They also wanted her to eat quickly so that none of them would miss their mealtimes. After Jane had agreed to all of this, she was shown through the large house ending in the master bedroom.

"I think I should stay in another room," Jane explained to the slave, a middle-aged woman who wore a tight green dress over her athletic body.

"I don't think so. We've never had a woman here. His wife was never here if that is what is troubling you. He'd want you to sleep here. Especially if he comes back, am I right?"

"I don't know," Jane said because it was all just too overwhelming. Was she really doing this with Jei now, his lover, mother to his hybrid child and then probably his wife. Could she really find it in herself to do this?

The slave looked at her incredulously, "What do you mean, 'You don't know'?"

"Forget it . You're right. I'll stay here."

"I know I'm right," replied the slave, "I'm not the maximum class fool."

"Thank you for your instruction," Jane said sarcastically. And thought to herself, something humans always said to one another, 'And slave definitely doesn't mean "slave" in the Alliance.'

"Anytime," the woman said as she began walking out of the room, but at the last minute, stopped and turned back, "Lieutenant, many written messages have come for you about House Human, apparently your charges have been very naughty. So naughty in fact that even the High Priestess wants to see you."

"You shouldn't read other people's personal messages," Jane said annoyed.

"You shouldn't be staying in other men's beds that are

not your husband's or a slave artist's, but here we both are. The lovers' bracelets go against the gods you know. I've left the messages in the library downstairs. The High Priestess expects you tomorrow. Bless the gods for their wisdom," the slave said as she walked out.

"Let the gods be blessed," she said casually and investigated the master bedroom. It was all stone with huge floor to ceiling windows overlooking the rest of the compound. She wondered if Jei was a self-made man of if he had inherited this.

Jane went into the large stone bathroom and took off her uniform. She wanted to have a shower and just go to bed. When she was naked, she looked at herself in the large mirror. Her body showed no outward signs of being with child and she had to admit, she had kind of known, but this pregnancy was so different. She almost wondered if James hadn't have said anything if she would have been six months gone before realizing it.

Jane stepped into the shower and the water turned on but then she jumped out again, saying "Cold, cold, cold," under her breath. "Shower, temperature to 40 C."

"Unable to complete request due to health restrictions."

"Override."

"Only Admiral Jei of House Rega may override."

"What's the maximum temperature?"

"The maximum temperature is 30C."

"Okay, 30C," Jane said as she stepped in again preparing herself for the lukewarm water, at best. She showered quickly and then brushed her teeth with the laser toothbrush she found in the bathroom and put on her Earth pajamas. Then she got into bed. She was shivering. The room was kept at 15C for Jei. She addressed the computer, "Please raise room temperature to 20C."

"Maximum temperature 20C," the computer said.

Jane leaned back and thought, *Well, at least something is close to the correct temperature.* As she lay in the bed looking up at the stone ceiling, she realized she had not prayed yet today, so she grabbed her IC, and quickly went through the large house looking for the shrine she had seen before. She had forgotten her extra prayer candles for her pajamas, but she would pick some more up tomorrow. Onboard ship, the rules were much more relaxed about praying every day and the fleet had conveniently set up statues around different areas of the ship, so it counted if you just passed one and were supposedly thinking of a prayer at the time you walked by. On planet though, your IC monitored your prayers, and everyone had to pray at least once a day.

She heard the slaves curiously coming to follow her as they spotted her in her human pajamas. All Alliance people slept naked and they would have thought nothing of it if she ran down naked to the shrine, but pajamas were odd to Alliance eyes. It went against the gods and health to wear clothing at night according to Alliance doctors. As Jane entered the large shrine, a slave followed her and then nudged her in the back with some candles. Jane turned.

"Here," said the slave as she handed Jane some specific prayer candles for the pajamas. "The Admiral has provided you with all a human would need."

"Thank you," she said and thought, *Just like a good pet owner.* And Jane knew now, this was what Kara found so irritating about Alliance men, they were always thinking way too much instead of just doing their own thing and allowing women to get on with what they needed to do themselves. However, in this instance, she was grateful for his foresight as she didn't want another fine for something so ridiculously small.

Jane entered the shrine and found the black and green statue of the goddess of home. She was young and beautiful and had hair about the same length as Jane's now. After reciting the standard prayer, she couldn't help but add, "I'm sorry I've not been here for a while. I've been off planet. I hope you can forgive me that too." Then she lit the candles in front of the statue and went back to bed. She was so cold, tired and emotionally exhausted, she just wanted to jump under the warm covers and sleep.

As Jane lay there in bed, she wondered what it would be like to be married to Jei. What marriage would be like in general. After a few minutes she got up again and went to her bag to retrieve the purple ring he gave to her. She put it on her hand and looked at it as she lay in his bed in his house thinking, *How does this feel? Do I feel like I am cheating on Jim? Do I feel like I am using Jei only to see Jim and my human family again?* After many minutes contemplating this all, she took off the ring and set it on the bedside table, all the time looking at it as she drifted off to sleep.

9

A Change of Plan

The next morning Jane woke up and it took her a few seconds to remember where she was. At first, she thought she was in a fancy hotel on Earth. And Jei's bed had been so comfortable after being on Beta ship *Ilo* she had slept through the morning meal. She had missed two meals now and was starving, but unfortunately now it would be three hours until the next meal.

She checked her IC and saw she had a message from Jei.

Why aren't you eating? There should be some food from Earth there.

Jane smiled imagining him, one-minute concentrating on important issues in the Alliance fleet that would affect trillions of people in the galaxy and then the next worrying about her missing two meals.

I'm tired. I went to bed early and slept late.

She was shocked to get a message back immediately.

I understand. I hope things are getting resolved with Babette. Please don't miss another meal.

Jane smiled.

If your bed hadn't been so comfortable and house so welcoming, I wouldn't have.

Jei replied,

I prefer my home on the Second Alliance Planet, it's more luxurious. Maybe you will too?

Jane smiled at that but didn't reply right away. She wondered for a minute if James would give her the forget-me-not forever. She was sure James could do it, but would it be right? Jane got up and got dressed thinking about all of these things. She replied back,

Maybe. We will see.

She knew that James's medical report would have reached him by now as he was the father of their unborn child. They were officially lovers. But she knew Jei well enough, he was waiting for her to mention it. She had to give him that, he was patient.

When Jane made her way downstairs her two guards were waiting for her. Gio nodded to her and then they escorted Jane to the Grand City Temple. They stood outside the High Priestess's compound near the back of the temple with the other guards. Jane entered and was escorted by nuns to the High Priestess herself in her private meeting rooms. The walls were lined with the black statues of the gods and goddesses. Jane bowed, "I have come to seek your guidance High Priestess. May the gods speak through you today."

"You will know the gods' will by the end of our meeting," the High Priestess responded in the set reply and motioned for Jane to sit before her in a black wooden chair. "Jane, I've been as patient as I can be with some of these human women, but they are not praying every day and they flaunt the courting ritual as if it were a joke. You must get some control, or I'll have no choice but to begin inflicting real punishments as if they were Alliance women."

"Your punishments don't work," Jane said thinking about Babette. "So, I don't see how increasing them would make these women follow the law more by making the punishments worse. Humans are secular. We don't believe in religion. I think exceptions must be made. You cannot beat people into believing in a religion."

"You mean to say, you used to not believe in religion until you were enlightened and realized that you were the Lost people of the Alliance Empire, right?"

"Of course," Jane said and bowed her head respectfully.

"What are you going to do about it as Head of House Human?"

"I've had a vision from the goddess of home," she lied. But she did think a human goddess would be helpful.

"Oh," said the High Priestess sitting on the edge of her chair now, clearly interested.

"Yes, she revealed to me a new goddess. A human goddess who would represent the Lost People. This will inspire the human women to become more religious and to pray. "Jane was fabricating this as she went along. She hadn't even considered it until now.

"What does this goddess look like and what is her symbol?"

"I don't know what she looks like, but her symbol is an Earth and Alliance fruit, the peach," Jane was proud of herself that she said that without even cracking a smile.

"Will you testify to this?"

Jane held her finger over her heart, "Yes."

"No doubt this truly is a vision Jane. Gods be blessed. I have been praying for the Lost People."

"Gods be blessed," Jane replied hoping this would satisfy her.

The High Priestess considered this for a minute. "I will add this new goddess after I pray on it. From you, I hope to see a great improvement in your wards praying and adherence to the laws. And this includes you too Jane. If the human women's behavior improves, I will install the Lost People's goddess into our patheon."

"Praise the gods."

"Go and may your path be blessed."

Jane walked out and nodded to the gods' statues as she left and thought to herself, *It cannot be this easy.*

"This one needs to be taught a lesson", the god of War thought.

After her visit to the Grand City Temple, Jane met Frank and his niece Jade in the Immigrant Ring to discuss plans for her restaurant that she planned on calling, 'Human Food.' When Jane had asked her why she had chosen such a ridiculous name she had explained, 'Alliance people wouldn't understand any subtilties and it's what they will call it anyway, so why not?' Jane couldn't fault her logic, but still, for every other human, it was a slap in the face, like calling the restaurant 'dog food' or something else degrading. But Jade countered her again, 'Are you telling me you are not going to eat at the only human run restaurant in the Capital City because of a name?' And again, she was correct. Jane would eat there and frequently.

After lunch and promises from Jane of messages to be sent to gain favor for her new restaurant, Jei's guards arranged for Jane to get back on her way to the *Kzi*. Gio and Sra escorted her as far as her transport from the *Kzi* and then said their goodbyes.

Jane got into the transport and waiting out on one of the main routes to pick up with a fleet ship heading in the direction of the Kzi. She had had to travel for a day in the transport to get to this place and wait. When she arrived at the rendezvous point that evening, there was a human pirate ship there, the Styx, it was one of the many other ships waiting for someone or something.

Jane checked their information. Of course, they called themselves 'traders' but everyone knew what they really were. And they said that they were waiting on some passengers and then would be traveling to the Solar System. She rubbed her eyes and had to look at it twice. They were going back to Earth, to home. Her heart leapt. *They are heading to Earth*, she thought. *But you can't go*, she reminded herself and tried to settle back into her life and what she was supposed to do. But she kept looking at the human ship every time she checked to see who had gone and who had come to the rendezvous point.

Every hour she waited she wondered more and more if this was a sign from the gods to return home. She knew these 'traders' would take her. She had some UCs and if necessary, she could trade the ring Jei had given her. Two hours, three hours, then after ten hours had passed, she couldn't help herself, she contacted the human ship.

"Styx, I couldn't help but notice that you are going all the way to the Solar System," she said into a blank RVM to the other ship.

"Hello Lieutenant Jane," a voice said and then a human man's face appeared on the RVM. Jane was surprised. She hadn't seen another human man except for Frank who ran the Earth Store in some time. "We are indeed headed to Earth. Frank wants more supplies and there are some straggler women who want to come and join House Human."

"Oh really?" She doubted these extra women were

legally sanctioned by the Alliance as she hadn't heard anything about it.

"You don't know?" the man asked innocently.

"I've not heard anything about it. Do you mind sending over the list of names so that I can cross check them?"

"I've no objection to showing you. We are both humans after all, and we know this game." He hit some buttons and said, "I've sent the names to you. They've all paid a hefty price and no doubt you will see some of them when they 'apply' to House Human."

Jane didn't look at the list yet but asked, "What do you think the Alliance will do if they aren't allowed in?"

"You know better than I do, but I suspect they will be set adrift."

"Have you brought over human women before?"

"Yes, I thought you would have known?"

"What?"

"Look this isn't a secure channel," the pirate said then. "Why don't you come over here and we can talk?"

Jane looked at the time and since she still had a couple hours before her rendezvous. So, she agreed.

Onboard the traders' ship she was surprised to see a mixed human and Alliance crew and a few that were clearly hybrid teenagers. The man she recognized from the RVM approached her. He was middle aged with dark hair and a hard face.

"Please come into our conference room so that we can talk."

Jane nodded and followed him into the room. A hybrid young woman tried to follow them until the man told her to stay out. She was clearly dismayed and so was Jane she wanted to look at this young woman more closely. To think about how the growing hybrid inside of her might look. To possibly find some sympathy for her and keep her from what life altering decisions she might make in the next few minutes.

Inside the small conference room, they sat down, and the trader introduced himself, "I'm Captain Hester, this is my crew. We often do runs for Frank. We were told by the Ambassador to Earth that these new human women were sanctioned. However, if you have no record…" he trailed off.

"I don't think so. Is this the new Ambassador to Earth?"

"Yes, but this isn't' the first time we've been lied to."

"Judging by your crew I would say that you just kept the other women then?"

"Ouch," he said. "Don't jump to so many conclusions. No, we didn't but they didn't want to return to Earth so all the women went elsewhere in this area of the galaxy."

"Doing what?"

The Captain shrugged his shoulders, "I'm not their father, I don't know."

"Don't you feel any remorse about that?"

"No, they pay the money and I transport them here. I have documents stating that they are sanctioned by the Empire. I don't need much else."

"But you just said you know they are lying."

"You, of all people, know how it is with the Alliance, sometimes they are lying sometimes they are not. Either way I get paid."

"How honorable."

"I don't care what you think, that is not even why I brought you over. I am trying to do you a favor."

"What favor?"

"Did you even look at the list I sent you?"

"Not yet."

Hester brought up the 3D projection between them and flicked through a number of different pictures and then stopped on one, "This is why I am doing you a favor."

Jane almost fell out of her chair, "Ellie?" On the screen was her eldest daughter Ellie's standard picture. "Oh no."

"She paid and is already headed to the rendezvous. I thought you would have known about this. That you would have organized it. I thought you were here to talk to me about it when I saw your transport."

Jane shook her head. "I didn't know. Have her sent back to Earth. Don't take her onboard. What do you want? UCs? I can give those to you."

Hester replied, "I can't do that. I'm not even going to see her. We are headed to Earth not away from it. She's with some colleagues. This isn't a commercial travel line. And she's left without expatriate papers. She'll be jailed by the human government if she returns and is discovered. You know that the government would love to make an example of her given that you are her mother."

"What do you mean by that?"

"Don't play the innocent human with me, Jane. Lover to the Admiral of the Fleet, ring any bells?"

Jane looked at him blankly.

"It's been all over the news. Your daughter was probably bullied a lot for it. You know there is a lot of racism towards the Alliance especially from human men lately. People are calling you an even worse traitor than Kara Rainer, didn't you know?"

"No," Jane whispered. She was thinking of her children now. The children she thought were safe on Earth. The children she thought she was protecting. The ones she thought were living normal lives. They hadn't mentioned anything to her about bullying, but then she tried to remember the last time she VMed with them and it was a few weeks ago. They had sent written messages, but it's so easy to lie in those.

Jane was at a crossroads now. She could either allow Ellie and her other children to join her in this prison or somehow return Ellie to Earth. She felt the latter was the best course of action, hopefully this racism towards the Alliance on Earth would pass, but she knew that she had to save Ellie from making this mistake.

"I will pay you whatever you want to take her back to Earth when you pass the other ship."

"First, I have no plans to pass the other ship that will have her onboard. And second, I know House Human is poor. You don't have those kinds of UCs to make this worth the risk to me."

"Admiral Jei does. He is my lover. He will give me UCs."

"That is as it may be, but there is still nothing I can do."

Jane frowned, "I don't believe that. Please, this is my daughter, I don't want her to be a prisoner here like me."

Hester laughed, "Are you really a prisoner?"

"Yes, I can't leave."

"Have you tried?"

Then is struck Jane, she had never tried. "Take me with you and I will find a way to get to the ship carrying my daughter."

"And then what?"

"I'll return her to Earth and face the consequences. I'll stand trial as a traitor." Jane knew that this would mean a life imprisonment but at least Ellie would be safe and their lives a bit better knowing she came back to face her punishment.

The Captain looked her over skeptically, "But what about me? You're not a lowly human woman who's changed her mind and is leaving. I'll be killed if I help you escape."

Jane looked into the man's brown eyes, "If it was your daughter what would you do?"

"Just tell me this, are you really a prisoner here?"

"I was taken against my will, yes."

"In every regard?"

Jane knew exactly what he was asking, she didn't want to say this because she knew it was a lie, but she needed to stop Ellie from ruining her life at all costs. Jane looked Hester in the eyes and said confidently, "Yes, in every regard."

Hester considered this. He had a daughter and he would never want her to become an Alliance man's wife and so he said, "I'll take you as far as our next rendezvous. Leave your transport here. It will look like we abducted you. Just in case, I don't want all of us to die. And I'll need every UC that House Human has as we will have to buy a new ship immediately."

Jane took both of his hands and said, "Thank you Captain Hester, I will be indebted to you forever."

He smiled, "It's been a while since I did something truly dangerous and it's nice to have that rush of adrenaline again. Besides 'abducting' the lover of the admiral should bring in some nice UCs and at the same time I can keep another young human from sacrificing herself to a race that doesn't deserve her. I'd say this is a win-win for everyone as long as we aren't killed first."

"Thank you."

"Come on," he said rising, "Let me show you a bunk. It's small and there's no toilet, but it's all human-made, if you remember what that looks like?"

"It's only been a year."

"A long Alliance year my dear," Hester replied. "Here

we go," he stopped in front a room so small she could touch both sides at once, but it did have a little bunk and nothing else in it. "You stay here, and we will just go. I'll organize the rendezvous to get you where you need to go."

Before Jane could thank him, he was gone. She entered the small room that smelled of familiar human scents, of unwashed human bodies and closed the door behind her. She sat on the small bed and thought about Ellie. And wondered how Jim could have been so stupid to let her escape or have access to the amount of UCs she must have needed to fund such an illegal trip across the galaxy.

Jane thought about Jei then and whispered, "I am so sorry." She wished she could tell him why she was doing this. She looked at her bracelet and wondered what the consequences for leaving a lover was. She didn't think it would have the same consequences as leaving a marriage partner, but then she remembered the extra fine for the geriatric kiss and shivered. If she was brought back to the Alliance and it was deemed that she left freely, she would no doubt be killed.

In the middle of the night, Hester entered her room and said, "Jane, get up. You're transferring ships. The *Marianne*, will take you to the ship that's carrying your daughter."

Jane stood up, she had nothing to change into and nothing to take, "I'm ready."

Hester and his crew escorted her to the hatch to enter the other ship and they all wished her well.

"Thank you all for your help," and then she had to stop herself from thanking the Alliance gods as well.

"Humans help humans," one of them said.

Another replied, "Always."

And Jane walked through the hatchway with such a heavy heart about what she had done with Doctor Anu she decided she would never return to the Alliance. She had not been able to make up her mind before as she loved Jei so much and as long as she didn't think about her human family, she had been content. But now, after seeing her own people, she knew how wrong it all was. They were not the Lost People. It was just a ruse for a powerful civilization to get what they wanted, and they had wronged her. And she had not been strong enough to escape until now.

The Captain of the *Marianne* was a young woman with freckles and red hair.

"I'd like to say I'm not shocked every time I see a human in one of their uniforms, but I can't help it. You look like a traitor."

"I'm not," said Jane defensively. "I didn't choose this."

"I'd have killed myself before putting that on," the Captain spat.

"Well, you're not me. And you probably don't have a family back on Earth either. Now I'm risking everything to save my daughter. Are you going to help?"

"Yes, that's why we're here. We're going to rendezvous with the *Diablo* and then return you and your daughter to Earth. It's not going to be easy. Already the Alliance has been alerted to your abduction. Hester needs to turn and cross the border into Jahay space. We are all risking a lot for you. Well actually to save your daughter and to see you tried as a traitor. Humanity needs that."

"Thank you."

"Thank me when you're on Earth and safely in prison," the Captain said and then turned and said, "Jes will show you your quarters."

A young man presented himself and showed her to the same kind of small room she had onboard the Styx. Although when he left, he gave her a warning, "Don't leave. We don't trust you. I'll bring you food and what you need. There's a toilet here," he opened a tiny door with a disgusting little toilet and nothing else.

Jei was on the bridge when Captain Ota received a message and sent it across the open computer screens in front of them.

"Humans," Jei said unenthusiastically as he read the report.

Lieutenant Commander Jane, House Human has been abducted by an Alliance-Human trading vessel called Styx.

"Where is the *Styx* now?" asked Jei. He was of course very troubled by this turn of events, but he would never let his crew know this. He needed to treat her as if she was any of his crew that had been abducted. If she was Alliance, he would have been able to show more of his concern but because she wasn't, he did not want to give any indication that it might not have been an abduction.

"They crossed into Jahay space a few hours ago, but they rendezvoused with another human ship called the *Marianne* a few hours before which is heading towards the Solar System."

"Who's closest?"

"Admiral Tir's fleet is not far. He could send one of his ships. The *Marianne* has about the same weapon capabilities as one of our supply ships. They would be nothing against an Alliance warship."

"Ask him to send a ship then. Not Captain Kara's and do not allow Captain Kara or any of the humans to see Lieutenant Jane until she's safe and had a chance to make her official statement."

"Aye, Admiral," Captain Ota knew exactly what the Admiral meant. He wanted to know if there was something else going on. If Jane was a spy and planning something more. If they all were. Humans were not to be trusted.

That night Jei looked at some of Jane's belongings in his wardrobe and asked, "Jane, what are you doing?" Jei suspected that she had gone of her own will. He was so hurt. He had to think there was another reason that she abandoned everything. That she wasn't just leaving him and the Alliance that there was something on Earth that had moved her so much that she would drop everything. He had checked her personal messages and there was nothing there to lead him to believe anything had changed in her life in the last days since he had spoken to her. When he checked the RVMs between her and the human ship it showed that she went there in good faith to return to her transport as she had taken nothing with her. Not even his ring. But he couldn't quiet his lingering feeling that she had left freely.

Jei knelt on his bedroom floor and prayed to the god of darkness to bring her back to him. They were lovers so this was not for the goddess of home to pass judgement over them. And as he was praying to the god of darkness, that god always demanded blood, he unsheathed his sword and cut his palm and let the blood drip onto the floor, "God of darkness, I call on you to bring my Jane back to me. She needs your guiding hand now."

Tir looked at the message from the *Kzi* and immediately ordered the *Fira* to intercept the *Marianne* and take Jane back to the Capital Planet for punishment. He would keep this from Kara for as long as possible. He didn't want her to be associated with this mess any more than she already would be. He always thought Jane was a traitor and hoped that the Admiral would make an example of her.

Captain Rerg couldn't believe it. He looked at his message twice and then ordered his helmsman to change to a new course, "We've got to retrieve one of our humans who has been abducted by her own people."

"Again?" another crewman asked.

"I wouldn't mind another human woman onboard," said another bridge officer.

Commander Daz rolled his eyes.

Rerg stopped the comments there, "This particular human is the Admiral's lover so dismiss any thoughts you have right now."

The bridge was quiet then. They would intercept the *Marianne* in about two hours. The little ship would be no match for them. It was nothing, but they all wondered what the Admiral was going to do to Jane when she was returned, as no one really believed she had been abducted. This was a dishonor not only to him but to the Empire itself and to all Alliance men.

When the *Fira* caught up with the *Marianne*, she of course opened fire on them. It did no damage. They casually shot back disabling the small human vessel with one shot. Then a transport was sent over to bring back Lieutenant Commander Jane and any other human women of marriageable age. After those passengers were safely onboard, the *Marianne* was set adrift with its male crew to live or die by their own skills and luck in this remote area of the galaxy.

Jane and the other women were kicking and screaming all the way onto the *Fira*. Jane was put in guest quarters away from the other humans. She had two guards outside her door and was forbidden to leave.

Commander Daz being considered their human expert on the *Fira* and was sent to speak with Jane about everything that had happened together with Doctor Hou.

Jane stood up as the door to her quarters opened. In

walked two middle-aged Alliance men. One was a doctor by his uniform.

"Lieutenant Jane, this is Doctor Hou and I'm Commander Daz. Please sit down," he motioned to the small seating area.

"I want you to start from the beginning," Commander Daz said while he took in her appearance.

"Wait," Doctor Hou said, "Jane, is there anything you would like me to check before we begin?"

"No, I've already been asked and one of your assistants attended to me when I came onboard."

"Yes," Commander Daz said deciding he would take a more casual approach now, "Why were you fighting us?"

Jane had thought a lot about what she should say now to make it look like an abduction, but with the Doctor there she couldn't lie. He would read her thoughts anyway. "It wasn't an abduction. I asked them to take me."

Commander Daz wasn't surprised and asked sympathetically, "Why would you do that?"

"I've a daughter and she paid some smugglers to bring her to the Alliance. She misses me so much. I was worried for her life, so I wanted to return her to Earth."

"She didn't tell you her plan?" Hou asked, he was reading her thoughts to make sure she wasn't lying now.

"No, I only found out by chance from the human captain while I was waiting at the rendezvous point. I guess he thought I should know. He was a father himself."

"I see," said Commander Daz. "And then what did you do?"

"I asked him to take me to her so that I could return her to Earth."

"But why would you need to go?"

"She left without any exit papers; she would be put in jail if I didn't return with her. I was going to barter myself," she left out, 'Just like Captain Kara did'. "My daughter's freedom for me turning myself in as a traitor."

Doctor Hou nodded to Commander Daz so that he knew that she was not lying.

"Where's your daughter now?"

"Was she among the women taken from the *Marianne*?"

"No," Jane began to sob, she was on a ship the *Marianne* was going to rendezvous with."

"It's our standard protocol to disable those ships and just leave them."

"For anyone passing? She could be sold into slavery or killed! You must find them, it's a human ship, the *Diablo.*"

Commander Daz looked at Jane and said solemnly, "I'm sorry we are already on our way back to the Capital Planet where you will have to defend your actions."

"Is there nothing you can do? I would do anything to keep her safe."

"I'll talk to Captain Rerg. Thank the gods you have been returned to us."

Two days later, on the Capital Planet, Jane was moved into a two-room apartment which was like a prison cell as she couldn't leave. She had been given fresh clothes but otherwise not much else. She had tried to tell people about her daughter and to bring her to her, but no one showed any sign of listening to her. Jane had no idea what was going on or what was going to happen to her. All she could do was sit in the cell and wait.

Jane was alone for two more days in the cell. Food was brought and taken away, but no one spoke to her. She had no access to anything but prayer and her own thoughts. And her own thoughts were maddening. She imagined the worst for her daughter and for herself. She had no idea what was going on outside her walls but suspected that it wasn't good.

On the fifth day, the guards opened the door and Jei walked in.

Jane stood when the door was opening not knowing who to expect but she had not expected him. She ran into his strong arms. "I'm so sorry. I'm so sorry," she murmured into his chest and ranking jewelry.

Jei held her. He had read her testimony and that it was verified by the Doctor that she had not been lying. He knew that she cared for her family deeply. He only wished she would have told him and then this would have all been sorted nicely behind closed doors. Instead she was going to have to face his punishment for leaving him as she was not abducted. He could kill her for it and that is exactly what his station and the Empire wanted from him. To see a human punished by Alliance laws. They were aching for it. Especially from someone as high profile as they were now.

"I know you are," Jei said gently. "I know you love your daughter."

"I just didn't know what to do."

"I know," he said, "It's okay."

"Can I go now?" she asked.

Jei realized then that she didn't understand what she had done. No one had told her the consequences of her actions. He looked at her sadly, "No Jane. You've committed one of the worst offenses in the Alliance. You left me and while pregnant."

"I wasn't leaving you; I was going to get my daughter."

"I know, but the law doesn't see it that way."

"What do I need to do? Receive punishment from the High Priestess?"

"Unfortunately, it's way beyond that."

"What do you mean? Just tell me, I can't even begin to guess."

"The punishment is death by my hand."

"Excuse me?"

"Jane, you know you cannot leave, you left me pregnant and as an officer and Head of House," he sighed, "I'm petitioning the High Council as you didn't know how many laws you were breaking chasing after your daughter."

"Is she safe?"

"Yes, she is on an Alliance ship now headed here."

"What? Jei, no I want her to return to Earth. I never want her to come here."

"What?" Jei asked surprised.

"She should be on Earth."

"She wants to be with you and you with her. She will live in the Alliance now. A room has already been allocated to her in House Human. I thought this would make you happy."

"Yes, I'm sorry," Jane caught herself, "I just wanted her to have a human life."

"This is a better life for her, don't you see that?"

Jane didn't answer.

Jei sighed. He had reckoned that when she saw their beautiful baby, she wouldn't be so negative against the Alliance but now he worried if they would even make it that far. "You need to be grateful."

"I am. She could be dead," Jane answered honestly. "Thank you."

"The Alliance is the best place for her, you are the Lost People. Say it."

"We are the Lost People."

"I am grateful, say it."

"I am grateful," Jane said and then sat down crying.

Jei sat next to her comforting her, making "Zzzz," sounds.

"Are you really going to kill me?"

"I don't want to."

"You're considering it?"

"I've no choice. What you did is terrible and I'm not just a regular man neither you a regular woman. All Alliance eyes are on us."

"How do we get out of this then? Is there a way out?"

"First, you must promise me some things."

"What?"

"You will marry me as soon as you are free to do so."

"Yes."

"You will have our baby and keep her onboard the *Kzi* with us. I don't ever want to be apart from her or you. I spent a life not knowing my own children or wife. I won't do that again given the choice."

"Yes."

"You will publically say that you were abducted."

"Yes."

"You will kill the Captain of the *Marianne*."

"I can't do that."

"You must. Human blood must be spilled and it's better by your hand. This is the only thing that will keep the masses at bay. Otherwise they will demand I kill you to satisfy their bloodlust for humans now. So many people believe the propaganda that you are poisoning the Empire. Especially with what happened with Babette."

"But,"

"A human life must be taken. Is hers more important than yours?"

"No, we are equal."

Jei looked at Jane questioningly, "Are you really equals? You are Head of House Human and an officer in the Alliance Fleet, she is a pirate captain who chooses to break the laws."

"There must be another way."

"No. I'll give you time to think about this. And know that I won't be the only one seeing you today for demands. A lot of people will try to use this to use you to do their bidding."

"What do you mean?"

"People who don't want to have a public duel but want to have someone killed will come here today and ask you to name that person as guilty."

"What?"

"Come on Jane, you know the Alliance law. Now is the time to make the best out of it. Make whatever deals you can to make sure you and your daughter come out of this alive and in good standing order with the Alliance people."

"How will I do that?" Jane asked nervously.

"Well, number one, say you were abducted. Number two, kill that human captain. Number three, listen to whoever comes to see you today and do their bidding if they can help you. Accuse and kill to save yourself. When that is done, marry me." He looked at her confused face, "No one who is a stranger to you will ask for help. It must all look legitimate. Now may the gods keep you safe."

Jei left and Jane just stood there in shock watching him go.

The next person to enter was James about 30 minutes later.

"James," Jane said as she walked in and they sat down.

"I'm sure Admiral Jei has informed you how all of this works?"

"Yes, what could you possibly want?"

"A deal. You tell me exactly what Doctor Anu and you did with the new 1,000 human women and I won't expose you. I'll say she tricked you with mind-control."

"I don't know what you're talking about," Jane lied.

"Jane, I don't want to have to hurt you. I could forcibly

search your mind now. I've paid off the guards, they won't help you. Now, are you going to tell me?"

Jane considered her options and then began, "Doctor Anu came to me with a plan to keep more women from being taken from Earth. She wanted embryos from the human women. Human embryos but as not to anger the gods they needed to be created in utero."

"Where did you get the human men to participate in such a scheme?"

"The Alliance Capital Planet and Space Ports," Jane admitted.

"Where are these embryos now?"

"Growing somewhere in artificial wombs."

"And do you feel the least bit guilty about this Jane?"

"Of course, I do, but it was a no-win situation. The idea was that we would say humanity offered these orphan babies to the Alliance. The idea being that it would be easier for them if they were brought up in Alliance families to integrate. And the children wouldn't know any difference and they would be brought up in loving homes."

"Loving? How can you be so sure?"

"You know what I mean."

"What about the male children?"

Jane just looked at James, "I can't remember."

"You must have asked," Dru knew that Anu erased her memory.

"I'm sure I did."

"I think Doctor Anu manipulated your memory. You must accuse her of these crimes which I helped you remember through the help of the goddess of home and she will be punished accordingly."

"Or?"

"Or what? Jane, this is another crime to add to your list. To prove your loyalty to the Empire. Do you think

Doctor Anu would sacrifice herself for you in this situation? If the situation was reversed, she wouldn't hesitate to kill you."

Jane considered this. She didn't know Doctor Anu all that well. She knew that James hated her though and that she had a personal vendetta against her ever since their first Alliance medical check. And she remembered then that she highly suspected that it was Doctor Anu not Rez that had tried to kill James with an Uli virus last year. "Fine. I will accuse her."

"Good," Dru said taking out her IC. She already had the contract prepared. "Just put your fingerprint here and I will see you soon. May the goddess of home show you mercy."

Jane didn't reply and just watched her go. She was going to have to kill two women now with her sword. *Great,* she thought, *I'm becoming a regular executioner.*

Five other women visited Jane that day, but she only accepted one other person's cause. It was Kes, Kara's mother in-law's case against a woman at the High Council. This woman was named Sah and thought that the human women would serve the men better as breeders in their own separate class. Jane didn't need the long story that Kes was giving her about why Sah should be killed. Jane had raised her hand and said, "Stop. I've hated that woman for a long time. I'll do it."

By the end of the day, Jane had agreed to kill three women to set herself free. She went to bed that night thinking that she would never be the same after this and that she was truly going to cross some lines she would never be able to come back from. That by the end of the next day, she thought with a heavy heart, she would be a full-blown Alliance woman, a killer for her own interests. A true Alliance barbarian. Jane wondered then if she would sit and tell her hybrid daughter with pride how she killed all these women to stay alive herself so that her daughter's father would not have executed her himself? It gave her the chills to think about it. Tears escaped her eyes as she tried to sleep.

The next morning, Babette of all people woke her up.

"Shh, don't speak," Babette said.

"But what are you doing here," Jane whispered.

"I'm not really here."

"How?"

"That answer is not for mortals; I have a proposition for you."

"I must be dreaming," Jane said sarcastically.

"If you choose to allow Jei to kill you, you will be made immortal. The human goddess you spoke of to the High Priestess, will be you."

"What nonsense is this?"

"If you choose life through murder, you will suffer in the Underworld as one of the dark god's servants for all time. The Alliance has lost their way believing the truth can be bargained with. You know this in your heart."

"I don't believe in the gods Babette."

"Become a god Jane. Become the god of humanity as you suggested. Save your people."

Jane sat up suddenly, but Babette was gone. She looked around the room and then said out loud to herself, "What a strange dream," but she couldn't shake the feeling that it wasn't a dream at all, it had been real.

An hour later, breakfast was brought to her, it was Alliance porridge. A few minutes later a formal uniform was delivered. She had never had one for the *Kzi*. She almost began to cry when she saw the handwritten note from Jei,

Don't let this be the last time you wear this, my pet.

She put on the uniform and felt naked without any of her ranking jewelry. It had all been taken from her. She didn't know why, but she hadn't had the energy to ask. When the guards opened her door, she was ready.

Jane was escorted into a large stone room she'd never seen before, a bit like a cross between an Alliance gymnasium and a temple. The walls were all made of dark yellow stone with no windows and lit by candlelight. The shape was like a square amphitheater with places for spectators all around the main stone square. Jane was led to the middle of the square arena floor and waited with guards on either side of her as the High Council officials, officers from the fleet and many other people she didn't recognize were let in and sat according to their rank. Then the humans from House Human were let in and put in the front row on the side. Jane noticed that Ellie was among them, dressed in an Alliance dress and James was right next to her. Jane knew this was a threat from James. If she didn't kill Anu, James would kill Ellie.

Ellie yelled out to her mother, "Mom!" Ellie had missed her mother so much. She began to cry seeing her there. They were so close, but yet she still couldn't touch her. Tears were welling up in her eyes again.

Dru leaned over and touched Ellie's arm to use her influence to make her quiet down, "Hush now, Ellie. You can't distract your mother; she has to focus."

Jane gave her daughter what she hoped was a comforting look. She wanted more than anything to run to Ellie and hold her tight, but there would be time for that later she told herself. Then she reflected that this was possibly the worst day of her life. She had wanted to keep her human family ignorant of everything she had done in the Alliance and now her daughter was going to be front and center for one of the most brutal aspects of this whole culture.

Jane had very little time to dwell on that though, soon a High Court judge entered with Admiral Jei and Captain Ota. The High Court Judge began, "Lieutenant Commander Jane of House Human, you were abducted and held for ransom by your own people. Now is the time to seek your justice and punish those who have wronged you. Will you do this under the gods' watchful eyes and the witnesses here today?"

"By the gods' grace I will," Jane answered and bowed.

"The gods will guide your hands. Let the punishments commence. Your lover will provide you with the means."

Jei walked over to Jane and handed her a short sword. He said quietly, "This is a new sword I had made especially for you. It's a good one. Remember, strike vertically down the back from the neck."

Jane nodded and looked into his concerned grey eyes. She wanted to tell him that it was going to be fine, but she couldn't because she didn't know if that was really true. She wanted to carry this out and walk out of this room after these proceedings, but she honestly didn't know if she could kill three people for her own life.

Jane looked at the sword he had given her. It was a much better one than she had had before, and she was grateful. She noticed this sword had a strange gleam to it in the light, but she didn't have time to think about that as the judge was talking again.

"Call the first to be accused."

The captain from the *Marianne* was brought into the square, kicking and screaming like a wild animal. She looked at Jane holding the sword and began roaring at her, "You traitor to humanity." She spit on the stone floor, "You'll be forever remembered as the woman who betrayed her people again and again to the Alliance! Traitor! Whore!"

Jane stepped closer to the young red-haired woman who was bound before her and on her knees trying to escape even now. "Do you have any last words for human ears? Any messages for your loved ones on Earth?" Jane asked trying not to let her emotions betray her.

The young red head spit at Jane and it landed on her tunic.

"By the gods I punish you for myself and for the Empire," Jane raised her sword with both hands on the hilt and aimed downward as Jei had told her to do. She struck the back of the red headed Captain's neck. A slow fountain of blood followed. After she was sure the woman was dead, Jane looked up at her daughter who was horrified. She wanted to mouth the words, 'This isn't me.' But that was a lie too. Then she looked at Jei, he nodded to her confidently that she had done this right. Then he motioned with his hand just a bit and she knew she must say something. Jane tried to remember if she had said anything after she had killed Nun, but she had blocked most of that from her memory, so she finally just said, "The gods have granted justice."

The High Priestess spoke again, "The gods are with us here now to pass judgement. Jane you act as their executioner. Is there anyone else who stands accused whose time has come to an end?"

Jane looked for Doctor Anu and she immediately tried to leave then but was held back by guards. "Chief Medical Officer Anu."

"Let the accused be brought down," said the High Priestess.

Anu was brought down and bound just as the Captain

of the *Marianne* had been. Anu's dress began to become wet with the blood on the floor.

Anu knew better than to speak yet though.

"Announce Doctor Anu's guilt," commanded the High Court judge.

Jane took a deep breath and mentally told Anu she was sorry. "Doctor Anu coerced the new 1,000 human women into breeding human babies to give to the Empire. She coerced me too. Doctor James of the City Hospital undid the memory alteration to uncover the truth. She has gone against the gods manipulating the production of children for the Empire."

The whole arena was in shock and people began screaming at Anu that she went against the gods and deserved to die.

Anu began to scream back, "I did it all so that we could live more peacefully and figure out why we're having this demographics issue. Now all my work will be lost, and we will never know. But hear me now and question how this started? It began from the inside. Our problem is here."

"Where are the babies?" the High Court judge asked Anu.

"I'll die first."

The judge looked to James and she came down next to Anu.

Dru whispered in Anu's ear, "I know it was you who tried to kill me, but now I'm killing you. I hope your soul roams the skies forever, never finding peace."

Anu said nothing to James but tried to avoid her touch. It was pointless as James was able to grab her easily and find the information by raping her thoughts.

After a few minutes, Dru pushed Anu away from her roughly and announced, "I know where the unborn children are. She has no more useful knowledge. She's ready for punishment, ready to explain herself before the gods."

James moved back and Jane held her sword and tried to kill Anu in the same manner, but she missed because her hands were shaking so much. She only managed to put the sword through her back. It was not a killing blow. Then it was difficult to get the sword out again. Jane had to stand on Anu's leg as she screamed to remove it, then she tried again and it wasn't exactly right but Jane could not try a third time so she watched a woman she had worked with for the last year slowly die by her hand, with a crowd of people yelling that Anu was a sinner to the last. Jane couldn't help but touch Anu's head after she had died and think, *Forgive me. One of us had to go.*

The whole thing was repeated again with Sah. Jane was even more tired now, so it took even longer for Jane to kill her. By the end of it, Jane was covered in the three women's blood. She knew she must look like a monster so she could not even look at her daughter. She felt ashamed of what she had done, but it was all for Ellie. All so that they could be together. Now she was finished. She stood there and waited for the High Court judge to say she was innocent.

The judge then announced, "The gods have shown us their justice today. Now there is only one more task you must complete Jane to prove to us that you are truly Alliance and that your heart will always be with the Empire."

Jane was so tired, emotionally and physically. She looked at the judge and hoped it would not involve killing anyone else, "I am ready to prove myself to the Empire."

"Let the gods rejoice. We will all bear witness to Admiral Jei's of House Rega and Lieutenant Commander Jane's of House Human marriage ceremony now."

Jane made eye contact with Jei and shook her head a little.

Jei walked over to her and took her left hand , covered in blood, in his and pulled out the marriage bracelets. He whispered in her ear, "This is happening. You can do it. It's the last thing you must do, then you and I walk out of here together."

Jane looked into his grey eyes, pleading with him. She couldn't do this.

He looked back at her lovingly, "I don't want to have to kill you, my pet."

Jane said quietly, "My daughter is here. I can't let her see this. I can't."

"You're doing this for her."

Jane shook her head. Tears were welling up in her eyes. She looked at her bloody hands and wondered who she was.

"She just saw you kill three people. This is only sex," Jei tried to make her feel better.

"Make her leave and I'll marry you in front of all of these people."

Jei looked at Jane and said, "I can't. All must be in attendance for the entire procedure. Jane please."

Jane turned then and looked at her daughter and pleaded with James mentally to have Ellie taken out. She knew James could hear her thoughts.

James just shook her head.

Jane closed her eyes as she thought about this. If she did this in front of Ellie, she would never forget it and it would possibly drive them apart for ever. But maybe she was damaged forever from what had already happened today, but all of that she could blame on the Empire and their strange justice system. This she would be doing voluntarily and would definitely look like she was enjoying it. She knew Jei would want to put on a show. His reputation had been damaged. If she allowed this to happen Ellie would forever remember her mother as the Alliance whore. No amount of explaining would change that.

Jane opened her eyes searching the arena looking for some kind of way out of this situation. She couldn't think of any. Jei had the bracelet posed over her left hand. He was waiting for her to give her consent. Then she remembered the dream with Babette, it had felt so real, would she really be made into a goddess. "Look into your heart Jane, you know what is right and what is wrong".

Jane took a deep breath and stepped back from Jei. She made eye contact with him but didn't speak for a minute then she said, "I cannot marry you here with my daughter in attendance."

Everyone began murmuring that it went against the gods and that she must. She had proven herself worthy. Everyone wanted to see them happy. People began shouting for their marriage.

Jei almost had tears in his eyes, "Jane, Jane, my lovely Jane. It's nothing. It's sex. What are you talking about?"

Jane tried to explain, "My daughter is here, and humans don't do this. We can't."

"The gods have put your daughter here so that you will prove to us you accept the Alliance in every way. Do you?" the High Priestess asked.

Jane looked at Jei with tears welling up in her eyes, "No, I cannot do this."

"Mom, no, do it!" Ellie cried out.

Jane shook her head and looked at Ellie and said, "No baby, you be a good girl. I've always loved you so much. Remember what I did here today. And you remember, I've never been a traitor to humanity. I've always tried to balance both worlds."

Jane got down on her knees then and put her hands behind her back.

Jei took his sword out, but before he struck her, he whispered in her ear, "Jane my sweet Jane, I will make sure that no one ever forgets you." He stood then and said loudly, "Today I must kill my true other half as she refuses to be completely Alliance in the eyes of the law today. However, let the gods look upon her kindly as she knocks on their palace door. Let this be a new beginning." Jei struck Jane down with one blow. He had killed so many times, but he felt like a good part of him died with Jane too in that moment. He got down on his knees and held her bloody body in his arms. He had loved her so much. He picked her up with her blood dripping everywhere and brought her over to her human daughter. "Say goodbye to your mother," he ordered her gruffly. "She did this for you."

Ellie screamed at the sight of her mother's dead form being held by her murderer in front of her.

"Say goodbye," he commanded her again and she did it only for fear of him.

Then Jei carried Jane's body outside to Doctor Rea who was waiting with equipment to save the fetus and have it transferred into an artificial womb that would be looked after on the *Kzi*. No female babies would be lost no matter what.

Thank you

Thank you for reading *Married to the Alien Admiral of the Fleet*, Renascence Alliance Series Book 4. I warned you it was dark. As the whole Empire is shocked, especially all the humans, by what has happened to Jane, Drusilla asks that her sister be brought over from Earth to the Empire. This is a short novella and if you would prefer to listen to it, Bridget Bordeaux does an excellent job at narrating the story and you can listen here: Abducted by the Alien Pirate Audiobook

I will include a teaser of the next book. Thanks again for joining me on this eight-part series into the Alliance Empire.

Best wishes,

Alma x

Teaser

Abducted by the Alien Pirate Excerpt:

"Oh, sweet little adorable human, what have you done to yourself?" Kol asked her unconscious form as he picked her up gently and carried her to the *Ora's* small sickbay. He was no doctor, but he could heal her small wounds with the medical palmer and check that the translator was working properly. It was common that it caused migraines in the first few hours of speaking and listening after initial implantation.

As Kol inspected her body with the aid of some simple medical devices, he noticed that she had a small tattoo above her right breast. He wondered if it extended lower but was not going to unclothe her to find out. However, as she was unconscious, he was not going to stop looking at it either. It was a small pink flower on a vine, and he imagined that it would be the sexiest thing ever if it extended down the side of her breast.

Jesse opened her eyes and saw a huge grey skinned

man standing over her with a medical device, immediately she thought he was doing some kind of experiment on her. There had always been rumors of humans being stolen especially by Alliance people for medical experiments. To prove they were genetically the same or some such nonsense. She never believed in the abductions until now. Jesse sat up immediately and kicked the large Alliance man. While he was stunned, she jumped off the medical bed and tried to quickly run out of the room. Her head was throbbing, but she knew she had to get away from him.

"Computer close med doors," Kol shouted and the doors closed right before Jesse could run out.

Jesse's nose broke as she ran into the closing door at full force. She sat down slowly on the floor from the pain and put her hand on her nose, blood was running everywhere." The alien came up from behind her and tried to help her to the medical bed, "Get off of me!"

Kol would not let go. He lifted her up to the medical bed and then applied the restraints.

"Let me go you zombie!"

Kol looked down at the human and said, "Listen pinky, you can call me whatever you want. I've heard a lot worse and from uglier and scarier people than you. It's almost adorable when you say it actually. Say it again Julia."

"My name is not Julia, zombie." She didn't want to call him a zombie again, but then a part of her couldn't help it and she just had to because it was the only terrible thing, she could think to call him in that moment. Then she wondered, "How do I understand you?" She touched her head answering her own question.

Kol stilled. *Had he taken the wrong human?* He thought he had double checked before he left the *Ora* on Earth, but maybe there had been two women in the forest. He immediately went over to the computer in sickbay and brought up her files and then did a DNA match. He was relieved when it was the same. She was Doctor James's sister, there was no question about it.

"I know your name is Julia. I know who you are. Don't be alarmed. I'm taking you to your sister. She wants to see you and has paid a lot of UCs for me to take you to her. And you understand me because I graciously gave you a universal translator."

"I don't have a sister."

"Funny, because science doesn't lie, people do," he said casually beginning to fix her bloody broken nose. She had blood everywhere on her clothing. "I have your sister's DNA you see."

Jesse was upset. She knew a bit about technology even though she had never used it. "Well, what can I give you to take me home? I don't want to go to see my sister. She is dead to me."

Kol stopped healing her and looked into her dark green eyes, actually attractive next to her pink skin and asked, "Why wouldn't you want to go? You were living in the worst squalor I've ever seen in a far-off part of the galaxy no one ever wants to visit. No technology, no nothing. Like an animal. Now you have the opportunity to be a part of one of the most influential families in the entire galaxy and live as you should live as one of the Lost People. The time for humans to shine is now with the maximum class in the Empire."

"I've no idea what you are talking about. I just want to go home. My life. My family, my friends. My squalor, I love it. Take me there. Say you couldn't find me. I won't tell anyone I saw you. I don't belong anywhere else but on Earth. I can feel it in my soul," she would have touched her chest if her arms weren't being restrained. "I'm dying the further away I get from Earth. I can feel it." She didn't know how to describe how her six sense talents for the otherworldly had diminished since she left Earth for fear, he really would want to do medical experiments on her then.

Kol touched her shoulder comfortingly, "It's nothing. Everyone feels that way the first time they leave their planet. Your body will adjust to the artificial gravity soon enough."

"What? That's it you don't care at all that you are ruining my life?"

"How am I ruining your life?" he asked in disbelief. "I'm making it exponentially better. The Earth's Exterior is so primitive, without technology or running water. You might as well be living like an animal. And when I entered your quarters to reassure you that everything was fine, you were acting beastly. You even threw a small brush at me. The best thing I can do for you is to take you to civilization and to give you the opportunity to become civilized, if that is possible. The doctors say it's possible," He said the last sentence more to himself than to her and brushed some hair back from her young face. "And I think you are young enough to be saved just like your sister was."

"I wasn't acting beastly. You left me unconscious in a cold and dark room I could not get out of. What did you expect me to do?"

"Wait?" he suggested. He really thought she might have slept through it all or just waited to see what would happen next. That's what he would have done. Then a thought occurred to him and he remembered, "I'm sorry it was dark. I forgot that humans have poor night vision. I also forgot it would be cold for you as well, I will turn up your quarter's temperature to 20C. I'm afraid that's the maximum temperature though. However, we are going to be arriving at Falcon station soon. We can buy you some new and warmer clothes there."

If you would like to continue reading, *Abducted by the Alien Pirate*, you can buy the book or read in Kindle Unlimited here: Abducted by the Alien Pirate Book